DARK INTENT

A B Endacott

Cover designed by Marcus Moltzer
Cover illustration by Nicole Sizer
Map illustration by Ellen Liu

This book is a work of fiction. Names, characters, places, and incidents either are products of the author's imagination or are used fictitiously. Any resemblance to actual persons, living or dead, events, or locales is entirely coincidental.

978-0-6481875-7-8

Books by the same author

The Second Country
Queendom of the Seven Lakes
King of the Seven Lakes

The Fourth Country
The Ruthless Land

The Third Country
Dark Intent
Coming soon

Dark Purpose
Dark Heart
Untitled (First Country)

For Mitchell.
For knowing that this story was going to be special.
For buying me Scrivener.
*For buying me a drink and making me talk it through properly
before I started writing.*
For never once wavering in your belief of me.
For every day.

.

"that is the question:
whether 'tis nobler in the mind to suffer the slings and arrows of
outrageous fortune,
or to take arms against a sea of troubles"

-Shakespeare, Hamlet

The City of Oranis

ONE

The bells woke her.

As she did each morning, Freya rolled over and nudged Symon awake. He moaned softly in protest at the early awakening and moved further away from her.

"Wake up. We have to get to the square," she said when it became apparent he wasn't going to move. He sighed in resignation and after a moment longer, he got out of their bed. With the wordless accordance of long-established habit, they orbited one another as they quickly bathed and dressed.

The first worship of the day was held before the sun rose, so the streets down which they hurried were cool and dark. People walked along with them, the final vestiges of sleep still clinging to their movements.

The square was one of countless others across the city. One only needed to walk a few streets before they came across another square. That meant that worship was possible at any time. Nobody had an excuse to miss a single prayer. As she stood alongside about seventy other people, their breaths collectively rising in the grey predawn, Freya thought for a moment how brutal the sudden clear space was in contrast to the elegant buildings surrounding it. Perhaps her thoughts were tainted by the knowledge that this square had been created only after the takeover. A building had been unceremoniously torn down to make room for it. The reminder of that destruction was present in the ground, which was paved with the same smooth white stone as the city's streets rather than the more beautifully coloured stones that graced the floors of the city's older worship squares. The spindly trees which bordered the square were another reminder of the fact that this square only existed to force Pious to live the Kade way of life. They were only a few years old, and nowhere near tall enough to provide the shade that people often enjoyed during moments of non-worship in the grander, older squares.

Wary habit had her observing the people around her, noting the faces of acquaintances, familiar faces, and the faces which she couldn't place. It was commonly whispered that ununiformed Guardians were in the crowd at nearly every worship in the Pious district, making sure they were worshipping as the laws decreed. It was ironic. As a result of the measures, Pious were the ones who worshipped the Kade gods the most dutifully. She wondered how many Kade across the city had left their beds that morning while it was still dark. Then again, they probably did not have the same incentives as the Pious. The lives of the Pious who didn't worship enough were inevitably made very difficult. They would suffer frequent checks by Guardians for any and all manner of infringements. If they didn't improve their behaviour to the satisfaction of the Kade, something inappropriate would be discovered, the punishment for which was a cancelled work licence, a requirement to re-train, or a restriction on movement – whatever was most inconvenient. Sometimes when a Pious was still particularly resistant to demonstrating how completely they had adopted the Kade way of life, the gas pipes that supplied their houses with heat and light would ignite without explanation. The house, and anybody who was unlucky enough not to get out, would be burnt to a charred wreck. And anybody who dared openly speak against such things disappeared. Although, such occurrences almost never happened now. The citizens of Oranis remembered well what had happened to those Pious who had refused to accept the terms of the new regime when the Kade had taken control of the capital six years previously. Those individuals had been dragged through the streets behind wagons whose drivers seemed to delight in the pain they caused. Almost all of the Pious had screamed that they would repent in a desperate bid to stop the torment. But by the time they offered their fealty, it was too late. They died within hours from the wounds inflicted by being dragged along the unrelenting ground. Freya had watched as those people relinquished their beliefs while their skin peeled away, and committed herself vigorously to the edicts of the Kade. The horrific sight was etched into her mind – into the mind of anyone who had been forced to watch. For a second, she could see only the image of Rohana, but she viciously clamped down on the memory, pushing it back into the space in her mind where such thoughts were safely buried.

As the square filled, Freya cleared her mind to commit her attention to the prayer. She'd heard it whispered that the Guardians and the Ordained could tell if you weren't fully focused on the rituals. Doubt often weighed on her about the truth of the claim; they were only people, after all. That being said, caution guaranteed longevity. So she emptied her mind of any thoughts that could be deemed even vaguely subversive and focused on the incantation. The Ordained moved through the square as they spoke, waving smouldering arax root back and forth. The slightly acrid scent washed over the space, sending everybody into the trance-like state that facilitated focus on a single task or idea. Freya inhaled deeply. Occasionally, those who were perceived to not inhale enough arax root were questioned. She had no desire to give anyone any cause to doubt her loyalty. To be doubted ensured life became difficult. So she sucked in lungfuls of the smoky air. Her thoughts began to slip and slide into what had become a familiar haze. The experience was akin to her memory of being drunk – intoxication was also not looked upon favourably by the Kade, and Freya had been drunk only once in her life, before the takeover when she had been a young girl and had snuck more than the single glass of ale her parents had permitted her. Now, she barely touched any fermented drink for fear of imbibing too much. She wanted neither to loosen her tongue to carelessness, nor to appear in any way counter to the ideals of Kade life.

The Ordained raised their voices in chant. The sound never ceased to be harsh to her ears. She had never been able to find the exact words to explain why. But then again, she had never searched too hard for them. The invocations today were mundane: for peace; for the Kade gods to evermore favour those who worshipped them; that Oranis and the Third Country would continue to enjoy prosperity. Her mind wandered into the familiar dark, cavernous space she had come to in prayer from her earliest memory. Yet this space where her sense of self was contained, where only her awareness of herself existed, while once comforting, was now somewhere she went only with reluctance. She assumed the reason she now found it so alien, so filled with an unfamiliar presence, was because she was here at the law's requirement rather than of her own desire. The act of praying that once had given her reprieve from her worries, and a sense of peace, now was a duty she undertook with a sense of dull intrusion.

She remained in the space of nothingness, of dark existence within her mind, and the words of prayer to the Kade gods filtered through her awareness. She was dimly aware of the Ordained as they moved through the rows of people in the square. The drone of their voices permeated everything as they spoke the prayers to their gods over and over. It almost felt as though they were trying to press the words into the ears of every person who stood there with that docile obedience procured by the law and the promise of violent reprisal if they did not obey. Finally, the sun touched the rooftops, sending a pink glow down into the square as the buildings' walls reflected the light. As the effects of the arax root began to wane, the Ordained ascended the raised section at the front of the square and raised their arms. "Behold.

They have blessed us with a new day!" Their voices rose as one before they fell silent. The crowd stirred, as though finally awakening. Freya looked to her left, at Symon. He was looking at his feet, his face impassive but for a small frown. She wondered, as she often did, what he was thinking. The crowd waited obediently until the arms of the Ordained fell – the signal of dismissal – before filing out of the square.

Freya and Symon walked back to their house, their feet falling into synchronised steps. It wasn't unusual for them to walk in silence but today she perceived a difference to the tenor of Symon's quiet.

"Is everything all right?" she asked.

He reflexively glanced around before answering. "Do you ever think that their incantations are an attempt to control us?"

She glanced back at him, surprised by the boldness of his remark. "Of course," she replied casually. "Why else would they reinforce that peace and prosperity are achieved thanks to the Kade's governance?"

Symon dragged his feet, his footfalls tumbling out of step with hers. The susurration grated on Freya's nerves. She didn't understand what he could possibly be kicking his feet against. The streets were paved with completely flat slabs of white stone that left no unevenness, save the gutters along their edges.

"Do you think they're brainwashing us, Freya?" His question came abruptly, uncomfortably.

She considered his question as they moved through the lightening streets. The glow of the rising sun seemed to breathe life into the city; Oranis was suddenly a symphony of tender pink, gold, and soft cream. She was as surprised by the suddenness of his questions as she was that he was sharing his thoughts with her. Symon was a self-contained, cautious man. "I hadn't really thought about it," she said, keeping her tone light as she tried to scan the shadows for ears that might overhear their conversation. She liked her house. She didn't want it burnt down in an 'accident'. Especially if she was still inside it.

"Think about it, though," he pressed. "They drug us every morning and evening at the prayers, and while we're drugged, they tell us how wonderful the Kade is. Surely that's brainwashing?"

Nervous now at his lack of care, Freya walked faster, practically running to their front door. "Symon, arax root clears the mind. It can't be used as a brainwashing tool." She opened the front door and stepped inside the relative safety of their house. She was profoundly glad to remove this particular conversation from the street where anybody could be listening.

"Are you sure?" he challenged as she closed the door firmly behind them.

"I'm a healer. I work in the Main Healing Centre. I have to know the properties of every herb in the Third Country. I would know if arax root could affect people like that." She desperately hoped the firmness of her tone dispelled whatever had brought on these questions. "What's brought this on, anyway?"

The motion of his shoulders was a half shrug that could have meant anything. He looked slightly to her left as he replied, his voice vague. "Just something I overheard in the tailor's."

"From a Kade official?" she asked, a sliver or curiosity aroused. Symon's skill as a tailor meant he made clothes for some of the Third Country's most powerful people. He often alluded to some of the things he overheard but was normally tight-lipped about the specifics.

He made a noise of affirmation.

"What did they say?" she asked.

"Perhaps I misheard," he replied.

"What did they say?" she repeated, feeling a lick of irritation at his reticence.

"Honestly, Freya, it's not that important."

Before she could enquire further, he walked into another room. The sounds of him readying himself for work told her that the conversation was concluded, and the likelihood that he would raise it once more was small. As far as she was concerned, that was fine. She didn't want to engage any further in a discussion that could get them both sanctioned. Or worse.

TWO

"Freyanna Kuch." She stated her full name for the Guardian at the door. This little, irksome ritual was as much a part of her day as the morning worship. As though instead of working there every day, she had never been to the Centre before, the Guardian looked studiously through the list until he found her name. She waited patiently, pretending that she wasn't bothered by this rigmarole. Today she found it particularly grating, found it difficult to dispel the resentment that bubbled inside her. It was as though Symon's comments from earlier in the morning were infecting her. She found herself fingering the green band sewn into the sleeve of her white healer's robes, as she often did. This band, sewn into every item of clothing that she owned, demarked her as Pious for the world to see. She wondered what would happen if she were to wear unmarked clothing like the Kade. Would anybody notice? Or would a squad of Guardians descend on her and lock her away for her dissidence? She shook her head. Such thoughts invited trouble. The sort of trouble that she'd worked hard for the past six years to avoid.

After an eternity of checking, the Guardian nodded and stepped aside, allowing her to enter her workplace. She moved through the atrium and foyer to the Healer's station to receive her assignment for the day.

"Morning, Freya," the administrator, Leita, said. From the way she said it, Freya knew that she was not going to like her task for the day. There was a guilty twist to the mouth, her eyes met Freya's then skirted away. "The Dark Gods' Followers managed to poison a shipment of grain with barat," Leita said, her expression a cross between sympathy and distaste.

Freya winced. The extraordinarily beautiful barat flowers could be used to make a particularly lethal poison, the effects of which were very unpleasant to witness, let alone to experience. "Fortunately," Leita continued, "few people received a lethal dose. But we have an entire ward full of people who have been affected. I need you to oversee the ward."

Freya caught her breath before it rushed out of her in a sigh. Working for a whole day among a group of people who were suffering the effects of barat poisoning was not a pleasant prospect.

"I'm sorry to put you in there, Freya, but none of the other Master-ranked healers can be removed from their assignments. And you know how difficult barat poisoning can be. It needs someone truly skilled to ensure the correct treatments are administered." She probably was genuinely apologetic. Leita was Pious, as the green band on her sleeve reminded everyone.

Freya's smile was one of resignation. "We can't control what people come in with." A tiny part of her wondered if she had been assigned to this unpleasant duty because she was Pious, but she told herself not to be stupid. There was a handful of other Master-ranked Pious working in the Main Healing Centre. Granted, most of them had been awarded the rank before the uprising, but they were there. Besides, despite the religious differences between Kade and Pious, healers did not organise themselves in response to petty grievances. Their priority was to save lives. The best went where they were needed, and she was now needed to oversee the diagnosis and treatment of a room full of poisoned people. Surely, the politics of her birth had nothing to do with that.

As she entered the long room, she could smell the sour scent of bile and rotting flesh that followed ingestion of the poison distilled from the decayed petals of the barat flower. She shuddered as she considered the viciousness of the poison, and the way it would eat through a person's body.

The ward was full of moaning bodies. Some of them, Freya saw with a mixture of pity and horror, were children. A healer of initiate rank approached her.

"Master Kuch?" He looked at her with an expression that suggested he believed she was capable of single-handedly curing every person in the ward in time for lunch. She never failed to be surprised that the reputation of her skill as a healer had travelled as far as the initiates. She nodded, even as her focus was mostly on surveying the room behind him to assess the severity of the injuries.

"We've ordered the patients from most to least severe and have readied the antidotes," the initiate said. He seemed practically breathless with excitement at being in her presence. She ignored his delight and nodded in satisfaction as she noted that indeed, patients whose symptoms were noticeably worse were on the right side of the room.

"What about treatment for the injuries sustained due to the poison?" she asked.

"We're still assessing what damage has been done."

Freya sighed and moved past him to the worst-affected patients. The initiate trailed behind her. She would have to start doing basic diagnosing work right away; not enough headway had been made by the four healers already in the room.

The man to whom she went first was middle aged. His features, which looked as though they were normally open and pleasant, were distorted with pain. He was moaning, but barely any sound escaped his lips. Freya put her hands lightly on his forehead, checking the warmth of his skin, his pulse, the regularity of his breathing. After barely a moment had passed, she straightened up. "His lungs are damaged."

"How do you know?" the initiate asked, leaning around her to peer at the man.

She frowned so slightly that it would have been almost imperceptible, trying to find a way to explain how she had arrived at her diagnosis. "I can just tell," she replied, unable to exactly put into words how his temperature, the look of his skin, the tenor to his breathing had simply told her what ailed him.

"But how?" he asked again, looking first at the patient and then at her.

She shrugged, uncomfortable with his scrutiny and slightly annoyed by his obvious display of curiosity. "I've been doing this a long time." She didn't snap, holding the impulse in check because the unmarked sleeve denoted him as Kade. Even though he was her junior and looked at her reverentially, it was unwise to speak insolently to a Kade. Nevertheless, the downward inflection of her voice made it clear she had more pressing things to do than answer his questions.

He nodded, and noted the lung ailment on the patient's notes, giving instructions to a nearby apothecarist to prepare the necessary medicine. Freya moved on after she'd heard enough to know the initiate, for all his wide-eyed wonder, was prescribing the appropriate treatment. She retreated into the half trance that was as familiar to her as breathing. Her focus was on moving from one patient to the next, examining them, and diagnosing how the poison had started to take root within them. Perhaps the most hideous aspect of barat poison was that it affected everybody differently, and as such, was incredibly time consuming to treat. For this reason, it was the perfect choice of tool for the anarchic Followers of the Dark Gods.

There was a comfort in the certainty that came with placing her hands on the sick and determining the exact cause of their suffering. The task was more familiar than breathing. Flushed skin, laboured breathing, damaged bodies drew her in until the task of tending to the sick filled her awareness. It was only with a dim awareness of the world around her that she noticed how quickly she was diagnosing patients. Freya was the highest ranked healer in the room, but even allowing for that, she far surpassed anyone else in the speed and certainty with which she determined where the poison had travelled. It was impossible to not feel the covert glances thrown her way by the other healers, the near reverence with which they treated her, or their surreptitious attempts to determine what exactly it was that she did that made her so singularly skilled. Her reputation for being unusually young to hold a Master rank, especially among the Pious, added to her reputation. She was accustomed to this scrutiny. It certainly bothered her from time to time, but she had become practised in ignoring it, by focusing on the task of helping people.

She paused over a patient and beckoned to one of the initiates. "This man has ingested too much poison," she said softly. The initiate frowned as he regarded the man before them. The patient didn't appear visibly worse than those on either side of him. Seeing the initiate's scepticism, Freya clicked her tongue in impatience. "The poison hasn't eaten away much, but he had wasting sickness beforehand, which has been exacerbated by the barat. He will die before the end of the day."

"What should we do?" the initiate asked, shifting from foot to foot, obviously chastened by his failure to see what she had.

Freya fiddled thoughtlessly with the green band on the sleeve of her uniform. "There's nothing we can do. Just...wait," she replied, her voice soft. She cast one more look at the dying man before moving on to her next patient, allowing her training to guide her in focusing on those who would live.

She finished examining the worst of the patients as the morning drew to a close. It was a task that would have taken any other healer at least four times that time. She summoned the initiate with whom she had first spoken. "How are those less severe patients?" she asked. She wiped the back of her hand across her forehead, pushing strands of dark hair out of her eyes.

"Well, the antidote is working effectively for most patients." It impressed her that he did not need to consult his notes. "Although, one of the children is in more pain than we would expect."

She went to the bed he indicated and looked down at the child who was quietly sobbing in pain.

"Why did they do this?" The words tumbled from her lips before she could stop them. There was something too heart wrenching about the girl's pain for the wall of her professional detachment to remain unbreached. The girl could not have had more than five or six years.

Even though she wasn't really expecting an answer, the initiate replied. "Because the Dark Gods only want chaos."

"There were no demands, no threats?" She gently placed her hands on the child's arm.

"There never are," the initiate replied. He was certainly more astute than she had first thought.

Freya shrugged. Even the Kade in their takeover had realised their limitations and had not made any attempt to subjugate the violent worshippers of the Dark Gods. Not only would it have cost a great many lives, but the Followers of the Dark Gods lived in inhospitable mountain caves in a far-flung corner of the Third Country. It wasn't worth trying to subjugate them. They only ever came periodically to attack the capital to try to sow anarchy, and for the most part, their efforts were defeated. There was a certain irony in the fact that they were the only ones who had really remained untouched by the Kade coup. Although, to them this was simply another government to topple in order for anarchy and chaos to reign.

Freya closed her eyes, her grip tightening on the girl's arm. "She's fine." As she opened her eyes, the girl took a deep breath and stopped sobbing. Her breaths evened out and her face smoothed back into the unmarked roundness of childhood. Freya released her grip.

As they walked away, the initiate's mouth opened to ask what she had done. Unbridled wonder was once more in his eyes, but Freya forestalled the question. "She needed to hear that to calm down."

Despite her explanation, the amazement didn't leave his eyes. However, any further questions went unasked as a gentle chime sounded, signalling the middle of the day. Two second-rank healers immediately left the patients to which they were tending and went to eat. Freya made no move to follow them.

"You should go and get something to eat," the initiate said.

"But there are still people here who I can help," she pointed out.

"Master Kuch, it's not right for someone of your rank to do all the work," the initiate spluttered.

"But they need my help." She barely kept herself from making a comment about the type of healer who prioritised their stomach over people in pain who they could help.

The initiate looked uncomfortable, torn between a sense of impropriety at the prospect of a Master-rank healer engaging in such work and a desire to not contradict the order of one of his superiors. "Please, go and make sure you eat. We'll be fine, I promise." He was all but begging.

With no small amount of reluctance, Freya relented. Even though she preferred to push through her hunger, deeming it less important than the lives of people who she could help, she recognised the truth that someone of her rank should conform to a certain set of expectations. Certainly, it would be rare for a Kade Master-rank healer to miss lunch.

Blinking in the bright sunlight, she walked through the city, relaxing as she heard the sounds of everyday life: people laughing, talking, arguing; even one brave soul singing – badly. The sound of people going about their daily lives. It was so far from the pain and sickness of the ward she had just left that it seemed unreal.

Whenever she walked through the city at this time of day it made her feel almost as though she were back in the days before the Kade had overthrown the governing Dual Accord in which the Kade and Pious had shared authority. Back then, she had been so impossibly young. She hadn't known the responsibility of instructing people in how they should care for patients. Nor had she known the accompanying weight of holding so many lives in her hands at the one time. Even though she had been only an initiate before the takeover, she had taken the exact same route from the Healing Centre, passing the halls of governance, moving through the winding streets to circumvent the grand shops and business houses, to reach the market square. Oranis really was a beautiful city. Its oldest buildings were constructed from light pink mezite, the rocks found in the mountains now inhabited by the Dark Gods' Followers. Due to their presence, the stone was now almost impossible to obtain. Somehow, that fact made the buildings all the more beautiful. The mezite glowed in the light but, despite the heat and brightness of the sun, did not produce a glare, unlike the white stones that had been used to construct more recent buildings. It meant that walking through the street, even on an overcast day, was a visual feast of architectural flourishes and beautiful warm light. Freya loved the city most at dusk, though, when the light liquefied on the walls of the buildings to a flaming orange and yellow. To her, there was nothing more beautiful than the way the city glowed in those minutes before darkness fell. She always tried to leave the Healing Centre in time to catch the city at sunset. As the sun slunk towards the horizon, the city felt like it was pulsing with those final few rays of light, drinking them in.

Freya smiled when she saw the throng of activity in the marketplace. Not even the watchful presence of the Guardians – and the subdued threat of violence that emanated from their insolent postures and the weapons that conspicuously hung from their belts – could detract from the market's beauty. To her, it was one of the most beautiful places in the city. It was an open space, ringed by white columns with carved vines winding around them. The columns' height made the space somehow intimate, despite the large area over which the market sprawled. Creamy aegat stone, threaded with bronze-coloured veins, paved the marketplace. In the times of peace between the faithful, under the governance of the Dual Accord, the space had been a meeting place for the religious guardians of both the Kade Ordained and Goddess's Children. Huge stone seats snaked through the square like rivers, bisecting walkways and forcing everybody to stop and decide if they would sit rather than simply walk on by, or at the very least, forcing them to pause and appreciate the beauty of their surrounds. On these seats the religious leaders had sat and spoken with each other. Over meals that they would eat with their hands like the most modest of their people, the two groups would debate theology, the discussions often continuing long after the food was gone. Anyone who wished could listen, even make their own interjections. Sometimes questions would be put to them, and the Goddess's Children and the Ordained would proffer their respective approaches. But now the Goddess's Children were no more, and the seats were only occupied by people eating the lunch they had just purchased.

That fact that it was lunchtime meant the marketplace was teeming with people. Traders called to the passers-by, trying to entice buyers for their wares, wafting tantalising fragrances under the noses of anyone who came close. The air was filled with a mix of mouth-watering smells and the sound of people talking, laughing, haggling. Freya stood on the edge of the market square, admiring the beauty of the space. For a moment, she forgot about the ward full of sick people, her sadness at the world that had been lost by the takeover. She was simply happy to watch the vibrancy of life playing out in the marketplace.

Then the market exploded.

THREE

Time seemed to slow as the explosion pushed the stalls apart in a spray of timber, food, and stone. The stones tore flesh apart with an indifferent brutality. The damage wrought by the timber was only slightly less horrific.

Freya had been lucky. She was only standing on the edge of the market. Still, she was knocked sideways by the blast, and a wave of heat washed over her, seeming to crack the skin on her face as she closed her eyes against the flying dust, against that awful heat. As she landed on the ground, her mind worked to piece together what had happened. Her thoughts crawled, refusing to align themselves into anything coherent. Then the screaming started. Those who could fled the ruins of the marketplace. They climbed through rubble and trampled people, desperation to reach safety making them indifferent about on what they stepped.

Freya struggled to prop herself onto an elbow, fearful that she might too be trampled. Then strong hands seized her, and she found herself looking up helplessly into piercing green eyes.

"Can you hear me?" the man asked.

With an effort, she collected her thoughts and nodded, gripping his forearms to stabilise her as he pulled her up.

"Can you move?" he asked, looking into her eyes. He looked at her so intensely that for she felt to him, she was the only thing in the square.

She took stock of her body and nodded again, taking a deep breath and steadying herself. As soon as he released her she swayed, still dizzy from the blast. Appearing to have anticipated this, his hands flashed out to steady her.

"Thank you," she mumbled, embarrassed as much by her instability as her own incorrect self-assessment.

He tentatively relaxed his grip, and when she didn't topple, let his hands fall to his sides. "Ok, I'm going to go and help people. Will you be all right?" He spoke gently, as though she were a startled animal. It rankled her. It gave her the incitement to find a balance and focus she thought had been shattered by the force of the explosion.

"I'm a healer. I'm likely better qualified to help than you." She pushed him aside and walked into the remains of the marketplace.

He followed her without comment, moving to her side to place a hand on her waist as she stumbled. She brushed it away, irritated by his presumptuousness. This frustration was something she clung to, able to comprehend it, able to control it.

A few brave individuals were already helping anyone trapped under rubble, shifting anything that had fallen onto people, or attempting to treat their injuries. Freya stood for a moment, trying to find a way to order the anarchic scene in her own mind.

Two men and two women were trying to lift a large timber beam. It looked as though it had been a support for one of the stalls. It was thick, and it had fallen onto a man. Instinct warned her that if they moved him, the man would be injured beyond help. "Stop!" she called out, the authority of a woman who was accustomed to leading teams of healers ringing through her voice. They turned to look at her, uncertain, instinctively awaiting her instructions.

"If you move that beam, you'll kill him," she shouted, picking her way across the suddenly uneven ground to them. "Go and get help," she instructed one of the men. She knelt and put her hands on the trapped man and as she did, the rest of the world dropped away. It was immediately obvious to her that several of his bones had been ferociously shattered. Any jarring movement would send the fragments into his organs. She looked down at the unconscious man and chewed her lip, casting around for anything to use, wishing for an initiate hovering next to her with a tray of instruments. "Get cloth from the surrounding stalls. We need things we can use for bandages and bindings." She threw the command over her shoulder to a man standing nearby, watching her with a dazed uncertainty. The man who had helped her was also giving orders, telling people to find anyone else trapped, but not to move them. He was smart, she thought, smiling tightly, before returning her total focus to the man at her hands. No matter how she considered it, there was no way to help him or move him without causing irreparable damage, or rather, further damage.

"I can't do anything," she whispered, more to herself, hating the helplessness that engulfed her along with the realisation. She didn't realise that the man who had helped her up was now kneeling beside her until he began whispering. "Great Goddess who is ever-present. As you watch over us always, watch over us now." She realised with a jolt that he was whispering the first prayer to the Goddess. She hadn't heard it spoken aloud in years, much less said it herself. The lilting familiarity of the old words compounded the shock caused by the explosion, and she felt her throat close up and her eyes burn. She was overwhelmed by a deep desire to just lie down next to this man on the ground with his broken, battered body, and forget everything. But instead, she found her mouth moving, shaping the words of the affirmation, a rhythm so easy it was hard to believe she had ever ceased it. "When you are strong, we are strong; when you are weak, we will give you strength; when we are weak, we ask for your strength. For we are one and the same; from the beginning of time it will be thus unto the end."

Freya closed her eyes, her mind an oasis of calm amid the chaos of what had been the marketplace, feeling warmth and stillness move through her. The spell was broken by the tramping of running feet behind them, followed by agitated shouts. She opened her eyes and turned to stare at this man who had so brashly dared to defy the strictest of the Kade's laws. He was looking at the man on the ground, seemingly unconcerned by the fact that someone may have overheard them uttering heresy. Freya's body trembled with fear, shock and, she was surprised to realise, exhilaration. The most basic of all prayers, taught to all Pious children as soon as they learned to talk, was a reset point to clear the mind and enable focus. It had done just that for her. She hadn't realised how much she had missed it and what it offered until that moment.

The man turned to her, calm and impassive. "You could heal him, you know," he told her.

"I'm a healer, I know what I can and can't do." Fear from the magnitude of their act, and anger at her inability to heal the man before her, made her snap, shattering the temporary calm that the prayer had given her.

He regarded her for a moment, as though he was scrutinising her very being, then shrugged. "Maybe I was wrong," he said, sounding very much as though he didn't think that at all.

More help arrived as the afternoon wore on. Teams moved rubble aside and pulled people free while Freya took control of the healers who arrived. She gave instructions while trying to attend to as many people as she could, diagnosing injuries in her impossibly quick way, and giving instructions to whoever was nearby, administering bandages and poultices, and doing anything else that needed to be done when nobody else could. It was exhausting work.

It was late in the afternoon when Freya paused, collecting her strength. She looked over her surrounds, grief at the desolation which had replaced a place she had loved so dearly lodging itself in her heart. Movement caught her gaze, and she watched a group of people nearly trying to clear a large piece of one of the stone columns that had fallen down. One of them was her rescuer. A dark stain of blood was spread across his shirt.

"Hey," she called, realising that she didn't know his name. At the sound of her voice, he straightened and looked over. He wiped sweat from his forehead, replacing it with a streak of dirt. Freya moved over to him, wary of tripping over the stones strewn across the ground.

"Is everything all right?" he asked, looking her over with an expression that she could only conclude was one of concern.

"I'm fine," she said, a vague sense of irritation blooming at his concern. "It's you that's the problem – you're bleeding." She pointed to the stain on his shirt.

He waved her comment aside. "It's nothing. I'm fine."

"I'm the healer, I'll decide what's fine," she said, gesturing for him to sit down.

He smiled wryly and sat on a piece of stone, looking up at her as she ran her fingers lightly over him, checking for injuries. Almost of their own accord, her fingers sought the cut on the back of his arm. It wasn't deep, but it was long. She peeled the torn edges of the shirt away from the wound, murmuring an apology as he hissed in pain.

As she tended to him, she studied him surreptitiously. He looked strong, capable, certain of himself and of what he could and couldn't do. She realised that he was staring back at her, and she blushed at the frankness of his gaze, busying herself by affixing a bandage to the injury. As she finished, he moved his hand to hers, stilling them. His hand was so large that it engulfed both of hers easily. She looked into his eyes uncomfortably. He was staring at her so directly.

"Aren't you just the most exquisite thing I've ever seen." His voice was warm and low, but also without any hint of glib charm. It was just a statement, as if he'd commented on the progress of the rescue efforts. Freya knew she should have moved her hands, but she found herself compelled to stay. His fingers were long, hinting at dexterity and cleverness; calluses suggested he was some kind of craftsman. But above all, she was aware of the warmth of his hand around her own.

"My name is Freyanna," she said softly.

"Ashtyn." The way his supplied his name was like the continuation of the rhythm between the two of them that had been created when they whispered the prayer together.

They stayed like that, immobile, neither sure of what to say, yet neither wanting to move. A crash of stones nearby made Freya jump. Ashtyn chuckled at her reaction, and raised his arm to calm or reassure her. But the crash had broken whatever had kept her silent.

"I'm bound," she blurted, looking quickly around as the old term – a forbidden term –spilled from her mouth. He seemed not to notice the danger she'd put them in. Then again, if his prayer was anything to go by, he didn't seem like the type to care. He blinked slowly, leaving his hand exactly where it was, and looked at her. Finally he spoke.

"He's a lucky man." He did not move his hand, and she did not try to pull hers free.

Another crash made Freya jump again. She jerked one of her hands free and grabbed Ashtyn's shoulder instinctively.

"My, you're jumpy, aren't you?" he murmured. His tone was so intimate.

The patronising edge to his words shattered whatever remained of his hold over her.

"This should be healed within a few days," she told him, pointing to the bandage as she extricated her other hand from his grip. As she left him, she unsuccessfully tried to put thoughts of him, and the heat of the intimacy between them, as far from her mind as possible.

As darkness began to fall, smoke and haze obscured any real vision of the sunset or whatever beauty it had gifted upon the city that day. All she could see, all she noticed was that the light was suddenly fading, and with it, the rescue effort was slowing down. Most people had been pulled from the rubble, but two people were definitely still trapped. Torches were lit as rescuers gathered around the pair. Freeing them required the delicate removal of a lot of stones and wood. Darkness fell, and the effort to free the two final people persisted on.

Freya stood uncertainly. All the people who had required her attention had been seen to or moved to a Healing Centre. She remained with little to do, watching the line of people wearily passing stones to one another as they cleared the wreckage. The shadows from the torchlight were distorted by the uneven rubble. The scene was eerily mesmerising. A Master-rank Guardian – the highest possible level of Guardian before being assigned to oversee areas of the city – came to stand next to her, surveying the rescue efforts.

"You've done a good job here tonight, Master Kuch," she said to Freya.

Freya inclined her head, accepting the compliment. "I was here when the accident occurred." She gave the Guardian a justification for her being there, even though none was really necessary. It was a habit of years under the Kade rule.

"Not an accident," the Guardian corrected her.

Freya took her eyes from the square and looked at the Guardian in shock. "What?"

The Guardian nodded. "Dark Gods' Followers."

Freya was rendered silent as panic gathered itself around her. The Followers of the Dark Gods hadn't launched an attack of this magnitude in the time that she'd been alive. She'd always thought of them as being a band of crazy anarchists who would occasionally make a half-hearted attack on small settlements within the Third Country. Those attacks would be swiftly rebuffed by the Guardians, and peace would return. For them to have poisoned a shipment of grain and then blown up the central marketplace of Oranis in one day, made them suddenly seem terrifyingly omnipresent. The promise she had been told her whole life, that they were relatively benign, seemed so unfair.

The Guardian interrupted her train of thought. "You should go home."

"But they're still trying to pull out two people." The prospect of leaving two people – two people who needed her help – made her feel more sick than the dust and blood and gore that had surrounded her for the afternoon

"You've been here for hours. You should get some rest," the Guardian told her, more firmly this time.

Although Freya knew the Guardian was correct, she objected in principle to being told when to leave. She was a healer. It was her responsibility to be there for as long as people might require her help. The prospect that the two people who were still trapped might be freed and not immediately receive attention was one she could not abide. However, it wasn't advisable to cross a Guardian, even if it had only been a suggestion. As always, self-preservation and the deeply ingrained instinct to not draw any attention to herself won out. So she mutely left the square. Before she departed, despite herself, she looked once more at Ashtyn. He was still there, helping to shift rubble. She wanted to say something to him, call out and thank him, have one more fragment of conversation with him. But instead, she turned her back on him and quickly walked home.

FOUR

Symon was waiting for her when she walked in the door. She smelled the food before she saw the bowls waiting on the table. The familiarity and quiet of the scene was overwhelming after the chaos and destruction of the marketplace. Symon's anxiety assailed her.

"I heard about the marketplace. Are you all right?" he asked as she closed the door behind her.

"I'm fine," she said, fatigue finally hitting her. Symon gasped as she walked into the full light. Almost curiously, she looked down at her clothes. She was covered in grime and blood. The filth had stained the white of her healer's robes a murky brown. She grimaced. "It's not as bad as it looks." She waved away his concern. Past the point of caring about propriety, she sat at the table, her muscles aching from crouching in odd positions for the whole afternoon. She tore into the food Symon had laid out, so hungry that she didn't even notice until she had downed several mouthfuls that it was tepid. With each bite, her hunger grew, and she realised that she hadn't eaten since the morning. That breakfast seemed like another lifetime ago.

Symon sat next to her, watching her eat. He would have consumed his own dinner long before. It was common that he would eat before her – she often stayed past the end of her shift to look over one or two patients, both to care for their wellbeing and to demonstrate her commitment to her work.

"How did you hear about the marketplace?" she asked once she had sated the initial surge of her hunger. The pace of her eating slowed, and she had enough space between mouthfuls to ask the question.

"The sound of the explosion carried across most of the city. People nearby told others who told others...you know how such things happen," he replied.

"Have the Kade said anything?" she queried between mouthfuls.

"A runner came to the store to tell the Kade official who was being fitted that there had been an incident in the food market. That was all we heard of the message before she left."

"An incident." Freya shook her head at the euphemism. "They would call it that, rather than what actually happened."

"What happened?" His voice was sharp.

Freya waited until she had finished her mouthful before responding. She thought back, reliving for an awful moment the confusion and horror that had pulsed through the very air. She had lived through so much horror that she had thought herself unable to be surprised by violence or gore. And yet, the senselessness of the afternoon's violence had shaken her profoundly.

"At first it seemed it was an accident – a freak occurrence. But it wasn't. It was a deliberate act of the Dark Gods' Followers. I don't know how, but that's what a Guardian Commander told me. They also poisoned a group of people this morning by putting barat in a batch of grain. I can't believe that they managed to do both of those things." She rubbing her eyes tiredly, then cursed as she discovered her filthy fingers had ground dirt into her eyes. Tears stung her.

Symon stared at her with an expression of undisguised shock. Freya wondered if he was thinking the same thing as her: that one reason many Pious had accepted the Kade rule was the understanding that doing so would give them stability and security. The thought that the Kade could not protect Oranis from the violent and random attacks of the Followers of the Dark Gods shook her. It also shook her faith in the Kade's appearance of total competence.

"Do you think that the Followers of the Dark Gods could overthrow the Kade? Are the Kade going to do anything in response?" Symon asked eventually. His eyes were restless, not staying on her but jumping around the room – the beginnings of panic.

She tried to stay calm, tried to concentrate on finishing her dinner. "I don't know. I didn't talk extensively with the Commander who told me – she spoke to me and then dismissed me." Her mouth twisted in bitterness as she thought of the people still trapped, the people she had been ordered to leave.

"Well, I guess the only thing that we can do is wait and see what happens," he said.

She couldn't tell from his tone what exactly he meant by that, and she was too tired to ask further. In any case, she couldn't be certain he would tell her if she did ask.

The bells woke her.

Groaning with fatigue, she nudged Symon awake, and forced herself to get up.

As she dressed, she noticed myriad small bruises and aching muscles from the previous day all across her body. It seemed she hadn't escaped quite as unscathed as she had first thought. Then again, she had sustained far less significant injuries than a great many people, so she supposed she should consider herself fortunate.

Together they walked through the darkened streets to the district square. The atmosphere there was more tense, more suspicious than usual. Everybody must have known about the attack. Even if they didn't know the explosion had been caused by the Followers of the Dark Gods, the prospect that such destruction could have occurred so unexpectedly was a frightening one. Freya couldn't blame them for their anxiety – it seemed unfair that they all worked so hard to escape the persecutory gaze of the Kade only to find their safety threatened by this new aggressor.

The Ordained stood at the front of the square as normal. This morning, though, it was obvious that rather than simply waiting for the square to fill, they were waiting for something else. Each of the three looked expectantly at a Master-rank Guardian who stood next to them watching the throng of people file into the area. That in itself was unusual. Guardians did not normally wear uniforms in the squares – they were meant to be inconspicuous. Certainly, Guardians never stood on the platform.

When the square was full, the Guardian stepped forward and the square, which was already hushed, fell into total silence.

"The incident in the marketplace yesterday was an attack by the Followers of the Dark Gods in an attempt to sow the seeds of chaos and fear into the hearts of the citizens of Oranis, and indeed, the Third Country." He paused to let his words sink in. Freya reflected that he was a good orator; the Kade would likely bring him into their governing body at some point, especially if he was already of Master rank. Despite her own rank of Master, she knew that her Pious birth would forever bar her from the ranks of true command. She wasn't sure if she resented it or was grateful for it. After the ripple of shock had died away, he continued. "For your protection, we must be sure that we can hunt down and eliminate any more of these planned attacks. Therefore, we are implementing a nightly curfew. Its commencement and conclusion will be marked by the bells. Guardian patrols have strict orders to neutralise anybody found outside during the curfew. We cannot guarantee your safety if you disregard this." He paused again, waiting to ensure that the edict and its implications were fully understood. Then he nodded and left the platform so that the Ordained could begin the prayer.

Freya struggled to clear her mind, surprised by the severity of the punishment for breaking curfew. This was a new approach for the Kade, one which sat particularly unpleasantly with her.

Guardian patrols were infamous for the way they harassed Pious on the streets during the first days of the takeover. Those who were suspected of disloyalty were taunted, intimidated, then beaten if they refused to offer a complete and satisfactory subjugation to the Kade. But the Guardians had never outright attacked someone without waiting for an explanation. This was a new level of brutality. It indicated that the Kade was worried. Only what she suspected was a particularly strong infusion of arax root let her slip into the state of mindless focus that meant she could think of the prayers and nothing else.

As Freya walked through Oranis on her way to the Healing Centre, she was acutely and uncomfortably overcome with the sense that the city of her birth, as familiar to her as her own self, was suddenly full of hidden threats. Every shadow concealed a person waiting to attack, every noise dissonant with the city's usual melody, another explosion. It didn't help her jangled nerves that she saw four patrols of Guardians. On the route she took most mornings, it was rare to see more than one. She warily watched them pass by, sensing their readiness, verging on eagerness, for violence. As her eyes were drawn to the weapons hanging by their belts, she shivered, imagining what damage the long, smooth wooden rods, or worse, the cruel sturdiness of the blades, would do to fragile flesh. She wondered how many people would be brought into the Centre with injuries caused by those efficient tools. Averting her eyes from the understated potency of the Guardians' threat, Freya moved through the streets at just under a run, her own imagination tormenting her with the terror of a Guardian patrol suddenly wheeling to focus on her, or the heat and force and noise of another explosion engulfing her.

She arrived at the Centre trembling, her breath coming in shaky fits and starts. She could barely give her name to the Guardian at the door. Her trembling increased when she saw the extra Guardians posted around the building scrutinising her, waiting for her to be deemed a threat, readying themselves for potential action. Gulping in air like someone just pulled from the verge of drowning, she stepped through the atrium and into the foyer, and tilted her head back so that gaze was fixed on the high windows that let in the sunshine throughout the day to fill the space with a constant glow. She squeezed her eyes tightly shut, feeling the serenity of the building, her sanctuary, settle on her. Finally feeling calmer, she moved to the command station.

Leita looked up as she arrived. She appeared tired, with the shadow of fear sitting under the fatigue. Freya wondered if she had gotten much sleep the previous evening, or whether she had been organising the healers to tend the large numbers of wounded who would have come in from the market. "Freya, the Chief Healer wants to see you," was all she said.

The trembling returned to Freya's limbs. She had never been called to the Chief Healer's rooms before; she hadn't heard of anybody ever being called in there. The Chief Healer's place within the Kade leadership made her an extremely powerful person. Under her command, the Healing Centres of Oranis were run with a smoothness and efficiency that had never before been achieved. Her first act once she had been given the title was to abolish the guild system through which Oranis's healers had previously been trained, and through which every other profession was still organised. There were no more master-apprentice relationships for someone wanting to enter the profession. Instead, anybody wishing to be a healer was placed through a system of rotating teachers, learning a little from many. It was a fine system to ensure all healers had a thorough knowledge and were spared the misfortune of having a poor master. Freya herself had been lucky, completing her training as an apprentice under a fine healer. But she knew others who hadn't been so fortunate, having to accept a place with less skilled healers. As a consequence, their healing was substandard and they had very little chance of being placed in good positions or being able to do good work. The Chief Healer also had revolutionised the apothecary training, and all healers were now trained to a higher standard and stricter discipline than ever before. Anybody who did not meet her exacting standards was removed from the ranks, and anybody who hinted at being dissatisfied with the Kade's rule couldn't sneeze without the Chief Healer knowing about it.

Freya walked to the Chief Healer's rooms, her mind racing as she tried to envisage why she was being summoned to speak with this formidable woman. She imagined accusations of continuing Pious beliefs and practices, or of being linked somehow to the explosion at the food market.

As she reached her destination, a near-inability to speak accompanied the violent trembling that overtook her. Her state wasn't helped by the fact that two members of the elite Guardian force who exclusively served the upper echelons of the Kade stood outside the sturdy wooden doors. Their lethality couldn't be missed. It screamed out through the relaxed alertness of their stance and the ruthlessness in their eyes. Freya knew that they would kill her without hesitation or remorse if she was deemed a threat to the Chief Healer, or indeed, the Kade. "I'm Freyanna Kuch. I've been told to come and see the Chief Healer," she told them, forcing the words through lips which felt numb with terror.

For an agonising moment, she felt herself being appraised. Then one of the guards opened the door and stepped aside to let her pass. As she walked through the doorway, and between them, she tried to make herself as small as possible.

The Chief Healer's rooms were lavish beyond anything Freya could have imagined. Rich, brightly coloured rugs covered every inch of the stone floors. Even with shod feet, Freya could feel how thick they were. The windows faced the inner courtyard of the Healing Centre, looking onto the carefully manicured garden. Freya could glimpse the pattern that the flowerbeds, lawns, paths, and trees formed – something she realised could only be seen from this exact perspective. The windows were framed by sky-blue curtains, complementing the reds and purples of the carpets: the three colours of the Kade, representing each of their three gods. Three discreet doorways were set in the wall opposite the windows. Freya wondered how far the Chief Healer's rooms extended.

The walls were lined with the same aegat stone as the now-decimated floor of the marketplace, although these sections of stone had even more bronze veins running through them. Low shelves hugged one wall. Scrolls and books were neatly arranged on them, interspersed with items of the finest quality workmanship. In the moment that Freya allowed herself to look, she glimpsed wooden bowls that were so thin that they were almost translucent, and tiny statues of the Kade gods no taller than a hand span, crafted with such finesse that the expressions on their faces were almost discernible even at this distance. There was more, but Freya's attention was caught by the woman who sat behind a desk at the far end of the room. The top of the desk was made of a huge slab of mezite stone and looked solid and sturdy. No-nonsense. The woman was looking at Freya expectantly. "Healer Kuch." Her voice was soft yet authoritative, and carried clearly across the expanse of the room. Freya tried desperately to control her trembling.

"Yes, my lady?" she asked, using the title of respect for Kade leaders. She offered the Kade salute, placing her hand over her heart and then drawing it down her abdomen. As she stood waiting for the woman to speak again, she surreptitiously ran her finger over the green strip of cloth on her sleeve.

The Chief Healer raised her finger and crooked it, beckoning Freya forward. Shaking so hard that she could barely stand, Freya walked across the great room to stop directly before the desk. The woman looked Freya over with a dissecting eye.

Freya felt as though she was naked under the Chief Healer's gaze, every thought and desire laid bare before this woman's scrutiny, to be leisurely looked through and dissected. She had never met a member of the Kade governance before, and she wondered if they were all like this. The silence stretched so long that Freya thought the Chief Healer would never say anything.

"I've heard a lot about you." The Chief Healer's tone gave nothing away about what exactly she had heard.

Freya didn't know if she wanted a response or not, but felt as though the Chief Healer was waiting for something. "My lady?" she asked uncertainly.

"Mm. Pious background, no family save the man to whom you are joined: Symon, a tailor by trade, and quite a fine one too. Entered into a healer's apprenticeship under the old guild system at age fifteen, finishing in just one year – remarkably quickly, I might add. Remained an official healer through the days of the uprising and Kade ascension. One of the first to declare loyalty to the Kade governance. Rose swiftly through the ranks to become the second person ever to be conferred the rank of Master at the age of twenty. Has served the Kade with dedication and hard work for the past six years." She stated the facts from memory. "You are quite an exceptional healer, Freya."

"Th...thank you, my lady," Freya stammered, surprised by the fact that the woman hadn't used her full name. She briefly thought about the way in which the Chief Healer had glossed over the deaths of her family, but pushed it aside. She half suspected that the woman could read her thoughts and felt it better not to dwell on what some may consider anti-Kade sentiment.

"No need to thank me, Freya. It's a fact." The ghost of what may have been a smile flitted across her face, but it was too quick to clearly discern.

Freya nodded uncertainly.

"You were also present at the marketplace yesterday."

Freya nodded again.

"From all accounts, you did some very fine work there." She was silent for a moment, regarding Freya. Contemplation wove across her features. Seeming to come to a decision, she took an abrupt breath. "How much do you know about the Followers of the Dark Gods, Freya?"

"They seek to create a state of total anarchy," Freya answered hesitantly. "Any form of ordered society is anathema to them, although I believe they are coordinated and ordered in their attempts to undermine society, which must be confusing to them," she added, the words tumbling from her lips before she could wonder if it was wise to make such an observation. The Chief Healer chuckled, evidently agreeing with Freya on that point.

"They've never successfully killed anyone in Oranis…until yesterday." Freya trailed off, uncertain if that would be considered a criticism of the Kate.

"You are quite correct. Especially about their organisation. They are led by a man called Zarech."

Freya dared to ask a question. "How do we know this?"

"You are quick, aren't you?" the Chief Healer murmured, seemingly more to herself than Freya. "Because we captured him." She looked directly at Freya in obvious appraisal.

Freya stared back at her in shock. "But…why would he be in Oranis?" she blurted, completely forgetting the position of the woman to whom she was speaking and the infraction of her informality.

Fortunately, the Chief Healer did not seem to think Freya's question impertinent. "It would appear, to ensure that the attack was executed successfully. A Guardian patrol caught him this morning trying to leave the city. He was badly injured during his capture. He also tried to take some form of poison – we think a combination of barat and something else – but we stopped him from ingesting enough for it to be immediately fatal. He is in this building right now."

"What is going to be done with him?" Freya asked.

"We want him to be healed," the Chief Healer said, as though it were obvious.

"But...why?" Freya's fear totally left her and bafflement rushed to fill the void.

"That is what the Kade has decided," came the firm reply.

"Of course." Freya had overstepped her station. The question returned to her: why had the Chief Healer summoned her?

As if reading her mind, the Chief Healer said, "I've called you here because you are to treat him."

"Me?"

"Did you not hear me when I laid out your rather spectacular skills?" Annoyance crept into the Chief Healer's voice.

"But I'm Pious," Freya pointed out, her fingers again finding the green strip on her robe.

"And? You can't be blamed for the fact that you were born into a particular community. We can only judge you on how you then respond to the situation of your birth. You have served us loyally and worked hard to prove that loyalty. As far as I am concerned, you are not a Pious. You are loyal, disciplined, and the second best healer I have ever met. You are an excellent choice for this task." She tapped her fingers on the top of the desk. "We need him to be healthy for the duration of his imprisonment. He is not to have contact with anything of the outside world. I don't even want him to know what the weather is. He is in his own room, one of the ones we use for quarantine. The entire wing has been cleared. He is quite weak, so you shouldn't need to be concerned for your safety, although he will be restrained at all times, and Guardians will be present outside the room. All you need to do is knock on the door to summon them. Try to avoid any discussion with him, Freya. We don't want him in contact with any more people than is necessary. Sedate him so whoever takes the night duty can't speak with him. I am trusting you with this task. Not even the Guardians are to speak with him. They will only be posted outside his door." The Chief Healer's voice brooked no nonsense or superfluous conversation.

"I will do the best that I can, my lady," Freya promised.

"I know you will. You start immediately. Until such a time as we are satisfied with his condition, you will be with him every day. He is your *only* assignment. Questions?" Something about the brutal efficiency of her orders made Freya feel, bizarrely, that she was a soldier.

Freya couldn't help herself. Curiosity overcame her fear and pushed her to ask one last question. "Who was the other person to reach the rank of Master at twenty?"

She smiled. "Me, of course."

It was clear that the Chief Healer had finished with Freya, so she turned and walked back the length of the room, through the heavy wooden doors, and out through the corridor to meet the leader of the Dark Gods' Followers.

FIVE

The quarantine wing hadn't been full for years. There had been little need for it as the standard of healing had improved dramatically under the firm hand of the Chief Healer. Treatments and preventative measures were now in place that meant no significant outbreaks of virulent diseases had occurred since the Kade takeover. However, even the vigilance and talent of the Chief Healer couldn't entirely prevent people from falling ill with something unpleasant and highly contagious. So the quarantine wing was often occupied by one or two people. But it was a far cry from the first days of Freya's training during the Dual Accord, when almost every room in the wing had been occupied. Walking through the wing had been an unpleasant experience back then, and the apprentices had unanimously attempted to get out of any duty that required them to go near that part of the Healing Centre. As Freya walked through it now, though, it was eerily empty, but for the four Guardians standing outside one door.

Freya walked along the corridor, her steps echoing with a loudness that left her uncomfortable. She wondered if the noise generated by footfall was an added security measure – anyone approaching would be heard well in advance – or if it was just a fortunate coincidence.

When she reached the Guardians, she stood before them, not knowing if she was supposed to introduce herself or simply go in.

Her question was answered when one of the Guardians opened the door for her. "Knock when you need it opened," she advised Freya, her eyes flicking ever so briefly down to the green band on Freya's sleeve as she spoke.

Stubborn resentment made Freya lift her head high and walk past the Guardian as though she were her subordinate, barely acknowledging that the woman had even spoken. It was only when the door closed behind her that she realised the handle had been removed on the inside. "Great," she muttered, looking warily at the man on the bed which was pushed against the far wall. His skin was smooth and sun-darkened. Pain was making his face taut, but lines that suggested a propensity for smiles and laughter framed his eyes. His hair was dark, threaded through with grey, but neatly trimmed. This tidy, calm man was utterly incongruous with the anarchy of the marketplace. The screams of the previous evening echoed in her head as she looked at him. Frowning, she stepped closer. He was awake, looking at her with a keen intelligence. Straps bound his hands and feet to the bed frame, which had been bolted to the floor and wall.

He spoke, making her jump. She could hear pain in his voice, but also humour. "Were you expecting a rabid madman?"

"Well, something like that." She answered reflexively, her healer's instinct to soothe, to build trust overriding the very clear instructions she had just been given.

He chuckled, the warmth and self-awareness in the sound quite unlike her expectations of a mass-murdering lunatic. His chuckle was cut off by a hiss of pain. Freya's training took over and she instinctively crossed the remaining distance to put her hands on him. She was aware of the extent of his injuries almost immediately. His self-control must have been spectacular for him to be so calm given the pain such wounds would cause.

A table of instruments, ingredients for medicines, and bandages lined the wall closest to the high, narrow window. "I guess they want me to do everything, then," she said to herself, glancing over at it.

"Either they want me to die, or you are very good," Zarech said calmly as she concluded her examination. Her initial assessment was correct; his wounds were extensive. That he was so calm and able to converse in the face of such injury was something she had never before encountered.

"Well, I guess we're about to find out."

She moved over to the table and began mixing medicines. This kind of basic work was the kind she hadn't done in quite a while. Master-rank healers had apothecarists to make up the medicines they prescribed. The sheer number of patients, and healers, that Masters were required to oversee made such menial tasks a waste of their time. Yet it was unexpectedly enjoyable for her to do something so fundamental. Her mind fell into a familiar meditative rhythm as she turned on the gas flame to heat the mixture, her hands moved in comfortingly familiar rhythms as she stirred the liquid. The world fell away as she focused on that which she had been born to do. She almost forgot who she was treating. Almost.

Once the mixture was ready, she turned back to Zarech, medicine in hand. "Will you tell me what poisons you took?" she asked him in the casual tone she reserved for stubborn, difficult patients.

He regarded her movements with keen intelligence, his alertness completely undiminished by his injuries or the pain they must have been causing. "What is it worth to you?"

"Nothing. It just makes my job slightly more difficult if I don't know what I'm treating," she replied. She had treated enough patients who played games to know not to offer him any emotional reaction. The trepidation which ebbed and swelled within her at who and what the man before her was, was held in check by the familiarity of this kind of exchange.

He smiled. "Tell me your name, and I'll tell you what I ingested."

Freya knew he was playing with her, but she gave him what he wanted. "My name is healer Kuch."

His smile grew. When he spoke, it was in a soft voice. "Your full name."

She considered his request. The prospect of telling him her full name made her uneasy. But she told herself not to be foolish. It was irrelevant if he knew her name or not. "Freyanna Kuch." Her voice rolled off the bare stone walls, making a mockery of her attempt to speak quietly.

"Well, healer Kuch, the particular draught I took had in it barat flower, a pinch of arax leaves, some leema juice, and of course, erisk venom." His tone was so cordial, conversational. It was as though he were discussing the recipe for a delicious meal rather than a cocktail of poisons, each deadly enough on its own, let alone in combination.

"Why them? And why so many, particularly given none of them are fast acting?" Freya asked, realising she was in danger of breaking the Chief Healer's command to speak with him as little as possible, but she couldn't help herself. It was such a bizarre thing to do.

"That, my dear, is my business. I may tell you in good time, but not today. Now, are you going to administer that delightful-looking draught to me, or shall we see how long it takes before these poisons work their way through my system?" He continued to speak with the same conversational tone. It unnerved her, given the condition she knew his body was in.

She held the cup to his lips and he drank the liquid, not even hesitating for a moment. She wiped his mouth clean of the small amount that had spilled.

"Thank you, that's most decent of you." He smiled kindly at her, his dark eyes twinkling.

As the effects of the sleeping draught took effect, she went back to the table and began work on the antidotes for the poisons in his system. She was almost as good an apothecarist as she was a healer, so it was only a few minutes later that she heard his breathing smooth out into a regularity that only came with sleep, and she was left to work in peace.

For several hours, she mixed and administered the delicate antidotes needed to stop the progress of the various poisons. His considerable physical injuries had been roughly tended already, so her primary focus was on ensuring that he would survive long enough for her to finish treating them.

The walls of the quarantine wing were thicker than average – when the Healing Centre had been built, the wisdom of the day had stated that it offered greater protection from disease. That design meant no sound from outside was audible. It was well after lunch hour when she realised she had not heard the bells that signalled the middle of the day. The respite from those constant reminders of the Kade's expectations on how she lived her life was some recompense for the task of caring for this unsettling man, at least. A rap at the door in the mid-afternoon echoed around the room, startling her as she prepared a delicate medicine – the fifth of the day. She made to cross the room and open the door, but then remembered the handle had been removed.

The door opened. A Guardian stepped into the room, his eyes steadfastly averted from Zarech's bed. "Sorry, healer Kuch, we can't hear anything from outside. You'll need to knock on the door to alert us to anything." She scowled at the suggestion that she hadn't remembered the instruction, but she said nothing.

"I wanted to check on you and make sure everything was all right – you didn't have lunch," the Guardian said. There was no courtesy in his tone, no true concern. The way he spoke was as someone who was perfunctorily checking on her because he had received instructions to do so.

Freya glanced at the sundial positioned on the wall to catch the light from the window and mark the hour, and noted the hour with some surprise. "Yes, I'm fine, thank you for checking. I often get caught up in my work," she said as curtly as she thought she could get away with. She was irritated at being interrupted for something so irrelevant as food. Irritated at the fact that his tone made it clear he didn't care about her wellbeing in the slightest and reminded her that the concern only existed because she was undertaking a task of some value. The Guardian nodded and retreated outside, closing the door and leaving Freya to her work.

It seemed only a short time later that a knock sounded on the door again. Freya irritably waited for it to open.

A first-rank healer Freya hadn't seen before came in.

"What?" She restrained the impulse to snap; her question was rude enough.

"I'm here to relieve you for the night watch."

That she had not even a slight idea of where to place him, no idea in which part of the Centre he usually worked, nor any memory of having worked with him. It worried Freya that she was becoming out of touch with the healers alongside whom she worked. She prided herself on at least knowing the faces of the healers who worked in the Centre, if not their names, too.

"I have instructions to watch over him for the night," he explained.

The Chief Healer had mentioned that someone would watch over Zarech during the evening. However, the idea of a first-rank healer – the lowest level for a full healer – simply watching over him until she could get back in the morning seemed a poor solution.

"That seems inadequate," she said.

"If his condition deteriorates significantly, you will be summoned," he answered.

Freya shrugged, sloughing off her irritation. Something about his manner seemed impertinent given the deference that even Kade healers normally offered her. But she wasn't going to ponder why this particular young man seemed not to be in awe of the famous Freyanna Kuch. In truth, she was relieved at not having to field any questions or admiring looks; even though their absence was unexpectedly strange. She finished preparing another sleeping draught for Zarech. "He'll need this to sleep through the night. Give it to him in one hour," she instructed. "Make sure you keep an eye on the time candle, the bells don't sound in here," she added, before she left him and Zarech.

It was only as she left the building that the intense concentration required to mix the complicated medicines, and the fact that she hadn't eaten, caught up with her. Resolving to ensure she ate lunch the next day, she walked outside into the early evening sunlight. The long rays cast a warm glow onto the city, turning the buildings' walls to liquid gold. A soft breeze played around Freya, and she was grateful for the refreshment it offered. While the Healing Centre was well ventilated due to the building's clever design, the stillness of the quarantine wing and Zarech's room had felt deeply unnatural. After being on her own and working in silence all day, Freya longed for the heat and movement of outside.

As she regarded the area, she felt a jolt to see Ashtyn, the man who had helped her up the previous day, casually leaning on a pillar of the building opposite the Centre. He was looking directly at her, the green of his eyes so vivid that she could make it out even from across the square. When he realised she had seen him, he walked across to her.

"What are you doing here?" she asked him.

"Waiting for you, of course," he replied, as though it were the most natural thing in the world. A smile played on his lips.

"For how long?"

"Oh, a few hours. I wasn't sure when you'd finish, so I made sure to be here all afternoon just to be certain."

"Why?"

"Because I wanted to see you." His smile broadened into an outright grin.

"You realise you could come off as strange," she warned.

He cocked his head, looking far more charming than he had any right to. "Hopefully I've kept to the grand gesture side of that line," he said playfully.

She wanted to not smile at him, but she felt the corners of her mouth moving up involuntarily. "What do you want?" she said, trying to show that she was impervious to his charm.

"Like I said, I wanted to see you. Are you all right after yesterday? You vanished and nobody I asked knew what had happened to you." His demeanour became serious as he looked her up and down in what she could only take to be a careful inspection for any injuries.

"I was dismissed by a Master Guardian." Freya shrugged as though it hadn't bothered her.

"You look tired." There was a sense of concern in the way he said it that left her uncertain how to reply. So she chose irritation.

"Why are you worried about me?" she snapped. She didn't need to be cared for like a small child. And she certainly didn't need someone she had only just met to be acting as though she did.

"That's my business," he said obliquely.

"Well, as you can see, I'm fine. If that's all then..." She stepped away. Hunger and fatigue pounced on her and she stumbled. Instantly, Ashtyn's hand was on her arm, steadying her. "Are you sure about that?" His tone was light but his grip was firm.

"I just didn't have lunch, that's all," she mumbled, annoyed at the utter failure to prove her own point.

"Well then, let's get you something to eat. I won't have you walking home in this state." He didn't give her an option and she didn't object as he guided her to a hana house. Oranis's hana houses almost never closed, feeding Guardians as they changed shift, healers who had to work through the night, and anyone else whose purpose found them hungry and on the streets of the city at odd times of the night or day. Freya smiled at the memory of her own time in a place like this during the brief period when she had been a healer of junior ranking, and she had been required to work on night shifts. Of course, those days were behind her now. Master-rank healers did not work during evenings unless there was a grave problem. Even if they were Pious.

She had never been to this particular hana house before, but it was cosy, lit by gas flames set discreetly into the walls, and furnished with solid tables that were divided from each other by screens affording privacy and quiet. Ashtyn steered her into a seat, then turned to the server. He conferred briefly with the man, exchanging pleasantries and enquiries into one another's health, and then ordered two bowls of broth and hana-grain loaves. She concluded that he came here reasonably often.

"I may pass on the hana," Freya said. "A shipment of grain was poisoned with barat by the Followers of the Dark Gods, and I'm not in the mood to be poisoned," she explained when he looked at her questioningly.

Ashtyn raised an eyebrow as he sat opposite her. "They have been busy, haven't they." Evidently the Kade had ensured that all citizens knew exactly who had been behind the marketplace attack. The announcements at prayer times would have made it easy for them.

"Do you always live in fear like that?" he tilted his head as he looked at her, the slightest challenge in his gaze.

Freya bristled. "It's a perfectly reasonable concern."

"You're a healer. You know how to make the antidote, don't you?"

"That's not really the point," she said, but was prevented from talking further by the arrival of their order.

"Come on, Freyanna. Live a little," he goaded as he tore off a hunk of the hana. He put it in his mouth, his eyes never leaving her as he chewed and swallowed. "Besides, if you must be killed by something, they do make a particularly superb hana."

Reluctantly, she took her own loaf, tore off a small piece and put it in her mouth. He was right; it was delicious. She soaked her next piece in the broth. It felt good as it hit her empty stomach.

"You look much better already," he commented. She stopped eating to glare at him.

He laughed. "Don't worry, I'm sure you can take care of yourself."

Once she had eaten a few more mouthfuls, she said, "So, I'm here and fine. Are you satisfied?"

"For now." His eyes glittered in the light from the lamps as he looked at her intently.

It was an almost identical expression to the intense way he had looked at her the previous afternoon. It had unnerved her then, and it was unnerving her now.

"Did you get those two men out?" she asked, looking to distract him from his scrutiny.

"Eventually. Although one had been so badly hurt that he died soon afterward."

Her mouth tightened into a line of frustration. "If I had been there, I could have helped him," she muttered.

"Nobody could have helped him, save the Gods themselves," Ashtyn told her firmly.

"The Gods?" she challenged, remembering his prayer.

"Well, one of them at least." He smirked.

Freya's eyes widened at his audacity. He noticed her reaction and laughed again.

"This isn't funny," she objected.

"On the contrary. I think it's hilarious." Ashtyn's smirk returned.

"What do you do that makes you so carefree anyway?" There was an obvious bite in her voice as she asked the question. It felt good to be truly brusque with someone, rather than watching herself for any suggestion of insubordination or discontent.

"I'm a gildsmith. I work with mechanics, making things like timepieces, a lot of toys, some jewellery."

"Who do you work for?" Freya was intrigued despite herself. The finesse required to make such things, not to mention the clever mind holding the design as it was brought to realisation, intrigued her. She had only ever really had an aptitude for medicine.

"Myself," he sat back, casually tearing at the loaf of hana.

"You can't be much older than me, though," she exclaimed. Normally, after an apprenticeship was completed, an individual would remain working with their teacher for several years until their skills and fortune enabled them to purchase their own workshop.

"I have twenty-four years," he stated matter-of-factly. "You?"

"I have twenty-two," she admitted.

"And yet you're a Master-rank healer. That normally doesn't happen to people until they reach thirty-five years at least, if ever," he pointed out.

"Well, I guess we're just brilliant people then," she snapped, her irritation returning in the face of his calm, and at the fact that he was correct.

"I guess so." He seemed either to be ignoring or quietly revelling in her irritation.

Fed up with him, Freya snapped, "What do you want with me?"

"To get to know you," he replied, still obnoxiously calm.

"Why?"

"Because you are exceptional. I like exceptional things." He leaned forward. "You have a fire and a fear coexisting within you that intrigues me." When she didn't reply, he added, "I also like puzzles."

She dropped her eyes, unable to hold his gaze.

"Why are *you* here, Freyanna?"

"Because you all but picked me up and carried me in here."

"You're an adult. You could have said no," he pointed out.

"I don't think I had a lot of choice."

"In life you always have a choice." He looked at her, his gaze unerring in its steadiness. "It's just that sometimes the other option isn't particularly appealing. It may be too unpleasant or too tricky. But it is always there. So tell me. Why are you here?"

Freya now did hold his gaze, feeling any glib or quick answers she may have had fade away under the frankness of his look. "I don't know," she admitted finally.

He shrugged, the intense expression melting from his face and being replaced by an amiable smile. "Fair enough."

Freya finished eating and pushed her plate away, amazed that she had eaten it so quickly.

Ashtyn stayed where he was, looking at her, his expression inscrutable. Finally he stood up. "Come on, I'll walk you home." He held out a hand to help her stand.

"Thank you, but it's not necessary." She ignored his hand and slid out from behind the table.

"I'd like to," he said gently.

She was too tired to argue with him. It seemed he would do what he wanted, anyway. "But only to the edge of the district. I'll be fine from there. Besides, you should be sure to get back home by dark. The curfew will be in place."

They walked together through Oranis. As the sun set, the heat drained from the city. Normally Freya quite enjoyed this time of night and the walk back to her home; people were usually languidly enjoying the end of the working day, slowly making their way home, calling out to people they knew. There was a calm and relaxation in the air that made her feel safe and secure. But tonight, an atmosphere that was weighted with concern all but choked the streets. Nobody really talked with each other, people's movements were too swift, too nervous. Everybody was hurrying with a determination that was counter to the delight in living that characterised the citizens of Oranis. And yet, despite all of this, the city was still unimaginably beautiful. On an impulse, she said so to Ashtyn.

"It was planned and built by craftsmen who themselves were inspired by the Gods," he replied.

Her breath caught at his mention of the Gods. She glanced around to make sure nobody could hear, then turned back to him. "Are you insane? It's dangerous for anyone, especially Pious, to talk about the Gods so freely." The Kade had even banned discussion of the gods worshipped by other countries in the Godskissed Continent. As far as they were concerned, the only gods that existed were the Kade three and even the slightest suggestion to the contrary was met with the most severe reprisal.

He seemed to want to argue with her, but thought the better of it. Abruptly, he stopped. "My workshop is up that street," he said, gesturing. He winced.

Freya's healer instincts took over. "What's wrong?"

"It's nothing," he said dismissively, "just my arm."

"The one you hurt yesterday?"

He nodded.

"Stand still," she ordered, moving behind him. She untucked his shirt from the waistband of his trousers, lifting it up so she could see the back of his arm and the curve of his shoulder, where the injury extended.

"If I'd known all I had to do to get a beautiful woman to undress me was to be injured, I'd have done it years ago," he said lightly.

"I'm sure your woman is beautiful," Freya murmured absentmindedly as she examined the bandage.

"I'm unjoined," he said, not using the Pious term of 'bound'. Freya was surprised by his caution, but glad of it, too. He clearly had at least some instinct for self-preservation.

"But you're twenty-four," she exclaimed.

"I've never been in a position to join," he replied.

"You own your own shop," she protested, her fingers probing the bandage. She murmured an apology as he flinched.

"Freyanna, there are better reasons to join than wealth. Why did you get joined?"

Freya's mind flashed back to the days of the Kade takeover. "We'd both finished our apprentice training. We...I...had nobody. My family had died. It was the best choice." She blinked, surprised by her thoughtless honesty. "I don't normally tell people that."

"My family was killed in the takeover, too," he said quietly, all traces of humour or glibness gone. She gently squeezed his arm in the best gesture of comfort and solidarity she could offer. He reached around to put a hand on hers and for long, dangerous moments, they stayed like that. Freya broke the spell by pulling down his shirt. "It's fine, but I'd like to come by tomorrow morning and take a look at it," she said brusquely.

"Would that be an inconvenience?" he asked as he tucked his shirt into his trousers.

"It's the least I can do for the man who fed me," she said.

They resumed walking, moving in an amicable silence. The commonality of having lost their families made her feel more comfortable around him. It lent them a shared sense of understanding, and she knew too well that this easy glibness was the weapon he had chosen to survive in this world. All too soon, they reached the edge of the Pious district, marked by a line of green stones in the road. The stones had been put there when the Kade had taken power. Before, there had been no obvious delineation between the districts at all.

"Where do you live?" she asked, assuming he would give an address in the Pious district. "I can come by in the morning on my way to work.".

"Above my shop."

"What? You should have gone home when we passed by it!"

He put his hands in his pockets. "It's fine. I have the time. And I can't think of anyone I'd rather be with."

She looked down, uncertain what to say in the face of his clear interest in her. She had told him she was joined yet he seemed undeterred. Perhaps he was just naturally flirtatious. But she couldn't quite believe that was true. She didn't want to believe that was true.

"Anyway, I'll see you tomorrow morning." He gave her the address and began to walk away, hands still in his pockets, the very picture of casualness.

"Ashtyn?" Freya called. He turned back, eyebrows raised.

"Thank you for making sure I was all right. I'm unaccustomed to someone being concerned about me like that. I normally take care of myself." She stammered at acknowledging something so vulnerable, blushing for good measure.

He nodded once, then turned and walked back along the way they had come.

Symon was in the living area, writing at the table. "Everything all right?" he asked as he heard her walk in.

"Long day," she answered with a sigh.

"There was a lot of talk about the attack and the curfew. A lot of discontent over the severity of the response. It's not as though any of us have done anything wrong," he called as she took off her shoes.

"You shouldn't talk like that," she said, her bare feet padding across the rugs. While not as luxurious as the rugs in the

Chief Healer's rooms, they were still well made, and better than those in most houses.

"I'm just repeating what I've heard," he replied. He gave no sign of any emotional reaction to her admonishment.

"And what you think?" She poured herself a measure of laarat liquor. She brought it with her to the table and sat next to Symon.

"That bad?" he asked, noticing her unusual choice of drink.

"I've been assigned to care for the leader of the Dark Gods' Followers. He was captured and badly injured," she said, idly examining the glaze on the drinking vessel. She sipped, feeling the kick as the liquor slipped down her throat.

Symon put down the quill and stared at her. "You?" he Incredulity flooded his voice.

She looked up, annoyed. "I am good at what I do, you know."

He was silent for a moment. "I know," he said. It sounded very much as though there was a 'but' which would imminently arrive.

Freya stood up, finishing the drink in one swallow. "I'm going to bed," she snarled, surprised by the unexpected force of her anger at his disbelief, and how it propelled her.

"Do you want food?" he asked, seemingly unperturbed by the heat of her ire.

"I ate on the way home," she answered as she walked out of the room.

SIX

Freya didn't know what time Symon came to bed that night. She was only aware of his presence on the other side of the bed when the bells woke her, like they did every morning. They walked to and from the morning prayers in a silence that Freya maintained through her chilly demeanour. Not that Symon made any attempt to speak to her. It had always been impossible to tell what thoughts traversed Symon's mind. The silence between them was only broken when Symon went to the kitchen to prepare breakfast, as he always did after the morning prayer.

"I have to leave early."

He stopped what he was doing and looked at her in surprise. "Why?"

Something in his manner made her anger from the previous evening blossom once more. "Because I need to study. Make sure that I'm good enough to care for Zarech!" she snapped. She marched out the door, not waiting to see how – or if – he responded.

The cool of the streets chilled her fury. She wondered why she had been so irate over Symon's reaction to her appointment as Zarech's carer. She supposed it wasn't so much his surprise that had upset her as his talk of dissidence. She had worked too hard for too long for him to jeopardise her life and everything she had achieved. But his reaction to learning of her assignation had stung, too, pushing her beyond the limit of her control. Perhaps she owed him an apology for overreacting. The last few days had rivalled the brutality and uncertainty of the days of the takeover, and had left her tightly wound. There were only a few places in Oranis where she could allow her anger free rein. The privacy of her home with Symon was one of them, but that didn't mean it was fair of her to use him as an outlet for her pent-up rage and horror.

The final vestiges of her ire gave her stride added swiftness and she reached Ashtyn's shop quickly. It was a stone building with wooden shutters tightly secured across a display window and a wooden door with a pristine coat of blue paint on it. While she waited for him to answer her knock, she wondered if she would get the chance to see the kind of work that Ashtyn did. If he had his own shop, he would have to be very skilled. It wouldn't have surprised her if he had been conferred the rank of Master within the gildsmith's guild, although she hadn't gotten that impression from him the previous evening. He opened the door and she couldn't stop herself from admiring the way he looked, his shirtsleeves rolled up, his ink-black hair pushed back from his face. His smile, when he saw her, spread across his face like the morning sun, touching every feature. "Good morning, Freyanna," he said, moving aside in an invitation for her to enter.

She smiled in response to his obvious delight at seeing her. "You can call me Freya, you know," she said, stepping into the shop. Despite the darkness of the closed shutters, she could see a few pieces on the shelves – instruments to measure time, some jewellery. She assumed most of his work was commissioned, and likely by clients who had a generous amount of funds at their disposal. A small wooden table stood in the middle of the room, two plain yet comfortable-looking chairs on either side. On the table was a stack of paper and several charcoal sticks. Meetings for commissions would be conducted there, the plans and designs roughly sketched out to the satisfaction of the client. Most of those clients would, of course, be Kade.

"Come upstairs," Ashtyn said, taking a few steps up a flight of stairs set in a recess in the wall next to a corridor.

"Is your workshop back there?" she asked, trying to peer down the hallway.

"Yes, but I've been working for a lot of the night, so it's not tidy," he said absentmindedly, his voice floating down.

"Do you have an apprentice?" she asked as she followed him up the stairs. Someone in his position normally would, but she couldn't see any evidence of another person.

"No. I'm not sure the work I do is suitable for having an apprentice around," he replied as she reached the top. Definitely not a Master, then. Before being conferred the title, an individual had to have taken on an apprentice. It demonstrated a willingness to become part of the guild – to pass on skills and knowledge. It was one of the things that Freya particularly appreciated about the Chief Healer's restructuring of the healers – while Freya did instruct people who were training to be healers, she hadn't been required to take on an apprentice of her own in order to be given a title of recognition. It would have been an enormous restriction on her time, as well as a significant type of responsibility that she simply didn't want.

The stairs opened out into Ashtyn's living area. Large windows lined an entire wall and, unlike the display window downstairs, they were not shuttered. The first rays of the sun crept into the room, and she glimpsed three other doorways. The room was beautiful: timber furniture, thick rugs, a table with another stack of paper on it. Something about the table made her itch to sit and write out the medicines she devised, something she did when she could. However, she rarely took the time to do it properly. Most of her notes were simply quick sketches, dashed out so that she could return to them later. The important information was all in her head, anyway. Yet there was a sense of invitation in Ashtyn's home that made her want to sit down, want to take the time to relax and write down her thoughts.

"Where do you want me?" Ashtyn asked. It was the first moment of uncertainty she had seen in him, scrawled across his face as he watched her take in his home.

"Just sit down anywhere and take your shirt off."

He sat on the edge of a couch.

Hesitantly, Freya put down her healer's bag and laid her hands against his skin. It felt as though she was touching him in a way that was far more intimate than simply as a healer touching her patient. She told herself to not be ridiculous, drawing on her training to slip into professional detachment. She clicked her tongue with impatience. The wound hadn't healed as much as it should have. "Have you done something that might have pulled it?"

"I should rest it, I know," he admitted.

She again made a noise of irritation. "Don't say you should. Just do it," she said gruffly as she put a salve on the wound. "Yes, it stings," she said as he jumped.

She waited for the salve to be absorbed a little before putting on a fresh bandage. "It should be fine, just *don't pull on it*."

He twisted around to look at her. "Thank you. I'll try to be good." His eyes danced with mirth as he tried to keep a straight face.

She made a noise in her throat that indicated a clear disbelief in his capacity or willingness to do so. He laughed, and despite her best efforts, the twinkle in his eyes made her smile back at him.

"What were you making last night?" she asked. She should leave, but the desire to remain speaking with him was too strong to immediately resist.

"Nothing special. A design I've been working on for a while. I can't quite get the mechanics right." He put his shirt back on as he spoke, ruffling his hair as he pulled it over his head.

"What isn't working?"

"It's supposed to be a design to get something to walk. But the gears I need to get the legs to move just haven't been right."

"May I see?" she asked.

"Well, if there were anything to show you, I'd let you see. I got closer last night than I ever have before, but the metals keep bending, or the gears aren't the right size. Inevitably all I'm left with is a lump of twisted metal." His calm frustration intrigued her. "But I can show you some of my finished work, if you'd like?"

At her nod, he crossed the room and opened a wooden cabinet. The cabinet's grain was prominent, the sap lines a dark contrast to the lightness of the wood. She put her fingers on the surface and traced the undulations of the rings, following them along the length of the top. It was curiously hypnotising.

"Do you know anything about wood?" he asked, watching her inspection before he started looking through the cabinet.

"Nothing. I don't even know anything about cloth. All I know is medicine."

"Is that all you've ever done?" He stopped his search to look at her.

"I started my apprenticeship when I was fifteen. I was so fascinated by the body, the way it was put together, could break, could be put back together again. Even in my spare time, all I did was think about medicines and cures, and how to help people who were sick or injured."

"You could think about crafting a bit like medicine. You take pieces that you couldn't possibly expect will ever come together, and you eventually turn them into something whole."

"I suppose. Seems like crafting has a higher success rate, though."

"If my struggles of the last few weeks are anything to go by, I doubt it," he said wryly. "Ah, here it is." He pulled out a tiny metal bird. The attention to detail was exquisite. It looked so life-like that, at first glance, it appeared as though it was about to take off. Freya looked in wonder as Ashtyn's finger brushed some unseen mechanism and it spread its wings as if to fly. "It's amazing," she said softly, not daring to speak more forcefully lest her breath somehow damage the bird.

"Kade officials love these trinkets. They give them to their children, or better yet, have them in their rooms or their houses to show to their friends," Ashtyn said acerbically.

Freya said nothing, enchanted by the pointless beauty of the bird. He was right, though, if the pieces she had seen in Chief Healer's office were anything to go by.

"It's such a waste of your skill," she murmured.

"It could be worse. I know an artist who only paints portraits of Kade figures or paintings depicting Kade magnanimity. And being a writer would be even worse – only ever producing work that venerates the Kade. At least I get to make more or less what I want," he said, the lightness of his tone a counterpoint to the dark truth of which he spoke.

"What's that?" she asked, glimpsing a wink of light on jewels at the back of the cupboard. It took the conversation away from the dangerous criticism of the Kade.

Ashtyn pulled the tray out and set it gently on top of the cabinet. Various hairpins rested on a dark cloth, the fine craftsmanship of their design obvious.

"I made them in memory of my mother on the fifth anniversary of her death. She had the most beautiful hair. It was thick and long and dark. She used to pile it on top of her head; she was so beautiful. I always promised her that once I'd completed my gildsmith's training, I would make her a set of hairpins. I always imagined what a set with bright jewels would look like amid that mass of her hair." He wasn't speaking to her so much as thinking aloud, voicing a memory to which she happened to be privy.

Freya didn't know what to say, so she simply looked at the slender pins. Each was set with stones that Freya suspected were of the highest quality. Some simply had one gem set in their heads; others had a line of tiny stones set along the length of the metal. They were quite exquisite. "She would have been the most envied woman among the Pious to have them," she said softly, remembering the massed ringlets of her own mother's and sister's long hair.

Ashtyn turned to look at her, his reverie broken. "When did you cut your hair?" he asked.

She wondered if she could hear a faint accusatory note in his tone, or if it was simply something that her own mind was putting there.

Self-consciously, she put a hand to the silky locks that brushed her chin, cut in the style that most Kade women favoured.

"When I was sixteen."

"Ah. The takeover."

She nodded. And just like that, they had returned to the dangerous currents of critique and intransigence.

"Did you do it as a sign of your allegiance to our new rulers?" There was definitely a note of bitterness in his tone this time. When she didn't answer, he took her silence – correctly – as a yes.

"Ah well, I don't suppose I can blame you. It's a smart move. Especially as my mother died screaming defiance at Kade gods."

"Mine too, and my sister and father," she whispered.

"I can understand why you cut your hair." He replaced the tray carefully, along with the bird. "Seeing that would be enough to scare anyone into submission."

Stung by his comment, Freya stood up. "Well, if you're done telling me you think I'm a collaborator—"

He interrupted her calmly. "But you are."

She stayed for a moment, rooted to the spot by shock and hurt. "So are you, Ashtyn. I'm at least aware of it." She kept her voice calm, but her hands trembled as she picked up her bag and descended the stairs. She drew the bolt from the door and opened it, hoping that he wouldn't come down to re-lock the store and it would be robbed by an enterprising passer-by.

She stalked irritably through the streets. First Symon, then Ashtyn. Everybody seemed to be critical of her when she was simply trying to survive. The smell of freshly baked goods wafting out of a hana house reminded her that she hadn't eaten breakfast and she detoured inside to buy herself a loaf. She ate it as she walked. It wasn't proper to eat on the streets – while the Kade hadn't passed a law against it, they certainly discouraged it – but she didn't care today. She even revelled in the tiny act of rebellion. Mostly, though, she just wanted to begin work and take her mind off questions of loyalty and betrayal as quickly as possible.

Once her name had been checked off by the Guardians at the entrance of the Healing Centre, she went straight to the quarantine wing. She was still brushing a few crumbs from her uniform as she consulted the first-rank healer who had taken the night shift. "Anything to report?"

"Nothing. The draught you gave him was very strong," he replied.

Her barely subsided anger bubbled over at the criticism in his tone. "Obviously it was strong. I wanted it that way when I made it." Her voice was ice and knives, that of someone who was of a superior rank and wanted to remind their subordinate of that fact. "Go, I'll manage here."

A chuckle from the bed as the first-rank healer left told Freya that Zarech had heard her outburst.

"How long have you been awake?" she asked, going over to his side and placing a cautious hand on his arm to appraise his condition. She reminded herself to make the sleeping draught for that evening stronger; he shouldn't have been awake yet.

"Long enough to wonder why they thought that idiot was to be trusted with guarding me," he said, regarding her with that keen intelligence.

She snorted. "I'm sure he's a perfectly competent healer," she replied, amused despite herself.

"There is a difference between someone who is skilled at their profession and someone who isn't an idiot," he replied, the wit making his voice dry.

"You come from a sect of anarchists. Surely such things make little difference to you." She shifted her focus from the progress of the antidotes to his physical injuries.

"I can still appreciate intelligence when I see it," he said. "Besides, anarchy is as hard to achieve as it is to maintain order when you have only fools to do your bidding."

"Maybe you should give that piece of advice to the Kade," Freya suggested, her assessment complete.

"Are you going to put me to sleep again today?" he asked.

"Your body isn't in as bad shape as yesterday, so I don't have to. I'm going to tend to your other injuries, then bolster the antidotes that are counteracting the poisons. The things I'm going to do may hurt. You may prefer to not feel them."

"But then who would provide you with conversation?" he asked, amusement still in his voice.

"I'm not supposed to converse with you; I'm supposed to treat you," she said, but without the degree of conviction that she should have.

"You can do both at the same time, you know."

"I've been ordered," she protested, but her heart really wasn't in it any more.

"I promise I shan't convert you to my cause to destroy any form of ordered society," he said, pulling his face into an expression of sincerity.

She snorted again as she walked over to the workstation to prepare the salves she wanted. Things had been moved and she let out a growl of frustration. "He *is* an idiot," she said, eliciting another chuckle from Zarech.

"So, Freyanna, are you going put me to sleep?" he asked again.

"Only if you annoy me," she replied, re-arranging the bottles and containers.

A few moments passed before he spoke again. "May I ask you a question?" he said.

"Well, you just did," she replied, her mind more on the task of putting the ingredients back the way she liked them than his question.

"Why are you in a bad mood this morning?"

She paused to look at him. "What makes you think that I'm in a bad mood?"

"Call it a hunch."

"I had a fight with two separate people," she answered after a brief moment of deliberation.

"Two? And the sun's barely up. You must be a busy woman."

"Well, I'm joined to one of them," she replied, turning back to her work, double checking to make sure that everything was set up the way she liked it.

"And the other?"

"Someone I met two days ago at the attack on the marketplace. The attack that I believe you are responsible for, by the way." Saying it reminded her that he had caused that destruction. She had been falling into a flow of conversation that had almost led her to forget who this man was. What he had done. Her hands paused in their movement, and for an awful moment, she was once more staring at the awful ruin of the marketplace.

"I'm sorry that you had to see that." His voice was soft. It sounded as though he genuinely felt that.

"Do you think I would care less if I hadn't been there?" she demanded, glaring at him.

"Perhaps," he replied.

She gave a laugh of contempt and returned to her work. He was silent for a time. She was grateful for that.

But he didn't stay silent forever, and his deep, courteous voice came across the room to her. "If you really think I'm that much of a monster, why not simply kill me? You have the means."

She put down the tool she'd been using. "Because that's not what I was told to do."

"And if you had been ordered to kill me, would you have?" He seemed genuinely curious.

"My business is not one of killing. So I guess we'll never have to find out." She went to his side so she could see his face. "Anyway, if the Kade want you all patched up, it's probably because they have something worse planned for you than a quick death at the hands of a vigilante healer." If she had been expecting him to look afraid, or give any reaction other than a smile, she was disappointed.

"You are Pious, yes?" he asked her after a moment.

She moved back to the workbench. "Yes."

"Why are you so invested in a system that killed those of your people who stood by their Goddess and forces you to humiliate yourselves even now?"

Freya did not answer him as she carried the salve she had just made and several other instruments to his bedside. His question was an uncomfortably astute one, accompanied by a look she could only describe as knowing. She had to work to push away the answers that sprang to her mind, none of which made her like what they suggested about her.

"This may sting," she said to him as she pulled the sheets back.

SEVEN

Freya limited herself to only providing terse responses to Zarech's attempts at conversation for the remainder of the day. Despite her best efforts to dissuade him, the knowing look in his eye remained, unnerving and irritating her with equal measure. He seemed completely unconcerned by her unwillingness to be engaged in conversation, and continued to offer intermittent comments about the weather, Oranis's architecture, the medicine she was using...anything and everything, really. The innocuous nature of his subject matter left her frustrated, and the anger she had so poorly controlled that morning simmered all day.

She again didn't break for lunch. His battered body had become a project that she wanted to fix as quickly as possible, then leave far behind. If she was really as good as people thought she was, she would have him fit for the Kade's purpose in half the time anyone expected, and then she could move on as though she had never met him.

The knowledge that she was going to go home to Symon added to her foul mood as she left the Centre. She was so intent on feeling angry that she almost didn't notice Ashtyn waiting for her. He was leaning languidly against the same pillar of the opposite building as he had been the previous day.

She went over to face him, her arms crossed. "What do you want?" she asked, weary and wary.

"To apologise for this morning." He spread his hands in front of him to emphasise his peaceful intent.

"I'm tired, Ashtyn. I didn't stop for lunch again, I had barely any breakfast. I don't want to play any games." She was too weary even to snap at him, although her ire was certainly roused.

Instead, her words came out almost as a plea, which only contributed further to her poor mood.

He seemed uncertain. The bright green of his eyes – so light in contrast to the dark of his hair – danced as he looked at her, and she could sense the myriad of things he wanted to say but for which he was struggling to find the correct words. Refusing to help him, she stood waiting for him to say something, enjoying his discomfort.

"If you haven't eaten, can I get you something to eat and try to explain?" he eventually asked.

"What's there to explain? You made your opinions clear this morning," she said.

"It's not that simple. Please?" He seemed on the verge of begging. She considered storming off, never seeing him again, forgetting that she had ever met him in the way that she was looking forward to forgetting she had ever met Zarech. But an overwhelming part of her didn't want that.

"Fine," she said, letting him lead the way.

They ended up in the same hana house as the previous day. The food was as delicious as she remembered. The mood, however, was far more awkward. She dipped a chunk of hana in a vegetable paste while she waited for him to speak.

"I'm sorry about this morning," he said finally. "The takeover...it wasn't a pleasant time for anyone."

"Yes," she agreed as he fidgeted in his seat under her gaze. "You don't have ownership of feeling bad about those days, Ashtyn. We all lost people. I don't go around being nasty to others because of it though." She tried, but didn't quite succeed, to keep the annoyance out of her voice. Perhaps the most terrible part of the overthrow was that it had been sudden. Most of Oranis – Freya among them – had woken one day to the sound of the city's bells ringing continuously. Smoke embraced the city – the smoke of the Guardian barracks burning, with the Pious Guardians who would defend the Dual Accord inside. The oily, ashy taste still rested on the back of Freya's tongue, an indelible memory.

Then the executions had started. Overnight, the Guardians loyal to the Kade regime had found highly-ranked figures within the Dual Accord who were either Pious, or those who were Kade and would not support the eradication of the equal governance. They were publicly executed. That, and the threat of the Kade Guardians who had burned alive the Pious alongside whom they had served was enough to keep most people docile. It had been a living atrocity for everybody who had survived through that horror.

"You're right. I'm sorry," he said, his eyes downcast.

"I don't really know what you need to explain about this morning. It was quite self-evident." Her frustration, not only at him, but at everything that had occurred that day, was on the verge of boiling over once more.

"Hear me out?" he pleaded. She took a deep breath and raised her hands, gesturing for him to continue.

"Do you remember during the takeover, once the Kade had seized control, and everybody had to swear allegiance to them?"

"I don't know if this is the place to discuss this sort of thing," she said in an undertone, looking around warily.

"Don't worry. Kade officials don't usually come here, and if they do, they are discreetly steered toward a separate section," he said.

Too tired to put up a show of questioning, protesting and then relenting, she simply answered, "Yes, I remember."

"Do you remember that people who still practised were turned in by fellow Pious who wanted to secure themselves good positions in the new order?"

She nodded. The informant network had aided the Kade's consolidation of power greatly, while leaving the Pious living in fear and suspicion of each other. It had been a terrible time.

"Well, that's what happened to my parents. I was living in a separate quarter to them to be closer to work, so I wasn't there. But from what I heard later, someone reported to the Kade that they heard Pious chants and prayers coming from inside my parents' house. So the Guardians stormed in and pulled them into the street, demanding an explanation. Explanation." He repeated the word, his mouth curling in disgust. She shared the sentiment; nothing anybody said had saved them from a gruesome death. "My mother apparently told them that she would never renounce her belief in the Goddess, nor would she ever stop worshipping her. So they executed my parents then and there. Ever since then I've had a particular disdain for those who sought to ingratiate themselves with the Kade." He shrugged, as though telling the story no longer bothered him, his eyes not quite meeting hers.

"Ashtyn, I'm not a collaborator like that. I would never be. But when I saw the choices that we had, I had to decide what was most likely to keep me alive. My family died for their practices, just like yours, just like a lot of people. Rebellion didn't get them anywhere. All it got them was a death sentence. I just wanted to survive. So I blended in." Her anger at his earlier insinuation still burned but, she sought to explain, to disassociate herself from the kind of person who had killed his family for their own benefit.

"I wouldn't be here if I thought you were the kind of person who would turn in people for their own gain," he assured her, still looking slightly over her shoulder rather than at her face.

"Do you know who did it?" she asked.

"Do you remember you asked me why I hadn't joined?"

She nodded, confusion stilled by her understanding that questions about the takeover often had complicated answers.

"The woman I was in love with also died in the takeover."

She was silent, waiting for him to continue. These stories were common, but each was a unique kind of pain. "We were never together, barring a brief courtship that she broke off, claiming that I wasn't what she was seeking. Yet every time after that when we were around each other, everybody could see the intensity between us. I suppose I always assumed we would end up together, despite everything. She was cruel to me. No, we were cruel to each other. We were young and proud and stupid. And I worshipped her ahead of even the Goddess, entranced by her cruelty and her loveliness. And then..." He shook his head.

"Did you ever tell her how you felt?" Freya was filled with a mix of sadness and curiosity, held by a fascinated kind of horror.

"So often. She never said she felt the same way. I think she enjoyed the power that she had over me. But I always believed that she did care for me. I honestly thought that once we put aside our childish games and grew up, she would say it back to me." He picked at the hana in front of him, breaking off chunks and then crumbling them into a pile on the tabletop.

"So what happened?"

"Like I said, she died, too." He laughed once. The sound was bitter.

"I'm so sorry. She sounds—"

"Awful."

Freya blinked in surprise at his certainty.

"It's all right, it was many years ago. I was utterly in love with her, but that doesn't make her a good person." He shrugged in a perfect show of nonchalance. "Anyway, thinking about that time, it's hard for me. And you remind me of her – the good bits," he added hastily, seeing her expression

"Thank you, I think," she said.

"Don't thank me yet," he cautioned. "She was the one who betrayed my family."

Freya's breath caught in her throat. "What?"

"Yes. Although it didn't serve her very well. She was killed in retaliation by a Pious who didn't appreciate someone turning in one of their own." His mouth was a thin line, distorted by bitterness.

"That's horrible," she said. She didn't know what else she could say. This candour was as intoxicatingly intimate as it was terrifying. Nobody in their society ever spoke with that sort of honesty. To do so was to give ammunition to those who might use it against you to further their own position.

"Horrible?" His tone verged on incredulity.

Exasperation fluttered through her. "Ashtyn, I barely know you. What else do you want from me?" Regardless of how attracted she was to him, she didn't know what he wanted, and even if she did, she wasn't sure that she could give it to him.

"But it feels like I *do* know you." His earnestness was disarming. "Don't you feel the same way?"

The truth was that she did. But she didn't want to admit the strange pull she felt toward him. Not because it felt disrespectful to Symon – she hadn't even thought of Symon during any of the time she had been with Ashtyn – but because of the way in which Ashtyn looked at her: an intense, naked frankness, that made her feel as though she would tell him anything. She was afraid of that. It was so incredibly dangerous. Freya had no intention of allowing someone to make her heart into a weapon to be used against her. Instead of answering, she studied her hana.

"If you don't feel that way, I'm sorry, I won't bother you again."

"Ashtyn, I've known you for three days," she protested weakly. "I've survived six years by not trusting people, by not opening up to people. Three days isn't enough time to do that." What she didn't add, but what she hoped he knew, was that the terrible penalty the Kade imposed on anyone who was caught committing adultery also gave her pause. Families were expected to stay together to raise children in the Kade way. It had been deemed by the Kade that if an individual was unfaithful, they were threatening the very fabric and stability of Kade society. Regardless of the Kade's true motivations – murky as they often were – the penalties imposed upon anybody whose infidelity was uncovered were very public so that their shame could be exposed for all to see. Once, Freya had seen a man stripped naked and made to stand during the entire morning prayer. Freya wondered what had happened to him after. She couldn't imagine he had been allowed to simply return home. The Kade had a way of making such people disappear once they became cautionary tales.

"Are you lonely?" His question brought her out of her reverie.

"I'm joined." It was a reflexive response that completely failed to answer his question.

"Are you joined or bound?" he asked, his eyes catching hers in a moment of perfect intensity.

Her breath caught for a moment. Kade practices brought two people together in a ceremony to join them for life. The Pious bound people together on the same journey. It arose from the belief that binding two souls together created a perfect unity both in love and spirituality. To be bound was to commit yourself entirely to one person. To be joined was to join your resources with another so as to better serve the Kade.

"We were joined in a Kade ceremony," she admitted, her eyes darting away from his green ones in discomfort.

"You don't have to humour me by staying," he said suddenly. His change in approach surprised her.

"You're my patient." She said the first thing that came into her head. She wanted to stay with him. Of course she did.

"Ah well, I'd best let you treat me then." It was difficult to know exactly what he meant by that.

"Ashtyn..." She was so unsure of him. "What did you expect?"

He shrugged. "I want to know you, Freyanna." He caressed her name in a way that was unbearably familiar, made more so by the fact that he now held her gaze. The intimacy of the way he said her name made her shiver.

"Why?"

"Because you ran into an area that was filled with danger without a care or thought for your own safety. Because you are so beautiful that the memory of your face makes me want to recreate the curve of your nose or your lips in my own work. Because you are charming, and I want to know what you have to say on so many things. I guess I'm an artist first and foremost, and something about you just...inspires me." He awkwardly stumbled to a halt and returned his gaze to the pieces of hana he was crumbling.

Freya stared at him, his frankness again rendering her speechless.

"But you don't know me," she eventually said, her voice barely more than a whisper.

"Exactly. I want to."

"What if I'm not what you hope I'll be?"

"What if you are?"

She looked away, unnerved by the conversation. But he refused to look away from her. It seemed that he wasn't going to simply let her avoid answering this question.

She was saved having to reply by the tramp of Guardians' boots. Into the hana house came six or seven Guardians, standing with the easy comfort that suggested the presence of many more nearby. The Guardian nearest the door waited until everybody in the hana house was looking at her before making her announcement: "A curfew is in effect. Everybody has a quarter of an hour to get indoors or be held by Guardian patrols." She waited a beat, allowing the menace emanating from her and the Guardians to fill the small room. The threat of being held was vague enough to leave the imaginations of the people in the hana house substantiating it with all manner of awful things. Then the patrol left, the sharpness of shock hanging in their wake.

"Will you have enough time to get home?" Ashtyn asked, the calm with which he asked the question a contrast to the poorly contained panic exuded by everybody else.

She shook her head, her mind trying to find a way to get herself home safely, in the impossibly short amount of time. "I guess I could..."

He cut her off. "Stay with me. It's fine. They aren't joking, and nobody wants to find out what they'll do if they find you out after the curfew is in place."

Fear of the punishment rendered her compliant. She followed him out of the rapidly emptying hana house. They joined the throng of people moving through the streets. Barely anybody spoke; Freya could only assume shared memories of the takeover were urging people to fulfil a routine they had all hoped they would never revisit.

When they reached his store, Ashtyn unlocked the door and held it open for her. As she stepped inside, the bells began to toll, signalling the final few minutes before the curfew. Freya had thought she couldn't hate the bells with any more purity than she already did, but the strangeness of hearing them at a time that didn't herald the hour made them eerie. It reminded her of the days when sudden curfews were common, and announced with no other herald than the ringing of the bells. At least as markers of the time, they were regular. In this purpose they were darker, more sinister. Freya shivered, drawing her arms around herself. Ashtyn turned from locking the door. "Are you all right?"

"It's fine. It's just...I don't understand why they would do this now."

"Any number of reasons. They may be hunting someone; they may have received a tip off about something. They may simply just want to remind us all that they *can* effect a curfew." He led the way upstairs, lighting the gas lamps as he went.

"If they're doing this to remind us they're in charge, it seems so petty."

He shrugged, and she watched the rise and fall of his broad shoulders. "Well, they've done worse."

Freya fell silent. As she entered his living area, she was suddenly aware of the length of the night ahead, and that she would be spending it completely alone with him. Following on so immediately from the very intense conversation in the hana house, she wasn't sure if she was glad that she was still with him, or afraid of reciprocating his intimacy, especially because half of her did in fact want to.

"Well, not much to do except make ourselves comfortable," he said, moving into another room. His voice floated out to her. "Do you want something to eat?"

"We just ate!"

"Can always eat more." He emerged with a tray of dried and fresh fruits, cheese and biscuits. He set it down on a low table and sat on a lounge nearby. After a moment's hesitation, she sat next to him.

"I *am* sorry about this morning," he said ruefully, arranging himself among the cushions.

"Given what you told me, it's not entirely unexpected," Freya replied.

"It doesn't mean that I have licence to go around being rude to you." He was matter of fact rather than apologetic now, not basting himself with self-pity but stating a truth.

"We haven't lived through normal times. That's affected all of us." She reached across the distance between them and put her hand over his. He smiled sadly.

"Do you ever wish that things were different?" he asked, putting his other hand over hers and squeezing gently. The warmth of his hands chased away the chill that had settled over her at hearing the bells toll.

"Of course. But life isn't so bad now." She relaxed into the cushions. It took her a heartbeat longer than it should have to remove her hand from his.

"What do you wish was different?" He looked at her with an expression not dissimilar to the one with which Zarech had regarded her, as though he were trying to pull her apart and see every piece of her.

As she considered his question, she looked at the way in which the dying rays of sunlight entered the area, warming the wood of the furnishings so that they glowed. It really was a lovely space.

"I wish a lot of things were different. But the one that frustrates me most of all is the fact that I have to always wear a green stripe. It's a constant reminder that someone thinks not only that I'm different, but that the whole world must be made to know that I'm different." She withdrew her hand from his and ran it along the green band on her sleeve.

He chuckled. "That's a modest change."

"Like I said, there are a lot of things that I'd change. But that's the one that I see every day when I get dressed. I suppose I'd also get rid of the bells."

"Why?" He leaned forward, eyebrows raised, the picture of a captive audience.

"Because unless something's wrong, they ring to signal prayer times in the morning and evening. Every single day."

"You don't like your life being controlled like that?"

"Not exactly. I think what I really hate about them is the fact that they tell us that we have to worship. It makes it...disingenuous. I mean, I have to worship the Kade gods, which already isn't something I do by choice. But to me worship and faith, they should be done because you want to do them, because you genuinely believe, not because someone is telling you to." She took a breath, surprised that she was so freely saying things that she barely even allowed herself to think, let alone voice. A part of her whispered to be careful, that this was dangerous. She was revealing exactly the sort of thoughts that she had been worried she would.

Ashtyn was silent, but the quiet was unexpectedly comfortable. Rarely in the company of another person did Freya feel she could relax the rigidity with which she maintained her wariness.

He leaned forward. "Would you mind not moving?"

She obliged, but raised an eyebrow. "Your hands, the way they're resting on your legs...I've been trying to make a figure, and I can't get the hands right. It's the one downside to working alone – nobody to use as an impromptu model. Do you mind if I draw yours? I think I see what I've been missing." There was a simmering excitement in his voice.

Freya nodded her assent out of surprise more than anything else. Of everything he could have asked of her, she hadn't expected that. She resisted the urge to move her hands from where they rested on her thigh.

He walked over to the table, sat on the chair opposite her and selected a piece of charcoal.

"Should I do anything else?" she asked.

"No, you're perfect like that." He sounded like she felt when she was working, only half concentrating on the conversation. His eyes darted between her and the paper in front of him, his hand sometimes moving quickly, sometimes making only a mark on the paper after a long moment of consideration. Freya fell into a half meditative state herself, looking around the room while trying to remain still.

Ashtyn's home had a comfortable atmosphere that made her feel as though she could curl up anywhere and be completely at ease. She wondered how long he had lived there; whether he had gradually moved everything in, acquiring one piece at a time, or if he had always owned all of the lovely pieces of furniture, left to him by the family that had been killed by the woman he had loved.

The light eventually faded entirely, and the area was lit only by the gas flames. Ashtyn put down his charcoal, stretched, and turned up the flames so that they danced higher in their mounts, casting light across the room.

"Finished?" Freya yawned. She was soporific from sitting still for so long. It was the longest period of time that she had spent sitting doing nothing in her recent memory. Normally when she was at home, she was doing more work – reading texts on medicines, writing down her thoughts, occasionally trialling combinations of spices and herbs that she bought from Oranis's spice markets.

"Almost. But I don't want to finish it without the proper lighting." He sat down next to her and picked up a piece of fruit from the platter.

She stifled another yawn.

"You can lie down if you want," he said, shuffling over so that she could spread out. Freya thought about arguing, but in the end her fatigue won out. She stretched out along the couch, her head near him, her feet tucked up, enjoying the softness of the cushions. As though it were completely natural, Ashtyn stroked her head gently, his fingers lightly moving through her hair. Freya made a soft noise of pleasure, enjoying the soothing sensation. She went to say something, but her eyes were too heavy; two long days and countless emotional burdens had worn her out. She fell asleep with his hand tangled in her hair.

EIGHT

She woke alone. Light streamed gently through the windows. A blanket covered her.

Running her fingers through her hair, she got up and looked for Ashtyn. She found a washroom, a kitchen, and his bedroom, all beautifully furnished and stringent in their cleanliness. But she did not discover Ashtyn. She crept downstairs. Not finding him in the store, she went through the corridor she'd seen the previous day. It opened into a workshop. Ashtyn stood at a bench, his concentration entirely focused on the task he was performing. She watched from the doorway, captivated by the intensity of his focus. His eyes were tight with concentration at the same time that his mouth – where her eyes lingered – was slack, his lips slightly parted. Seeing him without any of the expressions that projected the carefree, irreverent joker, was enthralling. A tiny smile suddenly played across his lips. "I'll be done in just a moment, Freyanna," he said. She jumped slightly in surprise. She hadn't thought he'd noticed her.

After a moment, he put down his work, examined it, gave a nod of satisfaction, and crossed the room to her. She wondered what he was doing – it didn't look as though he'd been using any tools, but where he stood blocked her full view of the workbench.

"I would have given you my bed last night, but you fell asleep so quickly and soundly that I didn't want to move you," he said, his eyes roving along her as though trying to gauge how well rested she was.

"It's all right, I slept well. Thank you." A sense of shyness rendered her uncertain of what to say. There didn't seem to be a particular etiquette for how to address someone the morning after they had offered you refuge in their home. Her thoughts stubbornly returned to the way his hand had felt stroking her hair. His calloused fingers had been gentle, soothing. Her gaze fell to the rough stone floor as she remembered the intimacy of the gesture. "What time is it?" she asked, clinging to something mundane and impersonal.

"Sunrise was about an hour ago."

She rubbed her eyes blearily. "I need to go to work," she muttered. She wondered if her absence at the morning prayers would be noticed. As much as it should have worried her, she couldn't quite find the energy to care.

"Do you work on the fifth day?" he asked casually.

"Mostly no, although my current assignment may require me to," she answered, making a mental note to find out if she was required to tend to Zarech on the mandated fifth day of rest. "Surely you'd know that Master-rank healers have the fifth day off."

"Of course. But you seem quite invested in your work," he said.

She didn't know if she was being insulted or complimented. "I should go," she said after an awkward pause.

"Not before you eat," he said sternly, putting his hands on her shoulders, spinning her around and guiding her back upstairs.

"I'm going to be late," she protested, but he ignored her. Fruit and a small grain cake were placed firmly in her hands.

"If you're not going to have lunch, you have to eat in the morning," he lectured, watching her as she bit into the fruit without even looking at what it was.

When he was satisfied that she was actually eating, he allowed her to go back downstairs. "If you do get the day off, come and see me?"

She nodded, pointedly chewing on the grain cake. He laughed at the gesture, and she rolled her eyes as she took another bite. His apparent self-styled mission to look after her should have been insulting, but there was something nice about knowing that someone wanted to look after her. It meant that she did want to see him on the fifth day, even though it was a dangerous idea. He smiled and reached out a hand as if to touch her, holding back at the last minute.

"Thank you for letting me stay last night," she said.

"Of course. You may come here any time, Freya." There was a sincerity in the way he spoke that left her feeling that the offer was a genuine one; she could come to him at any time and he truly would welcome her.

She smiled as she left, at the pleasant start to her day.

As soon as she arrived at the Healing Centre, she summoned a runner. She scrawled a message and sent it to Symon's shop, to let him know the curfew had caught her out but she would be home that night barring anything unexpected. She wondered if he had worried about her. She suspected he wouldn't have. Symon was eminently practical, and would have deduced that Freya hadn't had time to return home. He would have started to be really concerned only if she didn't come home that night. The truth was that she hadn't thought of him that morning until she had reached the Centre. She wondered if she should be concerned that Symon's absence was so unremarkable, even though she had never spent an evening or morning without him in the time since they had been joined.

Once she was outside Zarech's room, she asked one of the Guardians if she was expected to be there the during next day, the day of rest. Ashtyn's request to spend the day with her drove questions of Symon from her mind.

"I don't know, healer Kuch, but I can find out for you, if you'd like," the Guardian offered.

She nodded a brusque affirmative, moving past him and his companion into the room with barely a glance at them.

It was strange. Here, the Guardians were much less threatening. Here, they did her bidding. The previous evening they had seemed to occupy the whole space in the hana house. But here, they were simply shadows on either side of a door, awaiting her command, ordered to protect her.

"Good morning, Freyanna." Zarech was as courteous as he had been for the past two days, an unchanged image of serenity and control.

"Zarech," she answered neutrally, promising herself that she wouldn't engage in unnecessary discussion with him. Her failings on the previous days were, she vowed, the only ones that would transpire over the duration of the time she treated him.

"Tell me, what happened last night that caused such a flutter in my ever-dull night warden?" he asked once she had performed her initial examination.

"They enacted a curfew," she replied, using as few words as possible.

"Ah."

She glanced at him, curious to see if he had anything to add, but his face gave nothing away.

She expected him to keep talking, to persist in questioning her as he had done before. Contrary to her expectation, though, he compliantly opened his mouth for her to administer any medicine, and let her work on his external injuries in complete silence.

The day drew to a close with a lack of comment for which she was grateful. Zarech's extensive injuries were healing well, although they would still require at least another two fivedays before she would consider him healthy enough to leave her care; the damage the poison had wreaked upon his organs, and the extent of the beating he had sustained, especially to his abdomen, were interacting in unusual ways. The salves and medicines he required were delicate, needing to be made fresh and frequently. Only someone with a fine touch and significant experience could properly prepare them.

She moved through the emptying streets toward home. The atmosphere in the normally vibrant city was still uneasy. People glanced at each other suspiciously. It was reminiscent of the days of the takeover, where violence was everywhere, random and brutal. During that time, anybody could have been an undercover Guardian, or a Pious making a stand against the Kade oppression that was symbolic more than it was a meaningful blow against the Kade's consolidation of power. She shivered as she remembered the uncertainty of those days, the way the streets were so dangerous that every walk outside was a game of chance, when encountering violence was a question of when, not if. At least, she reflected, the Kade had ensured that the streets were safe not only from the threat of political violence but from any other crime too. The beggars were provided housing and food every night in exchange for doing work. Those who believed that they could make more through crime than honest work were swiftly apprehended. And as the city had settled down after the takeover, so too had the brutality of the Guardians. For most citizens, though, the memory of the past violence lingered, keeping less-pleasant motives in check. As she remembered, her hand went to the green band of cloth on her sleeve. It wasn't that Freya delighted in the Kade's rule; she had learned to live in safety under it. And in the past few days, that safety had been usurped, leaving uncertainty trailing in its wake.

Symon was sketching at the dining table when she arrived home. "I got your message," he said, barely lifting his eyes from the sheet.

"Sorry I couldn't make it home. I had only just left when the order came." She sat beside him, looking over his shoulder at the sketch. It was a ceremonial dress, for either a joining or an ordainment. As with all of Symon's work, even on paper it was beautiful. "It looks good."

"Hm. Something isn't quite right." He frowned, charcoal stick in hand, scrutinising the image. "Where did you stay?" he asked, eyes still on the page.

"At the house of a friend from the Centre." The lie slipped easily from her tongue. "Maybe make the neckline different?"

Symon considered her recommendation. "So long as you were all right. You're correct. A high collar. Her neck is delicate, so something that encircles it will be perfect." He amended the design with a few deft movements. He had already forgotten the question of where she had stayed the previous night.

"A joining robe?" Freya guessed.

"Yes. For the daughter of Kade officials. She was in the store today talking with her father." He rolled the paper up carefully. "They were discussing whether or not to start asking for inform-ants again."

Freya stiffened. "Why?"

"Because they think cells of the Dark Gods' Followers have been infiltrating Oranis, which is how they managed to blow up the marketplace, and how Zarech got in."

He tied the paper with a cord.

"But surely nobody in the city would work with the Follow-ers. And if there were, somebody would have come forward with some knowledge of it already."

"I can only tell you what I heard today. Even though they seem to forget I'm there a lot of the time, they don't let every-thing slip But I would hazard a guess that they want to prove they're in control – that they're the only ones who can keep us safe. Or they want us to believe that, at least." He went into the kitchen. "Dinner?" he called out to her.

"Yes please." She selected a sheet of paper from the pile Symon had left on the table and idly began to draw. Healers had to be able to draw plants and describe their properties. Freya liked to keep her skills sharp by sketching when she could find the time. One of the hurdles for many healers-in-training was accurately drawing herbs or parts of the body. Despite a lack of natural aptitude, she had worked hard to be able to draw with some degree of finesse, and found it surprisingly enjoyable. Perhaps because of Ashtyn's drawing the previous evening, she felt the impulse to create something of her own.

"How's your patient?" Symon asked from the kitchen. Either he was ignoring the anger he had evoked two days earlier or had forgotten it. Knowing Symon, it had most likely been pushed out of his mind by the intricacies of a particularly elaborate hemline.

"Much better. He'll be completely healed soon – much sooner than I think they expected, given the extent of his injuries," she replied, her hand moving across the page. Part of her was still musing over the prospect of informants once again actively moving through society. Informants like the woman who had gotten Ashtyn's family killed. As far as Freya knew – courtesy of the Kade officials who had Symon make their clothes – the only reason they had not aggressively recruited for the informant network was because it eventually became a way for people to settle scores. The Kade may have ruled through fear, but they had no interest in being taken advantage of to settle the grudges of others.

"What's wrong with him?" Symon asked over the clatter of dishes.

"He'd ingested a lot of poisons, and been severely beaten. I had to stop the poisons, and each required a different antidote. Then I had to tend to the physical injuries, as well as the organ damage the poisons had caused." She paused to examine what she'd drawn. A figure was starting to emerge on the page.

"Sounds complicated." Symon returned to the room with a bowl of stew in each hand. He looked down at the paper. "You need to be more definite with your lines."

"The treatment is complicated," she replied. "A lot of medicines need to be made and administered." She took the bowl he handed to her.

"Are you still experimenting with your own medications?" He sat down and pulled the page across so he could examine her drawing.

"Yes. I was thinking I may go to the spice markets tomorrow to get some more ingredients – I have the fifth day off."

She took a spoonful of stew and made a noise of appreciation. Symon had added moench vegetable to it, one of her favourites. It infused the dish with a rich taste. Symon was a fine tailor and an excellent cook.

"I have to go in to work to make this dress," he said. "They want it ready in four days." He made a face. "Apparently they think I can do anything."

"Well, you are very good," Freya pointed out.

"I can't defy time," he replied, spooning more stew into his mouth.

She shrugged. "Are you going to miss all four prayers?" The caveat to the fifth day of rest was that there were extra prayers. It wasn't strictly necessary to attend all four, but it was strongly advised.

"If I'm asked, I have an exemption. Apparently we have to pray to their gods, except for when they really need a new dress."

His acerbic humour made her chuckle.

"You normally tell me off for saying such a thing," he noted.

Freya set her bowl aside and pulled the paper back in front of her.

"Is everything all right, Freya?" he asked. The genuine concern in his voice startled her. Symon did not normally notice if she was out of sorts.

"It's just been a strange past few days," she said, picking up the charcoal stick and letting her hand flow.

"Ironically enough, now's probably the time when a sense of propriety is most important to keep away unwanted attention," he said. He let out something that was a cross between a breath and a laugh.

"I'm glad you think it's funny," she muttered, moving her hand more quickly now that she had an idea of what she wanted to appear.

On the page appeared walls, a street, doorways, shadows. Symon watched her drawing. "It's quite good," he said. She inclined her head, acknowledging his compliment.

After a few more minutes, he got up. "I need to work on this dress," he said, placing a hand on Freya's shoulder and squeezing it gently before moving into his workroom.

She only dimly heard the snip of shears cutting cloth, almost completely lost in the scene she was creating.

NINE

Freya did not go to see Ashtyn on the day of rest. She had wanted to, but she knew what going back to see him would mean, where it would lead her. She instead followed her usual routine of going to the spice market, attending prayers and tidying around the house. As the days flowed on, she neither saw nor heard from Ashtyn. As much as she was relieved that she didn't have to face that complication, she couldn't keep him from her mind, despite her best efforts.

Zarech continued to make various comments to her, but she adhered to her vow of replying to him with as few words as possible. Slowly he lapsed into silently watching her, those keen eyes tracking her every movement. She tried to pretend that she didn't find his unwavering stare unnerving.

His injuries were almost healed when two fivedays later, she came in to find new wounds all over his body. At first, she thought that they had been caused by him tossing and turning against his restraints in the night, but she realised quickly that there was no way such movements could have caused the deep purple bruises on his side, or the precise cuts on his face and arms. He watched with that same silence as she looked at the injuries at first in puzzlement, then unease.

"What happened?" she asked, uncertain if she wanted her suspicion to be confirmed.

"What do you think happened?" he asked, his face a mask of calm.

"I don't want to play games," she snapped.

"Well then, while you were gone last night, the first-rank healer who has been assigned to watch over me asked me some questions. As you know, he's not a very good healer. But he does show a lot of promise as an interrogator. When I did not give him the responses he desired, he expressed his displeasure...well, you can see how." He sounded as though he were discussing a meal he had eaten the night before.

Freya felt sick. Hers was a duty to protect and to heal, not to facilitate extended harm to someone, regardless of what they had done to others. The fact that she had been deceived, that the healer was in fact not a healer, made it all the worse. That was why she hadn't seen him before. She wanted to scream, to find this imposter and shake him, to march into the Chief Healer's office and demand this brutality cease. But she couldn't do anything. It wasn't her place to question how the Kade treated their prisoners. Indeed, she would have been naïve not to assume this was going to happen. But she hadn't thought she would be made complicit in torture. Going to the Chief Healer would be pointless; she was aware of everything that went on inside her Centres. She had given Freya a very clear instruction: tend to Zarech's injuries. It was almost certain that would extend to those injuries he sustained during interrogation. The extent of Freya's powerlessness was breathtaking.

"Are you all right, Freyanna?" Zarech asked. It was absurd that he was enquiring after her wellbeing after what he had been through.

"I'm fine. I was...just not expecting this," she said, breathing deeply through her nose in an attempt to slow the gallop of her heart.

"Really? You've lived under the governance of the Kade for six years, you've lived through their takeover. A casual beating surprises you?" A hint of scorn crept into his voice, but when she looked at his face, it was as calm as ever. She said nothing. He was right.

"You are very innocent, Freyanna. It is a hard thing to be after all you have endured. It is interesting..."

Freya looked at him to see if he would finish his sentence, but the thoughtful, calculating expression on his face told her that it was futile to expect as much.

She went back to work, trying to put the thoughts of what was being done to him from her mind. She couldn't do anything about it anyway. The absence of any other instruction or explanation from the Chief Healer made it clear that her task was simply to heal the wounds inflicted by his interrogation.

She was at the workstation with her back to him when he spoke again. "Do you think that I am evil, Freyanna?"

She continued working as she replied. "I suppose."

"There is very little pure evil in the world, you know," he said.

"Are you trying to justify your actions to me?" She tried to focus on her work, to pretend that he wasn't really there. To pretend that the Kade hadn't beaten a bound prisoner.

"I wouldn't insult your intelligence," he said. "I was just wondering what you thought about evil."

Freya now put down her tool and turned. "Why?"

"Because you strike me as a woman with interesting opinions. I like interesting things." His expression was unreadable.

Freya's irritation rose, spurred by the unsettling echo to Ashtyn's comment in the hana house so many nights before.

"I am not a thing. I am your healer. And until the job is done, I will act as such. But if you try to make me your play toy, I will drug you so that these last few days of your life are spent asleep," she said as calmly as she could.

"I thought as a healer you were opposed to taking a life, or deliberately harming someone. Surely to heal me so that I may be beaten and eventually killed may be considered evil. You know that last night will not be the only time."

The calmness with which he spoke pushed her temper over the edge. She strode to his bedside and looked down on his serene face. Her hands clenched into fists, her nails dug into her palms. "Do you know what evil is, Zarech? It's blowing up a marketplace to kill innocent civilians. It's poisoning a batch of grain that women and children are going to eat. It doesn't matter what your goal is – those things are inexcusable. Evil is putting your own beliefs above the needs and rights of others who *don't* believe that. It's hurting those people who don't take issue with what you believe, but just happen to believe something different. It's taking a thirteen-year-old girl and dragging her through the streets for her beliefs, dragging her through the streets as she screams for mercy. It's leaving her on the ground like a heap of garbage to die." She abruptly pulled herself back, shocked to find she was panting. Tears stung her eyes.

Zarech looked at her, still completely calm. "Are you still talking about me?"

His calm manner, the innocuous way he asked the question, it was the perfect nudge to send her anger – six years' worth of anger and frustration and grief – into a frothing frenzy.

With a furious scream, she picked up the chair by his bedside and flung it across the room. "I know what you're trying to do, and it won't work. I have lived through too much to be goaded into rebellion by the likes of you." Her scream echoed off the thick stone walls.

"Freyanna, there are bigger things than you and I in this world," Zarech replied, as calm as ever.

She didn't reply, simply drew in a ragged breath and turned away from him so that he wouldn't see the tears as they trickled down her cheeks.

She passed another two fivedays speaking to Zarech as little as possible. She hoped it would upset him, but he seemed content to say nothing. The beatings he sustained every few days left him with injuries so severe that she often had to give him sleeping draughts so that she could attend to them without causing further pain. At least, that was what she told herself. If she were being honest, it was also that with him asleep, she didn't have to feel him scrutinising her. Something about the way he regarded her felt similar to the way the Chief Healer had looked at her, as though she were looking into her very soul, to the secrets known only to her. Her discomfort was not abated by the fact that while she had still not seen Ashtyn, his presence in her thoughts had been near-constant. She knew that she shouldn't be thinking about him, that continuing to see him would be dangerous, but every time she thought she had been able to shake him from her mind, the memory of those beautiful green eyes haunted her.

She couldn't keep Zarech asleep forever, though, and the silence of working only in the one room with the one patient was eroding her ability to ignore him completely.

"Was she your sister?" he asked quietly, one day.

"Who?" she asked. Despite her vow to avoid speaking with him, his question was so unexpected, so without context, that she couldn't help herself.

"The thirteen-year-old girl who was dragged screaming through the streets." He repeated her words back to her with a certain sorrow that seemed too profound to be anything other than genuine.

She wondered how long he had been thinking about it and why he had chosen now to ask. She was taken by surprise: by his question, by his emotion, by the rush of pain the memory brought with it. That surprise made her walk across the room and sit on the chair by his bedside. Her body bowed as she remembered, and her head fell into her waiting hands. "Yes."

"The Kade?" he asked, as though he didn't already know.

She nodded.

"What was she like?"

Freya was silent for a moment. This was a memory she hadn't spoken about in so many years. But recently she'd spoken about a lot of things that she'd buried deep within herself. It was as though somewhere inside her, a dam was cracking and she couldn't do anything to halt it. If anybody else had asked her, she might have been able to give them a lie, or misdirect them somehow. But something about the way in which Zarech stared at her, the way he asked her, made her want to tell him. Perhaps it was because she knew he would never tell anybody else. Head still in hands, she began to speak.

"She was my younger sister. I loved her so much. She was an artist – or she would have been. She was truly gifted by the Goddess. She taught me how to draw." Not even caring at her transgressive use of the Goddess's name, she raised her head, propped her elbows on her knees, and rested her chin across her clasped fingers.

"As soon as she was able to walk, she watched out for me; defended me if someone was mean to me; helped me clean up if I made a mess; shared the blame for punishments, even if I was the only one who'd been bad. I remember once she insisted on being punished for eating a tray of sweets with me, even though she'd been out with my father when they were eaten." Freya gave a sad laugh as the memory embraced her.

"She sounds too good to be true," Zarech commented.

"Oh, Rohana was hard headed, and stubborn. As she became older, truly beautiful, too. When she smiled, it was as though the sun shone. She knew it, though. She used her beauty to get her way all the time. And she was petulant when she didn't get what she wanted. But everybody wanted to make her smile." Frey paused.

"What happened?" he asked, his gazed fixed on her, his expression somewhere between curiosity and anticipation for the horror of the ending.

Freya shook her head at the memory. "She was such a believer. She would pray to the Goddess all the time. When the Kade took over, she was full of indignation at the order to stop worshipping her. I suppose she was still a child. She believed injustice in the world would be fixed by a firm word to the right person. She told anybody who would listen that to not worship the Goddess was the worst thing we could do. One day during the random devotion checks – I don't know if you know about them?"

He nodded.

"Anyway, the Guardians pulled her up and they demanded that she recite the opening prayer for the Kade worship. And instead she called out the prayer to the Goddess."

"She certainly was brave," Zarech murmured.

"Stupid," Freya corrected, a bite in her voice at the anger and sorrow of the memory. "Anyway, if you know about the devotion checks, you know what happened next. They made me watch while they dragged the rest of my family through the streets along with her – they always left one person alive to watch their loved ones suffer."

"My dear Freyanna, I could never tell you how sorry I am that you had to go through it." His melodious voice was filled with a note that made her look at him with curiosity.

"It was the worst day of my life," she said, trying to regain her control, to put all of those feelings and memories back into the place where she had locked them away for so many years. "And here I am talking talk to a mass murderer about it."

"I can assure you, I have no desire to kill anybody. But sometimes our convictions require us to do terrible things," he replied.

She couldn't determine if he was an insane zealot or simply speaking an uncomfortable truth.

"But to do that....no, I would never condone anything like what happened to your sister and parents. And if any of my people were to do such a thing, they would be swiftly executed." There was a suddenly sharp tone to his tone.

"Yours is a harsh justice, Zarech," she said, her words a tired rasp. This talk of vengeance and killing left her feeling empty. Not angry, not sad, just empty.

"Perhaps. But given how we live, and in accordance with what we believe, it is fair." He shrugged, went to raise his arm, and when he found it shackled, clicked his tongue in impatience. "Talking with you makes me forget I wear these dratted chains. Freyanna, my nose is itching terribly, might I trouble you to scratch it?" It was the first time he had indicated discomfort. There was something indescribably human about it that subtly altered the way she saw him. She reached across the distance between them and obliged.

"Thank you greatly."

"You don't speak as though you're a member of a sect that seeks to cause chaos and anarchy," she commented, glad to seize upon the thought and the way it towed her away from remembering.

"There is order and purpose even in chaos and anarchy, my dear," he replied. "But you are correct – I was not born and raised in the mountains."

Freya was intrigued. "Where were you born then?"

"Here, in Oranis. I am Pious by birth."

"What happened?"

"The same thing that happened to you. At the very start of the takeover, my wife and children were dragged through the streets because of our faith. I was made to watch. I could not bear to stay here. So I left. And I found the Dark Gods."

"To lose your children...I can't imagine," Freya said more to herself than to him. Losing her parents and sister had been awful, but the prospect of losing a child was unbearable. In her time as a healer, there had been a handful of occasions when she had been unable to save a child. The grief their parents demonstrated – Kade or Pious, it never made any difference – was unbearable to watch. It made her own suffering look insignificant in comparison.

"Do you have children, Freyanna?"

She shook her head.

"Then you really can't imagine." His voice held no recrimination, just the truth.

"How do you go on?" Her voice was no more than a whisper.

"By leaving that man behind. I imagine I survived in much the same way you did." He closed his eyes.

Freya looked at him, trying to order her thoughts. "Do you ever think about them?" she asked finally.

"Every day." He took a deep breath, and opened his eyes, looking at her. "And what happened to you after your family was dragged through the streets, Freyanna? How did you end up here?"

"I had a choice, I could either live or die. So I chose to live. I became joined, I worked hard. I did everything I had to in order to fit in. What other choice did I have? I didn't want to go to the mountains like you, Zarech."

"But do you still believe?" he asked. Now there was an intensity to his question, as though he had been leading up to it for the many fivedays during which she had tended him.

"Do *you*?" She couldn't deny that she was curious.

"Oh, I've never not believed. I've just chosen to put my faith in a different entity. But you haven't answered my question, Freyanna. Do you still believe in the Goddess's existence? Or when you saw what the Kade did to your sister in the name of their gods, did you become unable to believe that anything could care about you and allow you to suffer so terribly?"

Freya licked her suddenly dry lips. "Yes, I still believe," she whispered, grateful for the fact that no noise could escape the room.

"Why?" he pushed.

When she didn't answer, he asked again.

She swallowed, unwilling to say, lest he think it foolish.

"Freyanna, why?" he asked a third time.

"Because sometimes our faith is tested," she replied.

Zarech's eyes brightened, fixing on her in an incisive way. "Ah, so you are a true believer then," he said, almost more to himself than to her. "Do you know what that means?" The sharpness of his interest felt like a knife's edge.

She shrugged. "It means that I believe the Goddess does exist?"

He fell silent, and remained that way for the rest of the day. She was keenly aware he was still observing her, but she didn't mind so much anymore. Knowing what he had endured made her think of him not as a man who was terrible, but a man who as a result of his experiences had been broken, changed, warped. She bade him a goodnight when her replacement came, feeling her skin crawl as she walked past the ersatz first-rank healer: Zarech's torturer.

As she walked outside she could not help but hope Ashtyn was there waiting for her. But when she looked to the pillars where he had awaited her those fivedays ago, they were empty.

TEN

The day of rest was like any other, filled with obligation and menial tasks. After the first prayer had concluded, Freya went to the spice market. Unlike the general open-air marketplace, this was housed in a great hall reserved for traders. She enjoyed exploring the market, losing herself in its myriad of halls where the light was stained orange by the building's stones. The traders whom she frequented would often put aside ingredients they thought she might find interesting, and it felt as though the expanse of the Godskissed Continent was laid out at her fingertips – strange plants, strange spices, all coming from countries that lived outside the scope of the Kade's rule.

The city had been calm over the many fivedays that had followed the attack in the marketplace, but the draconian actions of the Kade, executed mostly through the Guardians, had endured. There was an air of fear, of expectation. People seemed to be waiting for something else to happen, even if they didn't know what.

Guardians around the building oddly reassured Freya with their presence. As much as they represented violence, they represented a sort of protection, too. They were a part of a known. Despite the uneasy sense of understanding she had created with Zarech, if the Followers once more came into the city to wreak destruction and mayhem, she knew which side she would rather win.

She passed at least an hour, wandering among the stalls, chatting with the merchants, looking at what they had to offer and casually bartering with them over items which she ultimately decided against acquiring. Her fingertips for lingered a particularly long time over a drug that was popular in the Fourth Country; forget-me-not. The Kade disapproved of it and as such, it was all but impossible to acquire in the Third Country. While Freya had no meaningful interest in experiencing whatever forget-me-not had to offer, the shape of the leaves reminded her of the arax plant. She wondered if the two plants were related. Her mind skipped to the experiments she could perform on the drug to investigate such a theory. Ultimately though, she decided to not indulge her curiosity, for today at least. The trader who had set it aside for her promised he would have more across the next few fivedays if she changed her mind.

It was rare that she got the opportunity to speak with people outside the Healing Centre, so she relished the time she spent talking to others. It was a relief to not have to contemplate her work, the political elements that so characterised her world, or worry about saying the wrong thing to the wrong person. Spices and herbs were simple. They were what she knew; they were inoffensive.

She had just exited the hall when the bells for the next prayer rang. Obediently, she moved into the adjacent square. The area was once occupied by a large open pavilion where patrons of the spice market could rest. Freya could still vividly picture the maze of elegant columns, could still remember craning her neck to look up at the dark wooden underside of the roof, where birds would perch, cooing softly and then swooping down to claim crumbs dropped by those enjoying a bite of food. But the pavilion had been hastily removed by the Kade and made into a square for worship to ensure the traders and shoppers prayed with minimal interruption to their business. The sun now beat down on the ground where different patches of colour marked where the timber supports had once been. There was no respite from the day, no opportunity to rest and relax, to chat with friends, to pause and enjoy the day. There was only a place for the mandated prayers.

The Ordained appeared at the top of the square, silently waiting for everybody to finish assembling. Finally, they began chanting. Freya breathed the arax root deeply and lost herself to the rhythm of the prayer.

As the last words of the chant faded, shouts filled the air. Two Guardians roughly held a man who struggled with feeble defiance in their grasp. A third Guardian stood in front of him and screamed, "Why weren't you praying with everybody else?"

Even from her place on the other side of the square, Freya flinched. This sort of public spectacle hadn't been performed for years, but the memories of such unpleasant ordeals came easily flowing back.

"I was!" the man said, trying to break free.

Everyone in the square was watching in sick fascination. Freya trembled, reminded of the way everybody had watched a similar commotion with her own family years before. It wasn't just that people were afraid to avert their gaze, or leave such a scene; they were quietly enthralled by the brutality.

"You weren't. We saw you. Are you an operative for the Dark Gods?" the Guardian shouted, then kneed the man in the stomach. He let out a cry as much of surprise as of pain.

Freya felt nauseated.

"Confess!" the Guardian screamed, slapping him across the head twice. The sound of the impacts rang through the square. The man tried to speak but the Guardian drew her weapon and struck him with the flat of the blade, blood frenzy rolling off her every movement. The metal smashed into his side. Freya could all but feel his ribs crack. The trembling in her limbs became so bad that people were starting to look at her.

It was all too much. Unable to watch any more, Freya pushed her way through the crowd and ran through the streets, blindly navigating her way to the closest safe place she knew. In fact, it was the only safe place she knew. The door was locked, but she pounded on it until Ashtyn opened it. She fell into his arms, half delirious with the memories that the brutality in the square had evoked. She hadn't seen him in so long, but it felt like only the day before that she had slept at his house. He drew her inside and closed the door behind him, wordlessly holding her tightly, the circle of his arms making her feel as though he wanted to protect her from everything bad in the world.

"Do you want to know why I cut my hair?" she sobbed into his chest once she had recovered herself. "Not so that I would fit in with the women of the Kade. I'll never fit in with them. It's because submitting to the laws of the Kade made me unworthy to grow my hair in tribute to the Goddess. My faith wasn't as important as my life." Her voice was harsh, foreign to her own ears.

"What do you mean?" He pushed her back so that he could look into her face.

"As I watched my family dragged through the streets, I screamed out my renunciation of the Goddess. I am not worthy of her anymore." She couldn't look at him as she confessed the extent of her deepest betrayal. Her eyes fell to the rough brown top he wore.

"Do you really think faith is about openly proclaiming a belief?" His grip tightened around her arms.

"But your mother..."

"There is more than one way to show your faith. For my mother, the idea of not living her life in accordance with things that she had been taught were fundamental to her being, was intolerable. For people like you and me, that belief itself is the most important thing. I can't disagree with how my mother died, but I wouldn't die in that way."

"So what would you die for?" she asked, aware of the heat from his body and the way it broke in waves against her skin.

He drew her back to him and cradled her. "What's brought this on?"

It was a moment before she was able to actually tell him what had happened. "It was just like the days of the takeover.

Guardians were beating a man because they claimed he wasn't saying the prayer. I thought those days were gone. I thought that if I went along with what they wanted, they would leave me alone. But nobody's safe."

He rocked her gently from side to side. Symon had never held her like that. They had always been co-survivors, co-habitants, regardless of however they dressed it up with displays of affection. She liked the way that Ashtyn held her. He didn't ask anything of her, he didn't try to make her feel better or reason away her distress; he just let her cry.

"What if I told you it doesn't have to be this way?" he asked after a long time had passed and her tears had finally ceased to flow.

"Who's going to change it?" she challenged from within his arms.

"There are people who would act, who are making plans," he said.

"What do you mean?" Freya heard the wary edge to her voice, even as she tried to keep her voice even.

"That other people share your sentiment."

"How do you know this?" she asked, extracting herself from his grasp so she could look at his face, read whatever truth may be there on the sharp cut of his jaw, or the high arch of his eyebrow. He had alluded to this before, but she hadn't pressed him, afraid of dissidence.

"There are some who want to be able to worship, like in the old days."

"Ashtyn, what are you saying? Are you speaking about a rebel group?"

"If such a group existed, would you be interested in it?"

She noticed that he evaded answering her question. "I won't tell anyone about it if that's what you're afraid of," she said, exasperated. A small part of her noted the callous way in which her horror at the brutal treatment of the man in the square had been so quickly left behind. She wasn't sure if she liked that she could let such suffering slip from her mind so quickly. It was a dark intent that drove such callousness.

"It's a help to know," he admitted.

"So does this group exist?"

He looked at her, thinking for a long moment. "It does."

"Why have I never heard of it?"

"Well, we aren't going to be putting recruitment posters out, are we?" he replied, the hint of a smile touching the corner of his mouth.

"We?" She wondered just how involved he was in this movement.

He shrugged uncomfortably, clearly unwilling to answer the question. "Just think about it?"

She nodded, turning over his words in her mind.

"Do you want something to eat? You still look shaken."

Mutely, she nodded again.

Upstairs, she sat on the couch on which she had slept. He disappeared into one of the other rooms. The area was just as beautiful as she remembered, just as serene. He returned after a moment with a tray of food. Almost unthinkingly, Freya took a piece of cheese and ate it, swallowing without really tasting. Ashtyn watched her carefully, a slight frown on his face.

"Does he know about what happened to your family?" he asked eventually.

"Who? Do you mean Symon?" She picked up another piece of cheese and chewed it. It at least gave her something to do with her hands.

"He's the man you're joined to?"

She nodded.

"Then yes." He took a piece of dried fruit.

"I don't know. I never told him the exact details, but proba-bly." She shrugged, trying to shake off the grief and horror. "He wasn't there that day. But the day afterward, I told him that I would join with him. We'd been sweethearts for the last two or so years before that. He'd been courting me and wanted us to become bound even before the takeover. I'd been uncertain about it. The day when..." She paused, collected herself, and went on. "I figured if I'd publicly aligned myself with the Kade, I may as well live the life they wanted me to lead. I went to him and we were joined not long after I buried my parents. In the Kade way, of course."

"Have you been punishing yourself for the last six years?" he asked. She could see the empathy written across his face.

"I haven't thought of it like that." She looked away. She didn't need his compassion.

"Do you enjoy living like this?"

"Like what?"

"Under the rule of a group that not only prohibits you from worshipping something you actually believe in, but also forces you to worship something you actively don't want to. Being joined, not bound, to someone who doesn't make you happy. To a man who is content to live with you under the yoke of a group of people who will never let you amount to anything significant in life, and who never wants more for you than this." He took one of her hands in his, gently running his thumb over the back of her hand. "Are you content to stay with someone who will never move heaven and earth so that you, and any children you may have, will live in a world where you can worship the Goddess in all her might because that is what you believe in with every fibre of your being?"

She didn't move. "What makes you think that Symon doesn't make me happy?"

"Are you?" His hands tightened on hers. They were strong and warm; she could feel the individual calluses on his fingers. Symon's hands were calloused too, but only around the very tips of his fingers.

She didn't answer his question. She couldn't. She didn't know the answer, or want to admit the answer to herself.

Ashtyn leaned forward and kissed her gently, his mouth hot against hers. For a moment she indulged herself, enjoying the feeling of his lips against hers, leaning into him and his kiss. Then she pulled away. She immediately missed the sensation of his mouth on her own.

"Sorry, I thought—"

"No, I'm sorry. I'm probably sending you the wrong messages, turning up on your doorstep after this long and in such a state." She blushed, not meeting his eyes. She was afraid that if she did, he would see just how badly she wanted him to kiss her again. "I should..." She reluctantly pulled her hand from his and stood up. He stood as well, clearly flustered.

"Freya, I didn't mean..." He seemed completely unsure of what to say.

"It's fine, don't worry about it." Freya gathered her things and practically ran down the stairs and out of the store, her thoughts and feelings in complete disarray.

Unwilling to go back to Symon, she returned to the Healing Centre. The Guardians outside Zarech's door were clearly surprised to see her, but said nothing, merely opening the door and stepping aside for her to enter. The healer who was minding Zarech for the day quickly left the room, not brave enough to question why Freya was there on the day of rest. This was not the tormentor who masqueraded as a healer, but instead a second-rank healer simply assigned to watch over Zarech's condition.

Zarech was staring contemplatively at the ceiling. "Shouldn't you be at home, Freyanna?" He didn't seem surprised to see her.

"I wanted to check on you," she replied.

He let out a single laugh. "Do you lie this badly to everybody?"

She went to protest, then gave up, and pulled the chair to his bedside so she could sit next to him. "At least I know when I talk to you that my secrets will go to the grave," she said resignedly. He laughed.

"Come now, Freyanna. What's bothering you?" Those dark, incisive eyes fixed intently upon her.

She felt torn, wanting desperately to tell someone, while also aware that by telling him, she was giving in to whatever power game he was playing with her. The strain of wanting so badly to talk about what she was going through was ultimately too great. "Everything is so complicated."

"In what way?" His rich voice was so gentle. Some quality in his tone reminded her of her father, of the times when she would go to him when something had gone wrong and he would sit her down and they would work out together what to do to make it right. She missed him so acutely. Even after all this time, when she really allowed herself to think about him, her grief was still just as raw.

"After my family was killed, I agreed to become joined with the man who had been courting me: Symon. He's a tailor. We've lived together under Kade governance, each working our way to successful positions – to safety. Even though he's spoken out against the Kade recently to me, I guess we've always understood that this is something we just had to deal with. And I thought this was what I wanted – to survive and make the best out of what had happened. Then when I was at the market when it was attacked, I met someone, and he's made me question everything. And talking with you has made that worse. And I don't know what I want anymore." She looked at him, imploring him to understand what she was going through.

Zarech was silent for a moment. "You've been joined – not bound – for nearly six years then?" he asked. She nodded. "Why have you not had children?"

When she didn't answer, he asked a different question. "Have you tried?"

"Yes..." she began reluctantly. The efforts had been few and far between, but they had certainly taken place.

"But?" When she didn't reply, he asked, "Do you want children, Freyanna?"

"Of course I do."

"What aren't you telling me, Freyanna?"

She bit her lip. "I've been taking madras leaves."

He raised his head to look at her better. "Does this Symon know?" There was a sternness to his voice. She shook her head.

"Why?"

"I don't know." She spoke so quietly that even the echoey room, the words barely sounded.

"Freyanna, you've been secretly rendering yourself unable to have children. You can't not know your reason."

"Because this isn't the world in which I want to have a child," she said eventually.

"Do you love him?"

"Symon? I...don't know. Is it enough to love him?"

"I can't answer that for you." He shrugged, making his chains rattle.

"I wish you'd just tell me what you're thinking." She realised as soon as she spoke that she had crossed a line.

"Why did you come here, Freyanna?" he asked after a moment, his eyes boring into her. "Don't you have friends to talk to about this?" He sounded suddenly bored. It was the cruellest thing he could have said to her.

She thought of the people she called friends: acquaintances who she saw every now and again, people she'd trained with and swiftly eclipsed, or friends from childhood who had not quite as successfully integrated into the Kade's way of life. The truth was that underneath their pleasantries, she knew that there was no real friendship there. There was only resentment of her skill, and recognition that remaining close to her may provide a benefit at some time. That, or a quiet judgment of her behaviour following the takeover, tempered only by the fact that she was still a Pious and thus a member of the community, however much she had tried to behave otherwise.

"I think you just enjoy being cruel," she accused him.

"I think you enjoy believing that I'm something that you want me to be," he replied. "Never forget who I am. I am not some sick animal you're nursing back to health. I am someone who you are nursing back to health so that I can be beaten and interrogated all over again. I will give you truthful answers, but don't be shocked when you don't like what I have to say."

Freya fought a desire to cry. He was correct. She didn't know what she had expected in coming to him, but she should have known that he wouldn't hold her hand and tell her everything would be all right. To her horror, she felt tears well, and she fought to keep them back.

"I've upset you."

She sat silent, battling her tears.

"Freyanna, I decided six years ago that you can either live in the world that surrounds you, or you can fight for the world you want." His voice was gentle. The cold, cruel man was suddenly gone.

"Surely life isn't that simple," she finally choked out.

"If you truly felt as though I didn't understand you, you wouldn't be here speaking with me," he pointed out.

"I'm sorry, I should go."

"Well, it's hardly as though I'm going anywhere." He raised his arms as much as he could, making the chains clank pointedly. A humorous smile twitched along his lips then he sobered. "Do think on what I've said."

Silently, she nodded and left.

She emerged from the Healing Centre as people were returning from the third prayer of the day. Their chatter filled the streets. But they were careful not to speak too loudly, or walk too far from their companions. She had noticed it at the market too, although it had been less obvious, hidden by the lively negotiations.

As she made her way through the throng, she rebuked herself for becoming ensnared by Zarech's questions and games. Anger at herself for letting his quiet charm yet again draw her into conversation was only eclipsed by her anger at having let his comments get to her. The worst part was that those comments had the undeniable ring of truth to them, which was why they pricked her so painfully and burrowed under her skin with incessant intensity. She hated that she craved some kind of approval from him – no, not approval: absolution. He'd done far worse things than her, and yet she wanted him to tell her that she hadn't made the wrong choices. The truly sad thing was that this sense of a bond with Zarech only spoke to how lonely she was. That truth settled across her like a cold cape.

On her way home she passed the square that had been hastily converted to serve as a makeshift replacement for the general market. It didn't have the beauty of the actual marketplace, but the atmosphere was still there: people negotiating, arguing, stealing a moment to quickly eat one of the delicacies on offer. Amid the fear that muted the vibrancy of Oranis, life had persisted in the way that it inevitably did, and seeing it took the edge off the chill around her heart.

Symon was muttering irritably to himself when she arrived home and stood at the threshold to his workroom.

"I thought you were going to be in the shop," she said, standing in the doorway and surveying the work he was doing. A robe sat on a mannequin, almost completed. It was a shimmering sea of blues and greens, the skirt made of layers upon layers of material. "It looks stunning."

"Only if you don't know what it's supposed to look like. Another tailor did the skirt last night because I needed it done by today and of course they didn't do it right. The skirt needs to sit more flat. It's a ceremonial robe, not a tent," he growled from his position, kneeling on the floor. Symon was a perfectionist. While most other tailors got others to make disparate elements of garments, Symon would fanatically refuse to allow any other person to work on his clothes, knowing – correctly – that they wouldn't do it to his specifications and standards. It was only in cases when there was a truly pressing time limit that he would take assistance from another tailor, and even then, only certain parts. Freya could see what he meant, but only because she had been around him for so long. To anybody else, the robe would have been fine. Then again, Symon's reputation was that of one of the finest tailors in Oranis, and it was only through being so pedantic that he had acquired it.

"Have you tried—" she began, but he cut her off.

"I've tried everything. Short of tearing every piece of material off and starting again, this is as good as it will ever be."

She fell silent, staying in the room watching him for a few more moments. When it became apparent that he had all but forgotten she was still there, she left to finish reading a book on the creation and properties of compounds for the treatment of coughing disease.

She went out for the fourth prayer of the day and came back, food in hand from one of the nearby street stalls. She knew Symon would be too busy to cook, and likely too busy to even think about food. She brought the spiced wrap in to him, staying to observe as he sewed one of the sleeves on. She watched his hands work, their dexterity unmatched. His fingers were long and deft, but they had always spent more time touching fabric than her. It was something she had never minded, had even preferred. She had never thought there was a need for anything else.

The events of the day preyed on her mind. She couldn't stop thinking about the heat that had shot through her with Ashtyn's kiss.

"I'm going to bed soon," she said to Symon. "Did you want to join me?" Her tone indicated exactly what she had in mind.

Symon didn't even look up. "I need to keep working," he said, too focused on what he was doing to pay her, or what she had offered him, any attention.

Humiliation doused her as she made her way to the bedroom, wishing with a desperation that she had never before felt in nearly six years with Symon, that she wasn't alone.

ELEVEN

Freya and Symon did not speak the next morning. They orbited one another as they prepared for their respective days of work, never touching, barely communicating other than with the most meagre of gestures. It was a silence typical for the two of them. Long periods would often pass without them talking, although it was something she had only begun to notice recently. Today, Symon's preoccupation with the robe was total, while Freya simply found that she had nothing to say to him. A few times she opened her mouth to say something, but then whatever she had thought of always seemed to be too uninteresting for her to break his concentration. She didn't think he even noticed when she left for work.

Zarech appeared asleep.

"I know you're awake," she said. He smiled, though his eyes remained shut.

"May I ask a question?" he asked.

Moving the bedclothes aside so she could better check his injuries, she made a noise of assent.

"Did Symon worry about you when the curfew was abruptly announced all those fivedays ago? If I've counted correctly, I think it was about two and a half cycles." She was impressed that he knew how long he had been incarcerated. Most people who were in the Centre for an extended period quickly lost track of time.

"I don't believe so. Why?" She pulled the covers back. "How's the pain?"

"The pain is far less, thank you. It merely occurred to me to wonder what sort of a man he is."

"Why?" She quickly redressed the bandages on his most recent wounds. Carefully, she pushed aside thoughts of how those injuries had appeared. She had learned it was easier that way.

"Because you are a curious individual, Freyanna. A description of the man to whom you are joined gives me a better insight into you."

Freya thought for a moment. "Symon is a tailor. He's a very good tailor, in fact."

"That's telling me what he does, not what he's like," Zarech pointed out.

"Symon is...quiet, hard working. He cooks very well."

"Do you love him?" Even though he had asked it the previous day, it still surprised her.

"We're joined," she said reflexively.

"Not bound," he said, pointing out the significance of the difference. "He sounds like someone I'd hire, not someone with whom I would want to share my life."

"Why do you even want to know about me?" Freya moved to the workstation and selected the vials she wanted.

"Well, you are the only person with whom I can speak. Even so, it is curious that you have been placed in my path." He struggled against his manacles to sit up.

"What do you mean?" She was intrigued, even though a part of her warned that this was likely another of his games.

"Have you ever wondered whether or not the Gods are real, Freyanna?" Zarech asked. It seemed a tangent, but Zarech's tangents were always a part of some broader point. Granted, it was generally an uncomfortably astute point, but it also made it easy to be drawn into what he had to say.

Freya paused in her task. "It is not for me to question that which I don't understand," she replied as she resumed mixing the medicine.

"I thought you didn't like zealots." He sounded amused.

"I'm not a zealot."

A teasing note crept into his voice. "So what are you then?"

"A believer?"

"A believer who has never seen proof of the Gods' existence?"

His comment caused her to again pause her work. "When I was younger I sometimes thought..." Freya caught herself, shook her head, and continued her work.

"Go on," Zarech prompted.

"I suppose I sometimes thought that I had abilities beyond the ordinary. But that's silly, surely. All children think things like that, especially given the wild stories of what lies in the First Country, and the knowledge the monks of the Fourth Country wield that some say looks like magic." She brought the mixture to his bedside and held it to his lips.

He drank. Once he had finished, he looked at her with a calm certainty. "What if I told you that the Gods were as real as you or I?"

Freya snorted. "How do you know?"

"The same way you do. Because there are moments during prayer when I feel that to whom I pray connects with me, gives back to me even." He was utterly undeterred by her scepticism.

"Even if that has happened to me, it hasn't happened for years," she said slowly, considering what exactly he was saying.

"And when was the last time you prayed with any real conviction?" Zarech asked.

She didn't answer. He clearly knew what her response would be.

"Freyanna, why do you think you are such a good healer?"

"Natural talent and hard work?" she suggested weakly.

"Your sister, you said she was deeply devout?"

Freya nodded.

"You also said she was the most talented artist you'd ever come across. What was it that you said? 'Gifted by the Goddess herself'?"

Reluctantly, Freya nodded again.

"Do you really think that the two of you being outstanding in your chosen areas, *and* both believers, is a coincidence?"

Freya shrugged helplessly, half of her wanting to believe him, the other half telling her that he was completely insane and finally, here was the proof for which she'd been waiting.

"What are you even saying?" She had completely forgotten the next medicine she'd wanted to mix. Instead, she pulled up the chair to sit next to him. She told herself she would reserve her judgment until he had finished speaking, that she should at least hear him out.

"That the strongest believers are able to literally touch the Gods. And that in touching them, they come away with some of the abilities of the Gods themselves. The stories of people in the First Country who can bend the world around them to their whim, and of the monks from the Fourth Country – those are more than mere stories, despite what the Kade want you to believe about the world outside our own land." He spoke not just with the excitement of a true believer, but also with the certainty of someone who has experienced something completely extraordinary.

"But...surely if those things were real, we'd know about it," Freya protested.

"How many people do you think genuinely believe down to their very core?"

"I don't know...I always assumed a lot."

"*Think*, Freyanna. People live according to customs, not according to belief. There are only a few who genuinely believe, and as such, only a few who can genuinely commune with those whose existence transcends our own." He went to lean forward, then made a noise of irritation as his manacles restrained him.

He arranged himself as best he could. "Besides, do you not think that the Gods have politics of their own?"

"What?"

"The Kade. Have you not heard the stories of the spectacular abilities of those members within the Kade leadership? They are all believers. And they all do the bidding of their three gods in exchange for the power they are granted, which in turn enables them to rule in luxury and comfort. It is a very mutually agreeable relationship."

Freya thought of the Chief Healer, of the legends surrounding her abilities. "But what do the Gods get in exchange?"

"Power. What do you think prayer is if not power? Pure and concentrated energy. Even someone who doesn't believe in the way that you or I do, when focusing their thoughts on a particular god, gives them some form of power."

"How do you know this?" Freya wanted to refute him entirely, but too much of what he was saying made sense.

"Did you know what my position used to be before the Kade takeover?" he asked, clearly aware that she did not know. She shook her head.

"I was an Ordained of the Pious – one of the Goddess's Children."

Freya's eyebrows rose. All of the Pious Ordained had been slaughtered by the Kade following their takeover. "How did you escape?"

"Luck, mostly. I was out at the time that they came for me. I returned just in time to see them killing my family. I fled before they saw me." His face tightened into an unreadable dark emotion.

"So yes, I know a great deal about the ways of the Gods and mortals. And I have had the great privilege to experience this connection myself during my own prayers to my gods, of course. How do I know about the Kade's motivations for the takeover?

Why, through intelligence from the offices of the Kade themselves."

She gave a shaky laugh as she saw where his point was headed. "Are you justifying everything you've done, all of those deaths for which you are responsible, by saying that communication with the Dark Gods compelled you to do those things once you had forsaken the Goddess?"

"It is not for me to question that which I don't understand," he replied. His eyes sparkled with something akin to mockery as he returned her words to her.

"My beliefs don't require me to burn the whole world down," she hissed.

"And what if that were truly the desire of the Goddess?" he challenged. When she hesitated, a gleam of triumph appeared in his eyes.

"Freyanna." He said her name tenderly, paternally. "You don't have to believe me, but surely you know that you haven't been praying to an entity that does not exist?" He asked the question like any parent, already knowing the answer.

"What am I supposed to do then?" Thoughts and beliefs she hadn't allowed herself to feel in six long years swirled within her, threatening to overwhelm the person she had constructed to survive the world of the Kade.

"Does it not change the way you view the Kade?" he challenged. "They force you to pray to their gods to give them strength – that's what prayer and ritual do. In forbidding you from praying to the Goddess, they deprive her of strength. You kill her by forgetting her while empowering the gods of the Kade. And of course the Kade elite. They are rewarded with skills and abilities for their devotion. So devout are they that they would change our very social fabric in the pursuit of their gods' empowerment – and their own comfort, of course." He smiled as he spoke, a savage smile that distorted his face.

"You're manipulating me," she accused, unwilling to give him the satisfaction of seeing that his words had affected her.

He gave a little shrug. "It remains the truth, however it may affect you."

"I haven't forgotten Her," she said after a long moment of silence had passed between them.

"Oh?" His tone was at once sceptical and inviting.

She was still for a moment. Uncertainty and trepidation at putting voice to the deepest truth of them all warred with a desire to contradict what he had condemned her for. He was silent, clearly aware that it was only a matter of time until she cracked.

"If I cook, I'm preparing a ritual feast. If I walk through the market, I'm going to worship. She is infused into every part of my life. I didn't renounce her; how I could I? She shapes my very being." Voicing the completely heretical truth made her tremble. Her hand went to the green stripe on her sleeve, plucking and tugging at it desperately.

"How long have you hidden that, deep inside you?" He didn't give her the opportunity to answer. "The truth is like water. It erodes slowly, patiently waiting until it has worn away at whatever seeks to constrain it. At that point, all it takes is the slightest pressure to let it come pouring out. Water will always have its way, Freyanna, like the truth that lies within us."

"Who knows about this...connection between people and the gods?" Freya stood, seeking to give herself space to think. She was still struggling to comprehend that she had just uttered something that, if overheard, would ruin her.

"I honestly couldn't tell you. Anyone who is Ordained does, but beyond that, I couldn't say for certain," he said.

She suspected he was keeping back an educated guess. "I...I need some time to think about this." She looked at the high window, wanting to get out, away from the constraining, silent walls of the cell.

"All I want is for you to consider it," he said.

"I have to go," she stammered.

"Take the day to think." He sounded generous; bizarre given that he was the prisoner. Yet his suggestion was exactly what she wanted to do.

She knocked on the door, waiting impatiently for the Guardian to open it.

"Freyanna?" Zarech called.

She turned.

"It's all right to be scared," he said, his voice gentle.

The door opened before she could reply. She wheeled around to address the Guardian. "I feel unwell. I'm going to go home," she said curtly, in the tone of command and certainty she had learned to adopt.

He nodded, believing the lie without a second's hesitation. And why shouldn't he? Freyanna Kuch's reputation was one of utter professionalism and loyalty.

"I'll be back in the morning," she informed him before walking away.

Once she was out of sight of the Guardians, she all but ran down the corridor, out through the atrium and foyer to the heat and open air. She was a few minutes from the Centre before she allowed herself to begin shaking, taking deep, gasping breaths in a bid to calm herself. All around her, the noise and movement of the city pulsed. However subdued that life beat might have been due to fear and restrictions, it was still her beautiful Oranis, a city where for hundreds of years, scholars, artists, and tradespeople had met in peace. Where creativity had been allowed to flourish, where a thousand differing ideas had not only bloomed, but been encouraged to do so. Until six years ago. It was remarkable to her that the people still lived their lives so cheerfully, with so little interruption. In so many ways, the city's resilience and tarnished beauty made her love it even more. Simply standing in the street soothed her, and as she leaned against the wall of a building in an alleyway, she began to regain control of herself. She began to walk. As she allowed her feet to guide her, she considered what Zarech had said. She knew he was playing with her; she even suspected that he was manipulating her to fulfil some dark intent that he had conjured. But she had no idea what end he was seeking, and that, among anything else, kept her intrigued, even though she could barely admit it to herself.

Suddenly, she was standing at the edge of the marketplace that only a few cycles ago had been a thriving square. The area had been cleared of rubble, but was still unusable. The floor had huge chunks missing, and the seats that had run through it were almost completely collapsed. A group of workers were sorting through a neat pile of stones that had been carefully swept to one side. A Guardian was posted nearby, watching their efforts impassively. Freya was almost transfixed by the methodical repetition of the movements of the workers.

"Do you know what they're doing?"

The voice at her side made her jump, but she was somehow unsurprised when she turned to find Ashtyn standing there. The day had already contained so many surreal moments, it was hardly remarkable that he had found her.

"I'm sure you'll tell me," she said.

"They're looking for the pieces of the floor so they can put it back together again."

"Surely the pieces are too small to find, given the blast came from below," she said.

"Don't you think it's worth trying?" he asked her. When she didn't reply, he continued. "If the cause is the right one, shouldn't you take it up, even if the odds seem stacked against you?"

She didn't turn to face him. "Are you still talking about the floor?"

He didn't reply. For long minutes, they stood together watching the scene.

Eventually, he moved, breaking the stillness that had settled over them. "Come with me."

He didn't ask her why she wasn't at work; she didn't ask him how he had come to be next to her. She simply followed him. Only when they reached the city gates did she ask him where he was leading her.

He paused and turned to her, his green eyes dark and captivating. "Do you trust me?"

Her answer came without hesitation, without thought. "Of course." She should not. She barely knew him, and being drawn to him, feeling that they understood each other, meant nothing. He could be lying to her to achieve some hidden purpose. She also knew that her cynicism, this deep-rooted mistrust of the world, was a product of the Kade. She wondered if her survival had been worth the hardening of herself, the closing off of who she was from not only everyone else, but her Goddess, too.

They passed through the city's main gate, giving their names to be noted on the records of who exited and entered. Freya didn't even care that she might be drawing dangerous attention to herself by leaving for no purpose. It was strangely liberating to be so reckless.

Ashtyn struck out away from the road, moving across the plain that surrounded this part of the city with the certainty of those who had traversed the way many times before. When she had started her apprenticeship, Freya used to come to the plains which surrounded the city to gather herbs. But since the Kade takeover, she had rarely gone beyond the walls. Residents travelling outside the city without official purpose were viewed as agents of the Dark Gods or as malcontents. Suspicion was a dangerous thing to draw to oneself. Today, though, she had disregarded those concerns that bound her so tightly.

She basked in the unrelenting heat of the sun as it shone down unencumbered by the buildings. Zarech's words seemed to be imperceptibly eroding her unquestioning obedience to the yoke of the Kade, and she felt such little concern about being outside the city with no good reason, that the emotion may as well have not been present.

They walked until the city no longer loomed over them, but merely sat at a distance. Only then did Ashtyn stop. Freya halted a little way from him, turning to look back at the city that was at once her home and her prison. The nearest aqueduct, stretching across the plain and disappearing into the distance, was like a careless pencil mark across the landscape. She sat down in the long grass, lying back so that all she could see were the tips of the stems and the deep blue of the sky. The day was nearing its hottest part, and she enjoyed the feeling of the unadulterated heat soaking into her skin. She felt as though she had been locked away in the cool stone walls of the Healing Centre for so long that she had forgotten what it meant to be truly hot. A thud near her told her that Ashtyn had also sat down, but she didn't bother turning her head to find him. She was too lost in the strangeness of the day that had started with Zarech's revelation. Without any doubt, she knew he was telling her the truth. What he had told her aligned far too closely with knowledge she had been unable to put into words.

"What are you thinking?" Ashtyn sounded warm and relaxed.

"I've missed doing this," she replied drowsily. He didn't reply. She figured that he was waiting for her to continue. "I've missed who I used to be."

"Who was that?" A swishing sound gave away the fact that he was moving, maybe rolling over or sitting up to better see her.

"Someone better," she replied, still staring up at the blue, blue sky.

"Why did you change?"

"Because I was afraid of what the Kade would do to me." The scent of crushed stems surrounded her, tangy and sweet at the same time. It smelled like her childhood.

"You aren't any more?"

"No, I am. But..." She mulled over Zarech's claim that the Kade had used her to serve their own gods' power, at the expense of the Goddess. "Do you believe in the existence of the Goddess, Ashtyn?"

His answer came almost immediately. "Of course. Why do you ask?"

"Do you believe that we can touch her?"

Something about his reply made her think that he was choosing his words with extreme care. "I think that not everybody can, but certainly that it is possible."

"Do you think that she needs us?" She was assessing his answers, weighing him and every interaction they had ever had up against what had been said, and was about to be said.

He didn't reply for a very long time. The heat made the air shimmer. Freya breathed in and out, the warmth spreading to her very core. She suspected that his silence spoke to a knowledge on his part that he was deciding whether or not to share with her.

"What makes you think that she may need us?" he asked eventually.

Freya shrugged, causing a rustle. "Someone I met recently suggested it."

"And you believe it?"

She wondered why he didn't ask her with whom she had been discussing matters that were banned. "I do, yes."

Ashtyn didn't say anything, and Freya didn't push him. His response has told her all she needed to know about his own beliefs. Putting aside the enormity of what Zarech had made her realise, she was content to lie in the grass and just be. She didn't have to worry about who might see her, whether she was acting appropriately, or if she was about to be singled out for not worshipping enough, not being ashamed enough for being Pious.

"Why did you bring me out here?" she asked.

"Because you always look so trapped when I see you. There's more to simply living life within the city."

"It's easy to forget that, living with so much fear."

"Have you ever thought about just leaving it all? The Kade's influence may extend across the Third Country, but nowhere near as strong as in Oranis. You could just find yourself a farm, live out your days there in peace." The picture that he painted was undeniably tempting.

"Surely in a smaller community the Kade's rules would be more easily imposed. It would be more obvious if they were broken."

"True, but there are some places right on the borders of the Third Country, where that isn't the case. You could always go there. I mean, it would be a less luxurious life. For a start, the gas network doesn't extend that far. You'd have to use wood for all heat and lighting. But you'd be free."

"Why are you asking me this?"

"Because I want to know you, Freya, and I can't do that without knowing what you want." He sat up, breaking into the periphery of her vision.

She was silent, unwilling to answer the questions that he had put to her. It seemed as though everybody was only asking her questions, wanting her to give all of herself away to them, answer by answer.

"We should get back," she said.

"Freya, I'm sorry." The regret in his voice sounded sincere. "It's just...you make me think about that life. Not the life I live here in the city, with the...people I know, but instead a life with someone like you, simply living out my days in peace and contentment. You make me think that's possible." His clear desire for her coupled with the thinly veiled reference to the Resistance movement made her shiver. There were forces at work that were beyond her. She felt as though she were trapped amid strong currents, helpless to do anything other than struggle to keep her head above water.

TWELVE

Freya walked back to the city with Ashtyn in silence. With each step, the sense of oppression within her grew as the walls became larger. The prospect of returning to the city and all it contained – the fear, the violence, the repression – was unappealing. The freedom and heat of the plains made a part of her want to stay there forever.

Only when they joined the line to re-enter the city did she realise what a foolish errand her outing with Ashtyn had been. On exiting, she had told the Guardians at the gate that she was a healer and she was leaving to gather herbs. Any cursory investigation into her whereabouts or motivations for suddenly running off and leaving the city would demolish the flimsy lie, especially as she had told the Guardians at the Centre that she was feeling unwell. The consequences for the discovery of her lie could be huge.

However, they passed back into the city easily, their names once again recorded on the list among many others, swiftly disappearing into anonymity as the names of the people behind them were added to the records.

As they re-entered the city, the walls closed back over her, and she felt the return of the need to take care with her every movement. The liberation that she had felt on the plain was gone, as though it had never been there. She self-consciously looked at her robe. It was covered in grass stains. She glanced around nervously. If anybody recognised her, she would have a hard time explaining her dishevelled appearance.

They walked together, Ashtyn's pace as natural and unconcerned as ever. Rays of the sunset were beginning to kiss the tops of the buildings. Freya glanced into a school that they passed, her pace slowing. Children were beginning to leave, obediently lining up, neatly organised. She remembered her own time in a school like this – learning letters and numbers to the satisfaction of the teacher. It seemed like an eternity ago that the world had simply been a dualistic good and evil, categorised in a child's binary way of absolutes.

"Are you all right?" Ashtyn asked as she fell behind.

"I'm just wondering if things will ever be simple again." She shook her head to clear the melancholy.

He stayed silent, looking at her with understanding in his eyes.

Finally, their paths diverged. Neither wanting to leave the other, they both lingered in the street. Looking around and seeing nobody, Freya swiftly embraced him, sliding her arms around his waist and resting her head against his cheek. His arms closed around her in reply, pulling her closer so that there was no space between them. Then just as suddenly they withdrew from each other, not wanting to be caught in any display of affection. Even had they been joined, the Kade did not approve of such displays in public. Freya opened her mouth to say something to him, to thank him for the day, but before she could, he put a hand to her cheek, gently cupping it before turning and walking swiftly away. She told herself that there would be plenty of time to muse on him and the day once she was safely at home, and forced herself to put one foot in front of the other, away from him.

She spent another evening with a silent Symon. The robe totally occupied him, leaving him with no attention to spare on conversation. The robe was a work of art – of course it was, Symon had made it. As she stood in the doorway and watched him, she wondered why he put so much effort into a piece for an official who would never regard him as an equal, no matter how fine a craftsman he was. She nearly asked him what he thought about the Goddess and whether or not she spoke back, but didn't want to face the irritation that the interruption would elicit.

Zarech was looking expectantly at the door when she came in the next day. She nodded curtly to the first-rank healer as he stepped aside to let her pass. The familiar sensation of unease crawled across her skin as she walked past him. She wished she could say something to him, reprimand him in some way, but she knew it was too dangerous. His orders evidently came from an authority far beyond her.

"Is everything all right, Freyanna?" Zarech asked once the healer was gone. There was the faintest note of concern in his voice.

She stood uncertainly for a moment, then shook her head and began her work.

Hours passed, and neither of them said anything. Freya was lost in her uncertainty, and Zarech seemed content to quietly watch her. It was only when Freya spilled a medicine and swore viciously that he spoke.

"Do you want to discuss it?"

She looked up at him from cleaning the mess. "What is there to discuss? You have pointed out to me a series of truths that I lied to myself about for six years to stay alive and in a position of relative prosperity. In so doing, I betrayed not only myself, but she who I worship as giving me life and providing a meaningful shape to this world."

"There is no shame in doing wrong, Freyanna," he said. "There is only shame in recognising when we have been led astray, and then failing to do anything about it."

"I'm so confused about everything that I don't even know if I think what you did to those poor people in the marketplace is wrong anymore!" she cried, throwing the rag she had been using down on the floor and putting her arms around herself.

"So if you are confused, start with the things that you *can* understand," he advised.

She thought for a moment. "I know that Symon is a stranger to me."

"So what are you going to do about it?"

"What can I do?" She wanted desperately for him to guide her, to give the answers to all of the questions that he had raised within her. Surely he should be able to do that – he had been an Ordained.

"Stop living your life in accordance with the needs of someone else's gods." He spoke as though the answer were obvious but she was simply too young, too inexperienced, to realise it.

"How?" She despised how helpless she sounded, even to her own ears.

"Freyanna, if my daughter had grown into a young woman, I imagine she would have been something like you. But I hope with all my heart that she would have had the fortitude to not live in fear, denying what she truly wanted, what she truly believed, using ignorance and uncertainty as reasons for her continued misery. You have a fire in you, the fire of one who not only knows the truth, but believes in its power. Do you really want to live like this forever? A citizen forever asking permission to be the subordinate of people who have robbed from you the very right to worship your Goddess?"

She sat blinking. He spoke with a passion she hadn't seen in him before. She hadn't thought that he ever was roused to such emotional depths.

"Freyanna, when you know what you want to do, do it. Don't let the lives of your family be lost just so you can live in fear. Let their deaths nurture that fire and cause you to do something meaningful."

She didn't know what to say to that, and remained silent for the rest of her time with him. What he had said utterly preoccupied her. Not just today, but on all the days; all of the pieces of knowledge at which he had hinted. He had told her so much, and yet nothing at all. She couldn't discern if he had genuinely wanted her to know the truth, or if he had revelled in the discomfort he had caused her. Regardless of his motivations, it was irrefutable that he had picked at the threads of her, and she had begun to unravel.

As she went to leave at the end of the day, he called to her. She looked at him warily, wondering what would come next.

"I am glad that I met you, and I am proud of who I suspect you will be," he said.

She looked at him uncertainly from the doorway. He smiled at her, the sort of smile a loving parent gives a child. "Thank you for looking after me."

The irony of his thanks for healing him so that he could be tortured again and again twisted a blade of guilt inside her. She rebuked herself for caring about this man who had orchestrated so many bad things Something in his demeanour made her feel cared for in a way that she hadn't felt since before her parents had died.

She couldn't help herself. "Zarech, may I ask a question?"

"Of course," he replied.

"Does it bother you that you're locked up like this?"

"Not overly. In a lot of ways, it is meant to be that I am here."

"But you're chained to a bed."

"There are worse things in the world than being in a comfortable bed with the delightful company of a good healer."

"I don't understand," she said.

"I don't expect you to." He arranged himself as best he could on the bed. "Good evening, Freya." The conversation was clearly over. It appeared he would only ever let her in so far.

She raised her hand to knock on the door to be let out.

"I do miss the stars though," he added softy.

She couldn't remove his words from her mind as she left the Centre. Even if he was toying with her, there was an undeniable truth behind his words. She wasn't content to go on living like this – constantly looking over her shoulder just in case she were inadvertently placing a single step out of line. It was no way to live. To even call it living was a misnomer.

While her mind wandered, her feet took her through the streets with certainty. Suddenly, she was knocking on Ashtyn's door with only a faint memory of the journey through the streets. It occurred to her that he may not even be there. But he was, and he looked at her as though he had been expecting her all along. Perhaps he had been.

Wordlessly, she stepped inside, pulling the door closed behind her. He said nothing, waiting for her. Her uncertainty masked by her desire to fulfil Zarech's challenge, she put her hand up to his face, running her fingertip gently along his jaw line. He didn't move. He simply regarded her with the same intensity as he had on that terrible day when they first had met.

"Do you want me?" she asked, as though she didn't know his answer.

In response, he put his arms around her, pulling her closer to him.

"You know I do. What do *you* want, Freya?" His eyes didn't leave hers.

Trembling as much from desire as from disbelief that she was actually brave enough to disregard the rules that she had strictly lived by, she kissed him. She didn't care that adultery was an offence against the Kade. She didn't care that this was an act of dissidence. She didn't care that Ashtyn was dangerous. This was what she wanted.

She sighed as his lips touched hers, sending the warmth of the sun she had lain in the day before, through her body.

Passion making them clumsy. They barely made it past the top of the stairs. Afterward, Ashtyn stood, held a hand out to help her up, and led her to his bedroom.

They lay side by side on his bed, limbs entwined. He ran his hand over her body in a light caress, his eyes never leaving her. Freya couldn't help but suspect that he feared if he closed his eyes, she might vanish.

"What do we do now?" she asked. She laughed as he leaned over to kiss her. It was clear exactly what he thought they should do.

"I don't mean right now. I mean in the next fiveday, the next cycle, in the eons to follow: what do we do?"

"What do you want to do?" He kept looking at her as though he couldn't really believe that she was there next to him.

"Did you really mean what you said about a farm on the outskirts of the Third Country?" She could barely believe that she was suggesting it, but the more she thought about continuing life in Oranis, restricted and repressed, the more unbearable the thought became. She couldn't stay living a life of subjugation and fear. Not anymore.

"Are you seriously considering it? You'd leave the city completely?" he asked, excitement creeping into his voice.

"We could even go beyond the borders, if you were game," she offered.

"We'd have to leave the city with nothing. It wouldn't be luxurious," he warned.

"Would we be free from the Kade?" she asked.

He nodded.

"Then why would I ever say no?" She laughed as he pulled her to him. His arms were strong and warm around her. It felt good.

"When I first saw you, I would swear I heard Her whisper in my ear that if I didn't follow you wherever you led, I would be lost," he told her, bowing his head to kiss her shoulder.

"I don't think it works like that," she protested, laughing as he trailed a series of kisses down her arm.

"It might."

"If we go, we can worship Her freely." It was the first time Freya had really entertained the possibility. Voicing it aloud thrilled her. "Let's just leave. I don't want to be here, like this, anymore." She flung out her arm in a grand gesture, excited at the prospect of a future without fear; instead, one with the ever-calming presence of the Goddess truly with her. The idea that she would no longer be inhibited by the worship of the strange and harsh gods of the Kade thrilled her. She kissed him again.

They were lying together as the light dimmed outside, planning their escape and the life that they would lead, when explosions rocked the city.

THIRTEEN

The city had been transformed into a foreign land. Smoke filled the streets, disfiguring them; what once was familiar was now unrecognisable. Everything was suddenly silent, a stark contrast to the booms and crashes of the previous moments that had travelled across the entire city. The silence was eerie.

The Healing Centre lay before them in ruins. Parts of the building were still standing, but it looked as though they might fall at any moment. Rubble was strewn across the area, even along some of the surrounding streets. Nearby buildings had sustained damage, smooth stone walls spattered with craters. Freya and Ashtyn stood together, neither saying anything, simply looking at the destruction before them.

They had dressed in a flurry of clothes and agitation as soon as the explosions ended. Freya hadn't needed to say anything to Ashtyn. He simply handed her the healer's bag she had dropped when she had arrived, and they'd set off in search of the wounded. But neither of them had expected to find this.

If the marketplace after the explosions had been chaotic, what Freya was looking at was something she couldn't have dredged out of her darkest nightmares. Dust and ash filled the air, obscuring all vision for more than a short distance. That same dust and ash carpeted every surface. It settled on them, too, in their hair and on their clothes; it made them cough and their eyes water.

Bodies were strewn everywhere. It was impossible to tell who among them was injured and who was dead. Voices called plaintively, desperately.

Freya did not object as Ashtyn pulled her close and cradled her against him. She suspected that he was acutely aware, as she was, that she could have been inside the collapsed building, trapped or dead. Despite the danger that embracing each other invited, Freya leaned into him. Trembling overtook her limbs as she imagined herself working in the Centre as it exploded, what it would feel like to be thrown up in the air, her body colliding against unyielding, unforgiving, uncaring stone, to be battered, broken, and finally crushed.

Freya pushed the terror of the 'what if' aside, and instead focused on what she could do. "We have to help."

"It's dangerous," he said. "The rubble could shift, we can barely see, the rest of the building may fall down." He didn't say so, but his fear for her was written across his face.

"And?" She looked across the scene, years of training pushing away every emotion so that she could simply focus on what needed to be done.

"And you'll help nobody if you're dead." His worry for her made him sharp.

"I'll also help nobody if I do nothing," she snapped, yanking herself free of his grip.

"Freya..." He followed her as she strode purposefully toward the heart of the devastation. He could barely keep up with her.

A Guardian loomed in front of her, appearing out of the dust, the sudden appearance making her jump. "Where are you going?" she demanded.

"I'm a healer." Freya tried to move past, but the Guardian blocked her.

"Nobody is to enter this area without permission. Especially not Pious," she intoned. The calm response was at complete odds with the sounds of devastation around them.

"What! Why?" Freya's indignation made her blind to the menace in the Guardian's words. Ashtyn tried to draw her back, but she evaded his grasp.

"Nobody is to enter this area without permission," the Guardian repeated, looking down at Freya. "We have a response team to manage such events."

"A response team?" Freya had never heard of such a thing.

"Yes. A purpose-designed team to respond to incidents such as...this." The Guardian gestured to the utter destruction behind her.

"What is wrong with you? There are people who need help. I'm a healer. I can help them. I don't need to be a part of a response-team to do that." Freya's voice began to rise with anger. She didn't care that the shadows of other Guardians were prowling around the area and could hear her insubordination.

"Freya, let it go," Ashtyn advised her.

She ignored him. "Are you telling me that you're willing to let people die?" Her voice cracked, she was so angry.

"Leave or we will ensure you leave." For the first time, emotion had crept into the voice of the Guardian. She sounded irritated.

"I will not leave," Freya yelled, her temper finally overtaking her, driving all thought of reason or self-preservation from her mind. She went to push the Guardian aside and walk past her, but the Guardian grabbed Freya and flung her back. Freya crumpled to the ground. The stone was warm beneath her. The dirt under the hands she flung out to break her fall felt as though it was soaked in blood.

An animal-like snarl burst from her as she readied herself to spring at this woman who was standing between her and people she could help. Years of careful behaviour to keep herself the perfect Kade citizen were brushed aside by the horror and desperation that overtook her. But before she could do something which would mark her as an active dissident, Ashtyn knelt beside her and grasped her arm. His fingers dug into her skin.

"Freya, after the marketplace caught them unprepared, the Kade are not going to allow it to appear that they can't handle something like this without help from unofficial procedures. Just go straight home," he said, his lips brushing her ear, his voice urgent.

She opened her mouth to argue, but he forestalled her comment by holding up his other hand.

"There's nothing you can do if they don't want you here. Go home so you can help people tomorrow, and the day after, and the day after that."

"Let me go," she screamed at him, not caring that the Guardian was watching. Her shock and rage and helplessness made her crazed beyond reason. She struggled furiously with him, succeeded even in dragging Ashtyn down onto the ground with her, but his grip on her was like unrelenting iron. After several minutes' struggle, she lay in surrender on the ground, tears of helpless fury running unchecked down her face.

"Please, Freya. Go home," he begged.

Defeated, she nodded, brushing the tears from her face. He helped her up and they stood together, dirty, helpless, all the fight gone out of both of them.

"Find me tomorrow?" he asked, a hand brushing her arm. "I'll be in my workshop all day."

She allowed herself the indulgence of his lingering kiss on her cheek before turning her back on the people who needed her help and walking away.

Symon was already home. He didn't even ask what had happened when she walked in. He was rendered completely silent by her appearance. Dirt stained the white of her robes from when she fell, dust had settled itself within her hair, feeling gritty as it filtered down to her scalp.

"The Healing Centre was blown up," she said.

"Were you inside?" He crossed the room to scrutinise her, searching for any injuries. She shook her head.

"Do you want to bathe? Have something to eat?" He uncertainly put a hand on her shoulder. "You're filthy. Take off your clothes, I'll wash them."

She stumbled into the bathing room and lit the flame that would heat the reservoir of water. Symon followed her in, watching as she waited for the water to become warm enough to trigger the mechanism that would send it cascading down into the recessed area and then out through the slats in the floor.

"I'm not really hungry," she said, letting her filthy clothes fall to the floor.

"I'll go and wash these." He gathered the discarded garments.

"Burn them," she said, her voice harsh as she stepped under the water which began to trickle down. She couldn't stand the idea of being anywhere near clothes that had been marked by the dirt of the ruined Healing Centre. It was a reminder of her own powerlessness, the fact that she had been prevented from helping those who needed her.

He was wise enough to not argue with her. "I'll get you something to drink."

She was left alone. The water ran over her body. For a while she simply stood underneath it. Then she took up the soap and a washcloth. She scrubbed at her skin for a long time, even after the grime of the day had been removed. Even then, she swore she could still feel the dirt under her fingernails, on the strands of her hair, in her very skin.

Symon returned with a mug in one hand and a light shift in the other. He stood, saying nothing. She was grateful for that.

Eventually, the reservoir was emptied of warm water. She stood in the recessed area for a moment, staring blankly ahead, not bothered by the cooler air or the way it pricked at her skin.

"Here." Symon handed the mug to her. She sipped. The heated liquor, infused with herbs and spices, soothed the hard edges of her shock and anger. Only when she shivered did she realise the incidental fact that she was naked. She looked distractedly around for something with which to dry herself. Symon draped a towel around her shoulders.

"Is anything left of the Centre?" he asked as she rubbed herself dry with her free hand. She didn't really pay attention to what she was doing, rubbing the same place across her stomach over and over again as she pictured the terrible destruction of a beautiful building.

"I don't think so. Maybe a little." All she could see was the wounded lying on the ground – the wounded she had been prevented from helping.

With gentle hands, he took the mug and towel from her and gave her the shift. She slipped it on.

"You look exhausted," he said. The observation was devoid of any discernible emotion.

She shrugged, but went into the bedroom anyway, peeling back the blankets and slipping under them.

"Are you coming to bed?" she asked. It was only early evening, but she didn't want to do anything other than fall into an oblivious sleep.

"I should try to finish this robe," he said. "Will you be all right?"

She nodded. She was too numb to care about anything, let alone whether or not Symon was with her. She wondered how he could possibly work after learning that the Healing Centre had been destroyed. But really, she did understand. Symon's way to cope with things was to throw himself into his work. She was the same. But today, she hadn't been allowed to do that, so instead she had to sit with the shock and horror, something she hadn't been required to do for a very long time.

Gladly clinging to anything that did not reek of destruction and helplessness, her thoughts turned to Ashtyn. When she was with him, she felt fire sing through her veins. She had never felt that way about Symon. At most, it had always been an easy amicability, a shared set of values and behaviours rather than a shared passion for each other. She knew she should have felt bad about the afternoon she had just spent in Ashtyn's bed, but she couldn't help but see Symon as a stranger, someone with whom she lived, rather than someone with whom she shared a life. Try as she might to keep her mind clear of that horrible scene of destruction, those thoughts of Ashtyn collided against the memories of the Centre's remains, her anger at being prevented from helping people, and the sense of foreboding that was growing within her. For a long time, she stared at the ceiling, unable to sleep.

The bells didn't ring in the morning. Freya slept late without their peals waking her; she had fallen asleep long after Symon had finally come to bed. He hadn't seemed to notice she was still awake. She had said nothing, closing her eyes and feigning sleep until he lapsed into slumber beside her.

When Freya woke, the bed beside her was empty and cold. Sunlight permeated the house. There was no sign of Symon. Freya dressed, wondering at the silence of the house. Normally she was out by this hour, either at prayers, or the market, or at work. The thought of work led her to wonder what she would be doing now that the Centre no longer existed. She presumably would be relocated. The prospect made her feel strange. She had always worked at the Main Healing Centre; she'd always been too talented to be put anywhere else. Even her apprenticeship had been conducted under the tutelage of a healer who had a residency at the main Centre. The idea of going somewhere else, somewhere lesser, made her feel as though she was taking a step down. That being said, it really didn't matter what sort of step it was. She had always been told where to go, and she had always obediently followed the orders given to her.

She went into the kitchen and picked up a piece of fruit. In the horror of the previous evening, she hadn't eaten anything, and now hunger prowled within her. She raised the fruit to her lips, but the desire to eat anything abruptly fled. She stood in the kitchen, thinking about the way her life had always been the design of some other architect. For as long as she could remember, she had been driven by a curiosity to know how people were made. That had led her to be taught how to use that knowledge to heal, to put the body back the way it was supposed to be. She had always been told that she had to use her knowledge and skills to help people. In that moment, though, she had wondered what it would be like to do everything she had been told she shouldn't: rend apart perfectly healthy skin, force intact bones to snap. She couldn't help but suspect that it would feel good to shrug off her impotence and impose hurt onto those who dared tell her how her life should be lived.

Without even realising, she clenched the soft ripeness of the fruit, her fingers digging into it until the skin broke and juice ran unchecked down her hand. The flesh parted so obediently at the force from her fingers that there was quickly nothing but a pulpy mass in her hand. She looked down in sudden awareness and shook her head, surprised at this moment of brutality. She threw the mess away, cleaned her hand, and all evidence of the act was removed. She bent to rest her head on the coolness of the beaten metal of the sink, shocked not only by the dark intent that had overtaken her, but the force of it, too. "Where is this coming from?" she whispered to herself.

She jumped as Symon came into the kitchen. He saw her bowed over the sink. "Is everything all right?"

She straightened up, crossing her arms over herself. "Fine, just a little disoriented," she replied, the thoughts of destruction and brutality slipping slyly back into the shadows of her mind.

Symon remained looking at her but said nothing. She wondered what he was thinking. He was as inscrutable as ever.

"All right then," he said, before he left her alone once more.

She stood in the kitchen for several long moments, until knocking on the door snapped her out of her reverie and forced her to move to answer it.

"Yes?" She stood, uncertainly looking at the Guardians standing before her. One of them was a Master-level Guardian. The immaculate state of his dress reminded her of how perfectly the Guardians had been dressed last night, despite the debris and dirt.

"Freyanna Kuch?"

She nodded, conscious, of all things, of her bare feet.

"We have been sent to escort you."

FOURTEEN

Despite the near-paralysing fear that enveloped her, she found it within herself to ask the Guardians to wait while she put on her shoes. The Master-rank Guardian merely threw her a look that suggested he thought her an idiot. She took it as a yes.

She called out to Symon as she cast about for her shoes. He emerged from his workroom and raised an eyebrow when he saw the Guardians.

"Is everything all right?" he asked the Master-rank Guardian.

"We have orders to escort Healer Kuch," the Guardian replied.

"Why?" Symon threw a concerned look at Freya. It was a look that said 'what have you done?'

She shrugged at him, trying to appear unconcerned, despite the worry gnawing at her. She finished lacing her sandals and stood up straight, taking a robe from a hook on the wall and slipping it over the casual shift she wore. With movements that sought to buy her time, to give her a moment to collect herself, she straightened the fabric. She rubbed a finger along the green band that encircled her sleeve. Like a chain, she thought.

"That's Kade business," the Master-rank Guardian said to Symon, his voice unpleasant, discouraging any more questions.

Freya felt her stomach tighten. Someone must have seen her with Ashtyn and reported them. She wondered what she could possibly say in response to such an accusation. After all, it was true – she had been unfaithful to Symon.

"All right then." Symon gave Freya a parting look that indicated she was very much on her own. He went back into his workroom without another word.

The Guardians led the way through the streets, one on either side of her. Freya wondered what they would do if she ran. She considered it for a moment, too. If she was being arrested, the chances she would ever be let out were slim. But she knew she wouldn't get away. There was no point in running. So she marched along with them, waiting for them to take to her to whatever interrogation they had planned, and then to face whatever sentence was decided. Briefly, she wondered if she was going to be tortured like Zarech, or made to endure some terrible public humiliation – paraded naked through the streets like some of the adulterers she had seen. Perhaps both. Fear lurched within her at every step, lapping at her feet, her navel, her throat.

They were headed in the direction of the Healing Centre, or what remained of it. Freya wondered if there was a rescue effort in progress; were people still trapped under the mountain of rubble? She shuddered at the thought.

She was guided into one of the ministry buildings within the district. Freya didn't know its designation. People who had done something that deeply displeased the Kade often vanished into generic ministry buildings exactly like this one and didn't come out. It seemed that she was going to join the ignominious ranks of such individuals. She felt an uncontrollable urge to laugh. She had been right all along. Rebellion against the Kade would always be discovered and punished.

She was steered into the building, along a corridor with a high ceiling and a blue and scarlet rug. There were no windows. The only light was dim, provided by gas flames that burned in recesses cut into the stone walls. The flames were too far apart to provide any meaningful illumination. The thick stone left the interior of the building cold. Freya felt as though she were being led into the heart of a mountain rather than simply through a building. She wondered if she would ever see natural light again.

Eventually, they stopped in front of a door. The Master-rank Guardian rapped sharply on the wood and adjusted his already perfect uniform in an unexpected gesture of self-consciousness. Freya was still trying to quell her terror at what might be on the other side of the door when it was opened by the Chief Healer. Freya blinked in surprise. She had imagined a great deal during the walk, but she hadn't envisaged this.

"Ah, Estran, you've brought Freya." She stepped back. "Come in, please." Her courtesy was flawless. Completely unlike someone who was about to bring about accusations of dissidence and heresy.

Freya stepped into the room with steps shortened by caution and uncertainty. This was definitely not what she had been expecting. The room was equally as lavish as the Chief Healer's rooms in the Centre, although nowhere near as beautiful. The walls were a darker stone, there was only one window, and the curtain was half drawn, keeping out the sunlight that would have brightened the room. The curtain was sky blue, and the rugs were rich purples and reds. Freya wondered if all rooms in the Kade governing halls were furnished in Kade colours. A group of people sat in chairs and couches arranged in a loose circle in the centre of the area, and she felt their gazes on her as she crept further into the room.

She observed them from the corner of her eye rather than with a direct gaze. Several wore garments that were Symon's work. From the way they held themselves, she knew these were very clearly people accustomed to having their orders followed – the aura of power, or self-assurance, or even...carelessness which they gave off, left her reasonably certain of who they all were. The discreet presence of three elite guards spaced around the walls confirmed her suspicion that she was in the presence of some of the most senior members of Kade governance. She stood, uncomfortably aware of her status not only as a Pious, but simply as someone so very outranked by every single person in the room.

"Freya, please sit down." The Chief Healer closed the door, leaving the Master-ranked Guardian and his companion outside.

Freya sat in the nearest chair – a deeply cushioned leather armchair. She sank into it, feeling distinctly undignified, in addition to terrified, and amazingly enough – curious. Under different circumstances, she would have been comfortable in the chair. Her own home was furnished with plush furniture, but this was an unprecedented level of luxury. With a little shuffle forward, she sat perched on the edge of her seat, waiting for the Chief Healer to speak.

But it wasn't the Chief Heaper who spoke first. Instead, it was a man lounging against a wall to her right. He had a glass of something in his hand from which he sipped before he spoke. Freya suspected it was liquor. Her initial surprise that a member of the Kade governance would indulge in alcohol quickly gave way to a cynical acknowledgement of their double standards.

"You did a very fine job with Zarech," he drawled.

"Thank you." Her voice came out a strangled whisper. She wasn't sure what there was for him to sound so amused about.

"As a healer you would give our Elishe a fair contest," he continued, throwing a playful glance at the Chief Healer. She returned his look with a rueful inclination of her head.

"I'm sure you're too kind," Freya said cautiously.

A woman spoke. She was older than the Chief Healer, but had the same brusque authority. She wore robes of the Ordained. "You have served the Kade well, not only in your care for Zarech, but also in the last few years, Freyanna."

"I've tried," Freya said, pushing her recent treacherous thoughts aside. Allowing them to be known would only result in her being killed, possibly even in that very room.

"Zarech is, of course, dead," said the man who had first spoken.

Until that moment, the fate of the enigmatic leader of the Followers had managed to evade Freya's thoughts. The sight of the Main Healing Centre – for her, the epitome of stability and the adult life she had known – in ruins, had thrown all thoughts of him from her mind. Zarech would have almost certainly been killed in the explosion. He couldn't have escaped, not chained to the bed. And Freya couldn't see the Guardians outside his door being inclined to help him survive if anything of the quarantine wing had remained intact. Freya didn't allow herself any reaction to his death other than a nod. She couldn't.

"He ignited the blast, you know," the youngest man in the room said. He was stocky, with blond hair cropped close to his head, accenting the squareness of his face. He wore a far more ornate variation on the Guardian's uniform. He wore the menace and violence of the Guardians, too.

Shock trickled over her like icy water. "How?"

The bond man smirked. "We have our suspicions," he replied, overtly revelling in whatever knowledge he was not sharing with her.

"Was this his plan all along?" Freya asked, her surprise at this revelation giving her an audacity she otherwise would not have had.

The blond man stayed silent, his face going blank.

The older woman answered instead. "That is unclear at this point in time. During extended interrogations with him—" Freya inwardly cringed at the euphemism for the barbarous torture "— he alluded to many things, but was vague on specific details. Rest assured, the full resources of the Kade will be put to determining the precise elements of his plan and how exactly he managed to execute it. Contrary to the assertions of some, we don't know quite everything."

She threw a disdainful look at the blond man, who maintained his blank façade.

Freya noted in the back of her mind the politics within the room. It seemed that behind closed doors the Kade leadership had its own squabbles. It was an insight into their appearance of unity that she had never thought she'd get.

"We just know most things," the older woman added slyly, causing all of the occupants of the room, aside from Freya, to titter in knowing laughter. It was a smooth display of easy leadership, bringing the blond man back into the fold while serving to remind Freya of her place.

The Chief Healer waited until silence resumed before speaking. "You must be wondering why we brought you here today."

Freya wasn't sure if a response was even required, but she nodded regardless. The Chief Healer did not strike her as a woman who appreciated being left waiting.

"As you likely concluded, the Central Healing Rooms are no longer operational. It has required us to think about where we go from here."

"We need to redistribute people," the older woman said, a decisive tone to her voice.

"We need to restructure certain elements," the man who had first spoken added.

Freya looked around the room of powerful people, all of whom were looking at her expectantly. The previous disharmony was gone, replaced by an unsettling similarity and single-mindedness. Perhaps it was simply the way they carried themselves, or the fact that they had clearly discussed this matter prior to her entry, but she couldn't help but feel she wasn't speaking to a group of disparate people but instead a disaggregation of a single individual.

"We have an offer for you, Freya," the Chief Healer spoke, her voice crisp and efficient. "We would like you to take control over one of the Healing Centres. As part of that you would oversee training programs, organise people, report back to us on what goes on. You would do a little healing, although far less than you do now. I believe you have experimented in the past with your own remedies."

Freya was surprised and more than a little uneasy to discover that the Chief Healer knew this. She nodded.

"We would like you to continue with those experiments, but with our resources at your disposal, rather than simply your own initiative to impel you."

Freya sat still, uncertain if she was expected to speak.

"You don't have to say yes straight away. It's a lot to ask of you," the older woman said. Freya wondered if she heard a slightly condescending note in the woman's voice.

She cleared her throat. "Are you sure you are all comfortable with me doing this? I *am* a Pious." She was almost afraid to put voice to the reason they looked at her with that faint but discernible disdain.

"Your actions speak for themselves," the man next to her said, smiling slightly. She couldn't tell if it was a kind or predatory smile.

"Thank you," she whispered, looking down at her lap. Shame settled across her. Her actions were that of collaborator and adulterer.

"Don't thank us. We reward those who serve the Kade well. You have done that." The older woman spoke with a businesslike finality that left Freya in no doubt that she was dismissed. The Chief Healer opened the door. Freya felt the weight of observation on each step as she made her way to the door. The blond man started speaking to the older woman. They ignored her completely, apparently forgetting her presence now that they no longer had business with her. But the man leaning against the wall, and the man who sat next to him, both watched her as she walked across the room. To what end they were scrutinising her so, she wasn't exactly sure, but she felt like a small animal being tracked by a predator.

"We'll be in touch," the Chief Healer said as Freya reached her. "You did an excellent job with Zarech."

Freya smiled weakly at her and left the room.

Estran and the other Guardian immediately fell into step on either side of her, guiding her along the long, dark corridor. She noticed doors she hadn't seen when they had shown her in. Her terror must have made her completely blind to them. The tricks of her mind were just as bizarre as the encounter she had just experienced.

At the entrance, she took a few steps outside before she realised her escort was no longer with her. Evidently their job had been to find her, not to take her home. She stood outside on her own, looking at the clear blue of the sky strung between the buildings. She had been overtaken by such a strong certainty that she would never see sunlight again. She had never before realised how wonderful the feeling of the sun on her face actually was.

FIFTEEN

Ashtyn's shop was open, the unlocked door and unshuttered windows inviting anybody who passed by to enter. Freya hesitated ever so briefly outside it, then walked in, caution overthrown by the desire to see him. A bell tinkled somewhere in the recesses of the workroom. She had never heard it before, and she wondered why not. Ashtyn came into the storefront, his hands blackened from whatever work he was doing. When he saw her he hurriedly wiped them on his apron and took it off before he crossed the distance between them, pulled her close to him, and kissed her softly.

"Did you get home all right? I wanted to walk you home, but with so many officials in the one place seeing us together..." He didn't need to articulate the need to be wary of being discovered as an adulterer. The Kade's punishments against adulterers were so unpleasant that even someone like Ashtyn would want to think twice before conducting such a relationship in a public manner.

"It's all right, I understand. I got home fine." Freya smiled at his concern for her. She liked being cared for, for being worried about, even though she had survived this long without it. She found it strange that she had so violently resisted his concern for her when they first had met.

He locked the door and shuttered the display window too, sending them into abrupt darkness.

"Do you have to work?" Freya asked.

He came back to her, taking her in his arms. "Not if you're here." He lowered his head to kiss her. His mouth was warm as his lips gently explored hers.

He pulled away, a thoughtful expression drawing his features together, clouding his green eyes. "When was the last time you prayed?"

"Yesterday morning," she replied, confused as to why he would care about her prayer observance.

He shook his head. "I meant to Her."

Her expression told him all he needed to know.

"Pray with me."

She hesitated. She had been so sure that morning that she was about to be arrested. Should she really be committing an act of treason so soon after? Under his gaze, she arrived at the decision that her recent illegal activities had not been discovered. If she was discovered in prayer now, she would also be discovered in the house of her lover. Her fate in either instance would be a painful one. More importantly, though, a desire to return to the ways of her childhood coursed through her. The tumultuous events of the previous days had left her with a terrible sense of wrongness, and she wanted to pray to the Goddess in whom she had found comfort and strength from her earliest memory. She nodded, her eyes fixed on his, a trust she hadn't even realised she still had been reserving unfurling inside her.

Ashtyn led her upstairs into his bedroom. She sat on the bed and watched as he opened a chest and reached inside to remove a false bottom. Freya watched him, wide eyed. Seeing her look, he laughed. "Don't worry. I made it myself. Nobody would ever find it unless I showed them how." He removed a prayer mat and a piece of dried arax root.

"Where did you get that from?" Freya exclaimed, looking at the root. "That's fiercely controlled!"

"You *are* new to this, aren't you?" he commented, setting the mat on the floor and placing down a holder for the arax root. Freya realised she had been completely unaware of a whole world of subterfuge and resistance lurking within Oranis.

Memory guided Freya to sit cross-legged on the mat, placing her palms down on her legs.

Ashtyn ensured the covers over the windows were firm. "Have you ever privately prayed with arax root?"

"I was too young."

Ashtyn used a flint to light the root, then blew out the flame. He checked that the plant was smouldering correctly. "It's very intense. Just breathe," he advised her, taking a deep breath himself.

Freya inhaled the acrid smoke, feeling her thoughts begin to slip and slide in the familiar way. But this was entirely different to the prayers to the Kade gods, conducted outside in the squares under the watchful eyes of the Ordained. The sensation came upon her far more swiftly. Yet the slipperiness of her thoughts couldn't contain the budding excitement that for the first time in seven years, she wasn't going to be focusing on the Kade's alien gods while she prayed, but on her own familiar Goddess.

Ashtyn began the opening prayer. "Great Goddess from who we are created and to who we will return at the end of all things."

As though she had recited the prayer the day before rather than over six years ago, Freya spoke the second line, "To whom we give our strength, and are duly rewarded."

Ashtyn's voice joined hers and they spoke as one. "We open ourselves to recognise that which always exists; the eternal undying bond between us."

Freya began to whisper the first prayer, the invocation for strength, the words flowing from her mouth without stumble or pause. Slowly, her thoughts narrowed to focus not on the words, but on the meaning behind them, the connection that they formed between her and the Goddess. As her prayer came to its conclusion, Ashtyn commenced his own prayer: one for safety. A sense of calm enveloped her, calm such as she had not known in the longest time. As his prayer ended, she began a prayer for wisdom. And so they alternated, moving between each other to maintain a steady rhythm. Eventually they fell silent, both of them slipping into a trance-like state.

Freya felt herself move beyond simply the confines of what made her Freya and into a greater sense of herself and her place within the world. She saw how she, Freya, was in fact simply a small part of a greater whole. In that moment she was Freya but not Freya, there but not there. Time ceased to exist; physicality ceased to exist. The only thing she knew to be true was her thought, and its connection to a universe of other thoughts, all joined by the most delicate of threads. And ever-present was the cool, gentle presence that had always been in her life, even if she hadn't always been aware of it. She couldn't remember the last time she had felt so safe.

Gradually, she returned to her own sense of time and self. She looked around the room with a sense of wonder, as though she was only just seeing the world for the first time.

"Have you experienced that before?" Ashtyn asked, blinking slowly as though he too were seeing the world afresh.

"Never like that. I've felt as though I'd touched something else, but never felt so...so much a part of something greater than myself, beyond things I can comprehend. I've never experienced a total connection like that. Ashtyn, how often do you pray like this?"

"Not often. As you pointed out, arax root is pretty difficult to come by."

"Do you always need arax root to make that sort of contact?"

He shook his head as he stood up, his movements slow from sitting in the same position for so long. "I'm no expert. Nobody's sure – we don't exactly have any Ordained to consult."

She winced as she was reminded of Zarech's death. She didn't just mourn his passing, but also the loss of the last vestiges of complete knowledge regarding the religious practices of the

Pious. She would need time to properly consider what had happened to him, but now was not that time.

"But I think arax root isn't necessary," Ashtyn continued. "Although, I've heard that, even with arax root, some people struggle to find the connection."

She waved his comment away. "I'm sure I just got lucky. Maybe She's lonely."

He chuckled. "You're talking about the Goddess as if She were just you or I. I'm not certain that loneliness is something She'd experience."

"With so few people worshipping Her and praying to Her, of course She's lonely. Everybody's praying to the Kade gods." She remembered with a pang that it had been Zarech who had told her this. Without even realising it, what he had told her had become true for her.

Ashtyn was looking at her intently. "How do you know that?"

"It was one of the things that was told to me when I was younger." She shrugged with feigned nonchalance, unwilling to discuss Zarech with him. She was still trying to sort through her own confused feelings about the man.

He shrugged, seeming satisfied with her answer. She rolled up the prayer mat and handed it to him. As he put it back in the trunk and replaced the false bottom, she watched him carefully, but it was futile. It seemed he was correct. Unless he showed her, she wouldn't have known the hiding place existed. Even then, she suspected she would have struggled. It reassured her that despite his casual demeanour, he was careful and adept at keeping dangerous things secret.

"I'll be right back," he told her, picking up the tray of arax ashes.

"Where are you going?"

"I tip the arax root ashes into my furnace. Using a banned substance in heretical worship isn't something I want to be discovered doing." He smirked as he left the room, as though he was more amused by such an outcome than terrified.

Ashtyn returned a few minutes later. "Are you all right?"

"Yes, I'm fine. It's just a lot to take in." She smiled at him. She liked that he noticed the nuances of her moods.

"If it's not too much for you, I have one more thing I'd like to show you." He glanced to the timepiece fitted to the wall, his eyes resting on the shadow it cast.

She moved over to him, snaking her arms around his waist and reaching up to kiss him, long and slow and sweet. "Can it wait?"

He returned the kiss with no small amount of enthusiasm, but stopped before anything further could happen. "Later, I promise," he said, kissing her once more to prove he meant it.

Reluctantly, she let withdrew her arms, then followed him out into the street.

They were careful about the manner in which they walked together across the city. The little touches or glances that would mark them for all the world to know that they were lovers were contained. It felt so natural to want to take Ashtyn's hand and slip it around her waist, but Freya refused to indulge that impulse, to even allow that desire to linger. Even though the likelihood that anyone would stop them was slim, Freya couldn't help but shake the fear inspired by the knowledge that several members of the Kade elite knew who she was. She didn't like the idea that she was well known. It ruined her carefully crafted veneer of relative anonymity. Even though she was no longer sure that she wanted to be quite so subservient to the Kade, the prospect of attracting their attention in any way, let alone a bad one, made her uneasy. Especially given her relationship with Ashtyn. She didn't want to throw her life away so carelessly.

It took a while for them to reach their destination: a nonde-script merchant's warehouse. Freya regretted agreeing to be shown whatever this was. To return home at a respectable time, she would likely have to take one of the public carts. With an un-characteristic care, Ashtyn looked up and down the street to check that nobody was there, and only when he was satisfied that the cobble lane was empty did he knock on the door.

After a few moments passed, the door was partially opened. Upon seeing Ashtyn, a portly man gave an exclamation and pulled the door open wide enough to admit Ashtyn, and then Freya.

"Ashtyn, it's good to see you." The man greeted Ashtyn warmly with a merchant's burr to his voice, pulling Ashtyn into a fraternal hug that he enthusiastically returned.

"Bardan, you always act as though we've not seen each oth-er for several cycles rather than a few days." Ashtyn spoke through good-natured laughter. "I've brought Freya with me today," he added casually.

Bardan released Ashtyn to regard Freya. "It's a pleasure to meet you, healer Kuch," he said, taking her hand and pressing his thumb into her palm as was the customary Pious greeting.

"Please, call me Freya," she murmured, unnerved as much by the old rituals as the fact that Bardan clearly knew who she was. Yet another example of her carefully maintained anonymity in apparent tatters.

"Come through, we're all here. You're late...as usual," Bar-dan chortled, giving the two of them a knowing glance. Freya blushed, wondering exactly what Ashtyn had told him about their relationship. She glanced at him as she followed Bardan, a lick of irritation flickering through her at his presumption in sharing any information about his relationship with her with someone else. So much for concern over being caught as adulterers.

The building was exactly as it looked from the outside – a warehouse, filled with neatly stacked goods. Bardan led them along to a far wall, feeling on the stone for a moment until a panel slid back to reveal a descending corridor. Freya looked at Ashtyn. "I suppose you made this too?"

He inclined his head, grinning. "I helped with the mechanism."

She rolled her eyes, still irritated with him for sharing information about her without her knowledge or consent.

Bardan led them down the corridor and the wall panel slid back into place behind them, throwing them into almost total darkness. The walk was a short one, ending in a small room filled with several people. The furnishings and brightly coloured rugs looked well-worn, but the room felt comfortable and inviting. The occupants turned expectantly at their arrival. Freya stood under their collective gaze. She had a bizarre sense of déjà vu, reminded of being in the room with the Kade officials only a few hours previously.

"Freya, this is the resistance movement," Ashtyn said.

SIXTEEN

A woman with flaming red hair stepped forward. She extended her hand. "Freya, it's a pleasure," she said, smiling in a tight sort of way. Despite her warm greeting, something about her evoked a sense of iron.

Freya extended her hand in response. This time, she was unsurprised that the woman pressed her thumb to Freya's palm in the Pious greeting. Freya returned it.

"Makkyd is our glorious leader," Ashtyn told her cheekily, placing a hand in an almost proprietary fashion on the small of her back and guiding her further into the room. She stepped slight away from his hand, uncomfortable with the display of intimacy, wanting her own space in which to feel overwhelmed. She had suspected his involvement with the Resistance, but confirmation of it felt like she had been scalded with hot water.

Makkyd shushed Ashtyn. "Hardly glorious, Ashtyn. Your charms are going to get the better of you one day." She gestured to a nearby seat, which Freya obediently took.

Freya was rapidly introduced to the eight other people in the room. They all, like her, had the green band on their clothing which marked them as Pious. She barely caught their names, but she did note that everybody with one exception warmly introduced themselves to her. Freya wondered if she was paranoid, but she couldn't help but feel that this woman, Lyssa, looked at her without outright dislike. She sat curled up on a chair, sleekly regarding Freya with large green eyes, which were several shades lighter than Ashtyn's. Freya was as startled by her elegant beauty as the fact that the coolness of her greeting was such a stark contrast to the warmth exuded by everybody else.

"Freya and I were together when the Healing Centre was blown up yesterday," Ashtyn said once the introductions were concluded.

Freya shifted in her seat, wishing he would have asked her before telling everybody that they had been together. She wondered why he was so forthcoming with information about her.

"What was it like?" The question came from a lithe-looking man, sitting half in shadow. "None of us were able to find anything out." Freya thought she remembered that his name was Sek, but she couldn't be certain. There was a brittle sound to his voice – there was a certain tension to all of them. It made sense, after what had happened the previous day. After what had happened over the previous six years, really.

"Chaotic," Ashtyn said, a dark edge to his voice.

"Difficult. I don't think the Kade ever expected that something like the Healing Centre would be attacked," Freya said.

"What happened?" Makkyd asked, her eyes hard and bright.

Freya's mouth twisted, her anger at being denied the opportunity to help those who could have been saved flaming to life. "They wouldn't allow anybody anywhere near the Centre, despite the fact that we could have helped. I tried to go and help, but I was told that a special group would deal with it, that I – and any Pious – should stay away from the area."

The silence which immediately followed her words held the tenor of anger. After a moment, Makkyd spoke, her voice even despite the flame sparkling in her eyes. "The Kade were made to look very inept at the marketplace. They didn't expect anything like that to occur. The fact that it was ordinary people that came to help left them looking utterly unable to care for their own people. They weren't going to let that happen again."

"So what did they actually do?" Ashtyn asked before Freya had the chance.

"They have put together a group with the specific purpose of responding to disasters within the city," Makkyd said. She paused, her mouth pressed into a thin, unimpressed line at the decision. Everybody waited for the 'but' that her tone made clear was impending. Freya watched the way Makkyd commanded their attention, the way she controlled the room with so little thought. "But their special response group hasn't – as far as we know – been particularly well trained."

"Does anybody know if help was given to the people that were injured?" Freya hadn't been willing to ask the room of officials that morning. It had been made very clear that it was not her place to ask such questions. Makkyd's inferences fuelled her worry that a great many people remained trapped under the rubble, needing help but not getting it. For half a second, she was back at the Healing Centre, hearing the screams of those who had been near or inside it when it blew up. Then she was back in the room with this group who sought rebellion, who wanted to take that sense of impotent rage and make it action.

Makkyd shook her head. "It seems that the ban against anybody who isn't authorised going near the site is still in effect. We believe select groups are being used to clear the rubble and pull out survivors, but they're expendable, in case any of the building's remaining walls collapse."

Freya didn't need to ask to know that those 'select groups' would be Pious workers. "What about the survivors – are they being treated?"

"Again, we have very little information. The city is in utter chaos. Nobody is where they are supposed to be, everybody's afraid, and the Kade officials are scrambling to assert their authority. But from what we've heard, no survivors have been pulled from the site as yet," Makkyd replied.

"If they had let me..." Freya whispered, cold washing over her as she saw again the bodies sprawled out of her reach.

"There's no guarantee you could have saved them," Ashtyn said, placing a comforting hand on her shoulder. This time, she was glad of his touch.

"In our line of work, we find it best not to dwell on who we could have saved, or too many 'if onlys'. It's best to focus on who we can save, what we can do," Makkyd advised.

Freya nodded mutely, overwhelmed by the driving purpose this woman espoused.

"Speaking of which, what can we do in the next few days?" Lyssa asked pointedly, staring at Freya as if to blame her for delaying discussion of that topic.

Attention shifted to Makkyd. "As I said, we don't have a lot of certainties. But it's likely that the Kade will implement a series of curfews and restrictions."

"Do they know what caused the explosion?" someone asked.

"It was definitely deliberate. None of our people know who triggered it, although if I had to bet, I'd wager Dark Gods' Followers. Nobody else would target a place of healing, not even the Kade," Makkyd said.

Freya stayed silent. She could have told Makkyd that she was correct, but the suspicious side of her, the part that kept her mouth shut to ensure her survival, would not permit it. Not yet. She stayed silent and watched, reserving whether or not to give her trust to these people.

"What can our network do to circumvent a restriction on supplies?" Ashtyn asked.

"How severe are the restrictions likely to be?" one of the other men asked.

"What, you mean there aren't restrictions now?" another person joked. The room erupted into bitter laughter.

The Kade's control of Oranis and the Third Country was orchestrated not simply through the threat of violence, but a careful organisation of nearly every aspect of life. The supply of essential goods such as foodstuffs – or information from the world beyond the Third Country's borders – was strictly controlled. The Kade had mastered the art of seizing almost every item that entered the city and stockpiling all goods that were brought into

Oranis in their own warehouses. The warehouses were impene-
trable and guarded so heavily that it would take an army to get
into one. The Kade's control of whatever came into the city was
compounded by fierce licensing laws for traders which meant
that they were paid to transport all their goods into Kade warehouses. The same goods that they brought in were rationed back
out to them to sell to the population of the city. While some of
Oranis's merchants were allowed to have warehouses, to obtain
one required a plethora of permits and taxes, and then what was
allowed to be stored in them was severely restricted. Craftspeople
had it a little better; people like Ashtyn were allowed to craft
what they wanted, but restrictions on materials in addition to
heavy taxes limited what they could make. Only the fact that the
Third Country was nestled in the heart of the Godskissed Continent, and thus was a good trading route, meant that foreign
traders tolerated these measures.

"We have some of our own supplies stockpiled. Would that
help you, Ashtyn?" Makkyd asked.

"Everything helps. Although thanks to the restrictions, I've
already become quite creative," he replied, causing a knowing
titter to ripple around the room. Freya shuddered, reminded eerily of the same sort of knowing laugh that the Kade members had
exchanged just that morning. She knew she was missing information; she was only hearing half a discussion. True, if she'd
been Makkyd, she would have given strict instructions to limit
what newcomers heard. Regardless, the realisation that Ashtyn
kept so much from her made her uncomfortable. His involvement
was obviously not casual, but in fact ran quite deep.

As she listened to their discussion, Freya gained an idea of
just how far the resistance movement stretched, comprising
sympathisers and allies across Oranis and even the whole of the
Third Country. Even Makkyd's comments about not yet knowing
the decisions of the Kade officials hinted at intelligence within
the Kade governance itself. Now she understood how Ashtyn had

obtained arax root. Of course, there had been whisperings of a resistance for years, but Freya had always assumed that it was simply a handful of disgruntled people who would gather in a clandestine location and grumble about the Kade, rather than a subversive organisation that had reach and influence to meaningfully counter the Kade.

She turned her attention back to the meeting, aware Bardan was talking.

"...we've been given a tremendous opportunity. If the Kade is scrambling to recover from this, we can move our own supplies so that we are better positioned," he said, to murmured agreement.

Bardan's intense expression reminded Freya that everybody in the room was dangerous and intelligent, no matter how jovial and simple they may seem. The way they carried themselves and the decisiveness with which they spoke reminded her too much of the Kade leaders to whom she had spoken only that morning; the people in here were more than average Resistance members. They were, she realised, the leaders of the Resistance.

"We'll meet again tomorrow to coordinate those movements," Makkyd said. "We shouldn't act without better knowledge of what the Kade are doing. Hopefully by then we'll have it." The firm inflection to her voice drew the meeting to a close, and everybody relaxed a little. Tension was still strong across the room, but the promise of action, to seize upon what had happened to the Healing Centre as an opportunity rather than a cause for panic, seemed to have dispelled the worst of the anxious mood into which Freya had first walked.

Makkyd turned her attention back to Freya. "What do you think of us so far?"

Freya would have bet all the money she and Symon had toiled to accrue under the Kade's rule that underneath the polite curiosity, Makkyd was appraising her, deciding whether or not to trust her. No real plans had been discussed in front of her and

Freya knew that wasn't a coincidence. Ashtyn might trust her, but Makkyd didn't. Not yet, anyway. If Makkyd decided that she really wasn't to be trusted, Freya doubted she would leave the room alive.

"Isn't this a conspicuous time to meet, in the middle of the afternoon?" she asked.

Lyssa threw her a sideways glance. "And sneaking around after dark isn't conspicuous?" she asked, contempt dripping from every syllable.

Makkyd chuckled. "Easy, Lyssa, she raises a good point. You're correct too," she added, seeing Lyssa opening her mouth to protest. Freya noted the easy but firm leadership and couldn't help but admire it.

"We meet at different times and on different days, sometimes in different places, too. A pattern is the easiest thing to spot," Makkyd explained.

Again, Freya noted the distinct absence of any specific information. "So what is it exactly for which you are fighting?"

Lyssa made a noise of contempt, and Freya turned to face her, aware that everybody else was listening intently.

"Obviously you seek to overthrow the Kade. But what then? A return to the way things were? Life wasn't perfect under the Dual Accord. And a lot of people don't believe that it's worth fighting for the right to worship a seemingly uncaring deity."

Before Lyssa could reply, Makkyd spoke. "Again, you're correct. I suppose we're fighting for what goes along with worshipping that deity: the way we live, the way we love, the freedom to choose who we are and how we are."

"But that's an ideal. It's not going to be a reality, surely. Even if you take power, you can't allow complete freedom for the Kade. Otherwise, what's to stop a different group staging an uprising of their own?" Freya pointed out.

"When did you get so cynical?" Ashtyn interjected.

Freya shrugged. "I'm not cynical, I just speak based on what I've observed." She leaned back, feigning nonchalance, prickling with the awareness of everybody's attention on her.

"She's right, you know," one of the men, Oltrem, rumbled.

"Of course she is," Makkyd said firmly. "But that doesn't mean that it's not worth fighting for an ideal. Better to aim for that and fall short than to seek to create an imperfect world."

Freya decided that she liked Makkyd, even if she didn't necessarily agree with her. She was a clever woman and a good leader, who knew how to inspire her people as well as control them. Freya had worked many times under the authority of people who could do neither, and when she had attained the rank of Master and all of the leadership responsibilities that had come with it, she had sworn to be the sort of leader that Makkyd was. She wasn't certain she wanted to join the Resistance, but she definitely didn't oppose their existence and arguments as she once might have.

The Resistance members left in ones and twos, their departures directed by Bardan and Makkyd. Lyssa was one of the first to leave, and she tossed a venomous glance at Freya on her way out. Freya raised her eyebrows in response, amused and perplexed that she could evoke such a strong sentiment in a woman she had just met. Observing the rapid exchange, Makkyd laughed. This was a woman not to be underestimated; she missed nothing.

Freya and Ashtyn left the warehouse with a certain surreptitiousness that lingered as they walked along the street.

"Do you have time to come back with me?" Ashtyn asked.

Even though she probably should have returned to Symon so as not to arouse his suspicion, Freya nodded. She craved time alone with him that wasn't filled with intrigue or disaster. Rather than simply the previous day, it seemed it was another lifetime ago that she had shown up at Ashtyn's door to be with him.

So that they could cross the city quickly, rather they took a public cart. For the duration of the journey, and the short walk back to Ashtyn's shop, they didn't speak. Freya liked that she didn't feel the need to fill the space between them with words. The streets were all but empty, even emptier than the day after the explosions had destroyed the marketplace. Freya wondered if the team was still at work meticulously and painstakingly sorting through the pieces of rubble to find the fragments of the beautiful, shattered floor, even as they could be put to better use pulling out those still alive under the rubble of the Healing Centre.

Once they were safely back in Ashtyn's living quarters, she accepted his offer to make her an infusion. She sat lost in thought while she waited, picking her way through recollections of the meeting.

She sipped the drink slowly. It was nice to enjoy the simplicity of something as basic as the flavour of a drink, to focus on that rather than thoughts of everything that had transpired across the previous few days. He sat next to her, his leg warm where it pressed against her. From the corner of her eye, she could observe him drinking and watching her.

"What do you think?" he asked finally.

She bought herself a moment by taking a sip. She chose her words cautiously. "The Resistance certainly is organised."

"I mean, would you think about joining us?"

"It's something I would consider," she said, unwilling to commit herself. This was his cause, not hers. She wondered what else about this group he kept from her, like his exact role within it. He had divulged very little to her, but if the meeting had been indicative, she strongly suspected he was a key member of the Resistance. It sat uneasily with her that she knew so little about him. She had thought he was simple, without complications aside from an unhealthy irreverence for the Kade, not so completely enmeshed in this intrigue and rebellion.

"Can we not talk about this, please?" she asked, not wanting to think about it.

He put his mug down and put one of his hands on her thigh, the other hand sliding around her back. "Of course, I'm sorry."

"There's nothing to be sorry for, I just want to be with you." She put her mug down and reached for him, desperate to forget the world of shadows and secrets and just feel the comfort of his body against hers.

Freya eventually had to leave the warmth and comfort of Ashtyn's home. She moved through the streets like a thief, afraid that the places she had been and the things she had done that day had marked her in an indelible way that would scream out her treason.

Her house was as she had left it; a bizarre contrast to the changes that she felt had occurred within herself. Everything she had seen and done that day made her feel like a very different person to the one who had left the house in the morning at the behest of two Guardians. Symon's presence announced itself as soon as she stepped through the door. The smell of something cooking in the kitchen caressed her nose immediately, absurd in its familiarity. That familiarity was so far away from the subversive danger of the Resistance and her relationship with Ashtyn that she wondered if she had dreamed them. She had barely closed the door behind her when he came out of his workroom, hovering with a level of agitation that was unlike his usual impassivity. She had to look away from him as guilt for her infidelity surged through her, boiling and churning. She didn't regret whatever now existed between her and Ashtyn, but seeing the lines of concern on Symon's face reminded her that what she was doing was wrong not simply because it was prohibited by the law.

"What happened?" he asked before she even had time to remove her shoes.

"I got offered a position," she said, sitting on the bench and unlacing her sandals.

"A position? Two Guardians – one a Master – escorted you to be offered a job?"

"A whole room of Kade officials offered me the role. In their position, I'd want to make sure that I was delivered in a safe manner, too." She sighed the words out, the enormity of the offer finally settling upon her, making her feel so weary that she just wanted to go to bed and sleep for years and years.

"What exactly is this position?" Symon asked, shrewd calculation behind each slow word. Behind that was contained excitement.

"I would be in charge of one of the other Healing Centres, overseeing training, experimentation, that sort of thing." She stood and went to the kitchen, wanting to evade the speculation in his gaze. Symon followed her. She ladled out a bowl of the food he had prepared. When she asked if he wanted some, he shook his head. Uncharacteristically, he hadn't left her side. The unusual experience of his immediate presence was stifling.

"You're going to take it, aren't you?"

Freya wasn't sure if he was asking or telling her.

"Probably, I don't know. I haven't decided yet." Freya sat down and began to eat. As usual, it was delicious. After watching her for a moment, Symon sat, too.

"Freya, this is what we've worked for. This is the opportunity, the recognition. Everything we've done is finally paying off. This is incredible." He spoke with an excited intensity that she had only seen once or twice before.

"I thought you disliked the Kade," she pointed out.

"Of course I do, but that doesn't mean that I'm foolish enough to not want to do well in this society. I can't change anything, so I may as well work within the confines we've been set. Then maybe I can make my own life more comfortable. I thought you and I were of the same mind on this."

Her earlier guilt faded at his words as the faces of the Resistance members floated into her mind's eye. She wondered what they would say in response to his words. "So you're a collaborator?" she asked, using the word that Ashtyn had thrown at her so long ago.

He flinched, but didn't move. "I prefer pragmatist, but if you want to call it that, yes. No more than you are though." He shrugged, as though to emphasise his point.

Had he said that to her three days earlier, it would have been completely true.

"Doesn't it ever...bother you?" She pushed her bowl aside and looking at him across the table. She watched his face carefully, trying to discern what was going on behind his carefully controlled façade.

"Of course it does. I don't like being at the mercy of someone else. But you have to deal with what's been given to you, not the way you'd like life to be." His nonchalance threw her. "Why are you so interested now?"

Freya shifted uncomfortably. He was right, of course. The two of them had shared that unspoken understanding from the moment that she had come to him following her family's death, determined to survive in the Kade's world, no matter what the cost. And so they had lived in perfect Kade harmony, a law-abiding partnership. Now she had gone and changed all of that, first through her forbidden relationship with Ashtyn, and now by her attendance at the Resistance meeting. She knew on some level that the only reason Symon would be upset about her relationship with Ashtyn would be because it jeopardised their position within Kade society. She couldn't even begin to imagine how he would react if he found out about the Resistance. Certainly, it would not be positive. She felt as though the space between them was an impassable gulf. Although, it had always been. It just hadn't really bothered her before.

He was still watching her, waiting for a reply.

"I never really thought I'd be offered anything like this," she admitted.

He didn't seem to notice that she wasn't quite answering his questions. "We did what was asked of us and we're being rewarded. It's all we can ask for."

Freya wondered whether he would turn her over to the Kade if he found out about her connection to the Resistance, or her relationship with Ashtyn.

"What about the right to worship who we want?" she said, knowing full well that she should just let the matter drop.

"I thought you hated having this discussion," he pointed out.

"I thought you liked to."

At an impasse, they sat in silence. The minutes stretched out until Freya pulled the bowl back in front of her, picked up her spoon and resumed eating.

SEVENTEEN

"I made something for you," Ashtyn said.

Freya drowsily lifted her head to look at him. "Huh?"

He ran his fingers through her hair. "I made something for you."

She propped herself up on one elbow to look at him better, arching an eyebrow. "What is it?" She smiled, enjoying the way his fingers felt tangled in her hair.

"I have to get up to get it," he said, laughing at the look on her face at the prospect of him leaving her. "I'll come back, I promise," he added, extricating himself from the sprawl of their limbs. As he walked across the room, Freya's eyes roved appreciatively up and down the toned physique the absence of clothing revealed. He pulled something out of a drawer, keeping it concealed in his hands. Only when he had sat down on the mattress did he lay the laastram on the bed. Freya sat up suddenly and looked in wonder at the obvious craftsmanship that had gone into making the delicate item. She ran a finger down its links.

"It's beautiful," she said, awe making her voice quiet. The laastram was a Pious accessory, a series of metal bands placed along the length of the arm. Designed to be worn with a sleeveless tunic, the bands were linked by a fine chain. It was originally designed to be used to aid in stilling the mind, and giving the wearer greater control over their body. The individual was supposed to go through a series of movements without rattling the chain. The more fluid the movement, the better the meditative state and, of course, the better the connection to the Goddess. However, over the generations it had become a piece of fashion; worn decoratively as well as religiously. Then, its use evolved once more during the takeover when wearing them had been banned along with any other traditional Pious garb or practices. Pious who had fought against the Kade had worn it in skirmishes as a marker of their unwillingness to give up the Goddess. Amid the fighting, it had been discovered that they formed an unexpectedly effective shield against blades when the wearers raised their arms to ward off blows and the swords and daggers had met the solid metal rings rather than yielding flesh.

"Will you put it on?" he asked, almost shyly.

"I only have long-sleeved robes here," she said.

He grinned. "I think it would look good with nothing else on."

She crossed her arms and pursed her lips. She would not put on a religious object like a laastram when naked.

He laughed. "All right, I should have something." Still apparently feeling the need to remain exactly the way the Goddess had made him – which was particularly fine craftsmanship, in Freya's opinion – he once more left the bed and went hunting through his clothes, eventually throwing her a brown sleeveless tunic. Freya pulled it on; the material was coarse against her skin without the normal undershirt, and it was several sizes too big, falling almost to her calves, but it would do. She picked up the linked bands and slid them up her arm until they were settled firmly on her flesh and would not move unless she worked hard to dislodge them.

"How does it look?" she asked, adjusting to the weight and feel of the cool metal against her skin.

"Come and see for yourself," he said, gesturing to a highly polished piece of metal hanging on the wall.

She stood, looking uncertainly at her reflection. In front of her was a woman who looked like her. But this person was different. There was a determination about her that Freya liked; an intent to the way she held herself. "I like it. Why did you make it, though? I'll never be able to wear it."

"You could say, then, that you'll never be able to wear anything I make for you," he said. "I may as well make you something that has meaning." She touched the bands self-consciously. He had a point.

"Anyway, how about we call it aspirational." He smiled at her and she felt warmth bloom in her chest.

She reluctantly took off the laastram and stacked the bands so that they fitted neatly in her palm. For a moment, she looked at it, then with no small amount of reluctance, she offered it back to him. "It's beautiful," she said, touched that he would think to make her something. In some ways, the fact it was a piece that she could not wear made it all the more meaningful; he had put the effort into something simply so that she knew he was thinking of her. It was a beautifully impractical gesture. As his hand brushed hers to take the laastram back, she put her free hand around the back of his neck and pulled him toward her, kissing him tenderly. "Thank you."

With his free hand, he caressed her cheek. "You inspire me so, Freya."

She was left unsure what to say.

He replaced the laastram in its hiding place, then said, "There's a meeting this afternoon. Would you like to come with me? There may be something interesting there that I can show you."

She laughed. "The last time you said you'd show me something interesting, you took me to meet the Resistance. What could you possibly show me now?"

He threw her a mysterious look. "Well, if you come with me, you'll see."

Freya sat back on his bed, folding her arms across her chest. "I need more than that," she said playfully. It had been two full fivedays since she had been introduced to the Resistance and although they had seen each other several times since then, Ashtyn hadn't explicitly asked her to join him in attending another

A B Endacott

meeting. He had asked her subtly, but frequently, if she had considered joining them, and each time she had demurred, unwilling to step into outright defiance against the Kade. The Kade had made even fewer demands on her, with runners only arriving at her door on two days sending her to help in areas of the city where there was a shortage of healers. According to a message she had received from the Chief Healer, she would soon be assigned to run one of the city's remaining Healing Centres. Perhaps the time off was because the Kade was still scrambling to reorder the city so it was better under its control, or 'restructuring' as one of the Kade leaders had termed it. Or perhaps it was a reward for the years of hard work. She didn't care to think too much about it, still wondering to what exactly she was agreeing if she did accept the position the Kade officials had offered her. Not that she really had the capacity to refuse it. In the time when she had not been seeing Ashtyn, Freya had remained mostly at home, organising her notes or reading the medical tomes she had accumulated. The waiting was becoming tedious.

"Believe me when I tell you that you'll like it." Ashtyn picked up the clothes scattered around the room and gave them to her, pulling his own on with quick movements. As she regretfully watched his skin disappear beneath layers of clothing, she contemplated pretending to refuse. But her curiosity was too strong, so she dressed and followed him out.

She had assumed that they would return to the warehouse. Instead, they headed to the other side of the city, near the border of the artists' and builders' districts. Ashtyn knocked on the door of a building bearing a stonemason's sign. One of the women Freya recognised from the last Resistance meeting opened the door. Astrom, if Freya remembered correctly. The warmth of the smile she gave Freya as they walked in seemed genuine and Freya found herself smiling back.

In the two fivedays since she had first met the Resistance, since the Centre had fallen, the predictions made at that meeting had turned out to be unnervingly accurate. The Kade had put into place severe curfews and restrictions, nobody was allowed out at night, merchants were being regularly stopped and searched, and whispers of interrogations being conducted on 'people of interest' had travelled around the city faster than water. At this new meeting, Freya expected to be exposed to more of the previous discussion. She was mildly curious about what they may predict the Kade would do next, although that curiosity warred with exasperation that Ashtyn had brought her back to the Resistance. Contrary to her expectation, though, the workshop space into which she was led had been cleared of any furniture, leaving the room off-puttingly bare. The same people from the last meeting were standing around the edges of the room, quietly chatting. Makkyd greeted Freya in the Pious way, her thumb pressing into Freya's palm. "I'm so glad that you could make it."

"I'm flattered," Freya murmured.

"Have you told her?" Makkyd asked Ashtyn.

He shook his head, "I thought it may be easier to show her."

"Show me what?" Freya looked from Ashtyn to Makkyd, irritated at having yet something else hidden from her.

"Do you remember when you were telling me that when we pray, the Goddess draws strength from us?" Ashtyn began.

She nodded.

"And if that faith, that connection, is strong enough, the person who is praying comes away with some of the abilities of the Goddess?"

"Yes," she said cautiously. "I'm a good healer because of my faith. In a similar way, probably, that Ashtyn is a fine craftsman because of his." She was still truly coming to terms with exactly what Zarech had revealed to her, but it made too much sense for her to reject. The truth of his words filled her alternately with exhilaration and dread for everything that it implied.

"It goes a little beyond that," Makkyd said.

"I don't understand."

"Ashtyn?" Makkyd prompted.

"Watch." Ashtyn stepped into the middle of the cleared space. He took a small flat strip of metal from his pocket and held it in his open palm. For several moments, nothing happened as he simply looked at it intently, then the metal began to glow as if it was hot, first orange, then red. Ashtyn calmly twisted and moulded the metal as though it were mere clay, appearing to suffer no ill effects from the hot metal in his hands. Once he was satisfied with the shape, the glow swiftly faded. It looked as though the metal had always been that way rather than moulded by hand a few seconds ago.

Freya watched, astonished. "Did you just..." She was unable to say what she thought she had just seen, for fear that she had hallucinated. Even with what Zarech had told her, this was beyond anything she had imagined.

A smile moved Ashtyn's features into an even more attractive arrangement.

"How are you doing that?"

"With a little assistance from our Goddess," he said, excitement igniting the green of his eyes. Freya's pulse begin to thunder, the combination of the amazing feat she had just witnessed and the delighted expression on Ashtyn's face to blame.

"It's not entirely clear," Makkyd added. "Some of the most holy writings probably offer some explanation, but they've either been locked up or destroyed by the Kade. Similarly, our own Ordained – our Goddess's Children – would likely have known, but one of the first actions of the Kade was to kill them all. So there isn't much that we really know for sure." Makkyd's mouth pressed into a bitter line at the destruction done to the culture and knowledge of the Pious at the hands of the Kade. Freya felt a pang as she remembered that Zarech had been one of the Goddess's Children. He had known about these abilities – he had told her about them, and she hadn't truly listened to what he had been saying. It was entirely possible that he had been the last person alive who knew these secrets.

Ashtyn shrugged, closing his hand around the twisted piece of metal and slipping both his hands into his pockets. "In the way that our religious stories tell that immortal beings can directly affect our world in certain circumstances, we think that power is bestowed upon us in a diluted form. It takes a lot of work to actually do anything of worth, but it's a skill that can be used."

Freya went over to him and pulled one of his hands free, wanting to verify for herself that he wasn't burned. She ran her fingers over his palm. It wasn't even warmer than usual. She looked up at him. "Surely this is impossible," she said, her voice so low that only he could hear. But even as the words left her mouth, she knew she did believe this, that she had been waiting to see something exactly like this for a very, very long time.

"I thought so, too, when I first saw it, but here I am." He smiled, closing his fingers around hers. "You said the Goddess was disinterested in our world. Perhaps she isn't – perhaps she does actually leave her mark on the world. Through us." He closed his hand around hers and spoke as though she were the only one in the room.

She looked into the deep green of his eyes surrounded by creases made by his smile, and she felt her breath flee her.

Slowly becoming conscious of the eyes on the two of them, she pulled herself back to the present moment. "You were doing this in your workshop that morning after the curfew." She remembered how confused she had been that he had not been using any tools. Now it made sense.

"I wondered if you'd noticed."

"I should be able to do this too, shouldn't I?"

"You already do with your healing to some extent, if the rumours are to be believed," Makkyd said.

Freya again wondered how much Ashtyn had told these people about her. It made her uncomfortable to think that they knew everything about who she was, while she knew nothing about any of them.

More of Ashtyn's unusual comments began to make sense, trickling back through her memory. "You said to me that day in the market that I could heal that man. You knew."

"It was an educated guess. After you spoke the prayer with me."

"So he died, and I could have saved him." The realisation that every life she had lost as a healer was a personal failure wiped away the elation that had been building inside her at the magnificence of what she was being shown. Her eyes slid away from his as she thought of the man who had been crushed under the rubble.

"Only if you had known what you could do. Even if you would have believed me then and there, it's unlikely that you could have done anything." His hand tightened around hers in emphasis.

"Think of the people you can heal now," Makkyd urged. "Don't look back, look forward at who you can save."

They were both correct, but it didn't do much to alleviate the bitterness that had pooled in the back of her throat. She pushed aside her distress for later rumination. She wasn't going to get any sympathy here. Everybody in the room would only repeat Makkyd's advice. With an effort, she swallowed and looked up at Makkyd's intent eyes, moving her attention and feelings to the excitement of discovery, for now at least. "What else is there?"

Bardan stepped forward, a half smile on his face. "Move back," he advised her, "I'm not always good at controlling it."

Ashtyn, still holding her hand, guided her so they were nearer the room's periphery. She watched as Bardan closed his eyes and whispered to himself. The faintest fragments of his words danced around her ears – he was whispering a prayer to the Goddess. Soon the sound of his whispers became more audible, borne by a faint breeze that had sprung up. It grew in intensity until it ruffled Freya's hair and tugged at the hem of her robe.

"Don't go knocking things over," Makkyd cautioned. A few people laughed.

Her comment made Freya consider what a powerful tool such an ability would be in a fight. It could be used to knock enemies over, or blind them. She shook her head, wondering why she had leaped to that thought first. It was such a violent idea.

The breeze became even stronger, then suddenly dropped away as Bardan opened his eyes and stopped whispering. "It takes a fair effort to sustain," he said, the dazed look of someone who had abruptly stopped concentrating with intense focus creeping into his eyes.

"Does everybody do different things?" Freya asked, her mind whirling with the possibilities.

"It depends. I'm a craftsperson myself like Ashtyn, but I'm a stonemason. I can manipulate stones, although I don't heat anything like Ashtyn does," Astrom answered. She had a melodious voice that made people want to keep listening to her.

"Perhaps it's simply because that's what we spend the most time thinking of, but it's mostly some kind of extension of our trades," Ashtyn added. "For instance, those who work on farms have reported that they can hear the plants singing to them, although that may just be country inbreeding." He chuckled.

Bardan let out a chuckle too, but was silenced by a look from Makkyd. "Don't encourage him," Makkyd said, her voice dry. "Artists are the most interesting ones, in my opinion. Lyssa can make ink and charcoal fly across a page."

Freya looked to Lyssa, who immediately shot her back a look of contempt. "I suppose you want me to show you."

"If you would be so kind, Lyssa," Astrom said, sounding entirely unruffled by Lyssa's poison tone.

Lyssa's features softened at the request and she inclined her head in assent. Astrom pulled a piece of paper and an inkwell from a table and put them on the floor.

Lyssa took three quick steps forward and kicked the inkwell over. Freya gasped as the blue-black ink spread across the tiles. Then, with a dismissive flick of her hand, Lyssa sent the ink surging back toward the paper. When it reached the edge of the page, it didn't sink in, but diverged into separate lines, almost like veins. After a few seconds, the lines formed the perfect shape of a scribe's pen. Only then did the ink settle into the page.

"Are you able to alter the image after the ink dries into the page?" Freya asked, intrigued enough to brave Lyssa's contempt.

"I've never tried, but I'm sure I could," the other woman responded, turning on her heel and returning to the edge of the room, leaving Astrom to stoop down and pick up the paper and empty inkwell, which she did with no apparent resentfulness.

"It's beautiful," Freya said, meaning it.

Lyssa shrugged, the unpleasant expression never leaving her features. "It's certainly more interesting than what I normally do. Making art that glorifies the Kade and their trio of gods all day is a waste of my talent."

Freya wanted to ask more about what the Kade had Lyssa do – she was well acquainted with the posters and murals across the city that depicted the trio of the Kade gods: heat, light, and strength, in their various incarnations and manifestations. She had always assumed the plays venerating the Kade and often portraying the Pious as malign or weak were written to inculcate the message of the Kade's superiority, but she had somehow never put much thought into who produced them. She had always assumed that the artists and writers who created such things actually did so out of religious fervour.

Bardan spoke before she could question Lyssa further "I want to see Freya heal." Despite being a bulky, fully grown man, he sounded like an excited child.

Panic overwhelmed her, driving consideration of murals and plays from her mind. "I didn't even know until a few moments ago I could do anything like this."

"She's right," Lyssa said. "For some of us, doing anything takes a long time."

Ashtyn turned to Freya. "Nonsense, you already heal people. That's why people under your care get better so quickly. Here." To Freya's surprise, he drew a short knife from a hidden sheath on his belt. Before she could ask him what he was doing, he pulled it across the skin on his forearm. Bright, red blood welled along the long cut. "It's only shallow, it should be easy." He held his arm out as though he hadn't just sliced himself open.

In shock, she looked at his face, then at the cut on his arm. "How am I even supposed to know what to do?"

"How do you know what's wrong with people?" he asked.

"I just...know," she stammered.

"So try." He shook his arm slightly. Some of the blood trickled down the side and dropped onto the floor.

Fighting her trepidation, she put her hands on his arm and closed her eyes. She tried to ignore the people in the room and instead focus on the hum of Ashtyn's body as it met her fingertips. The hum, now that she knew what it was, made sense, as did the dissonance to it: the cut that was right near her fingertips. She had always assumed everybody was aware of this sense that people gave off, and it was why people so often shied away from the sick – because their sound was so discordant. It was a revelation to realise this was a skill special to her, that she had been instinctively doing something her whole life without ever understanding. A shiver of exhilaration shot through her as she considered how much more about her craft she could understand now that this veil had been lifted. But locating the source of an ailment was something she could already do. She could *feel* her connection to the flesh under her fingers and she wanted to know what else she could do. She focused on the dissonant note of the cut and probed it with that extra sense. She could feel the rip in his skin, the neat way that it had been sliced apart, and thought about bringing the skin back together. Slowly, the dissonant note became weaker and weaker until it faded away completely. She opened her eyes and released his arm. Had there not still been blood smeared across his arm, it would have been impossible to tell it had ever been cut. The room broke out into a smattering of applause as Ashtyn held up his arm for everybody to see.

Freya was silent for a moment, emotions crashing and colliding within her. "Can anyone do it?"

"I'm not following," Ashtyn said.

"Well, would Kade followers have these sorts of abilities?"

"If their faith is strong enough, we assume so. Although, if they weren't instructed, like you, they may not understand their abilities and just think they have an unusually high aptitude in a particular area," he said.

She raised an eyebrow. "Even if it's like Bardan's?"

"You can explain away the wind picking up just as you lose yourself to anger as a very fitting coincidence," Bardan said. "If you don't tell people about this sort of thing, most won't go looking for it. Only the people who have knowledge of the holy writings and religious teachings know that this isn't coincidence or a trick of the mind, and actually work to hone these gifts."

His words about knowledge of holy writings pulled on a thread in her mind. "And the Followers of the Dark Gods, would they have such abilities?"

"We believe so. Why?"

"It might explain how the explosions in the Healing Centre were started," she said, delicately picking her way across her words to avoid revealing her protracted contact with Zarech. That was not a discussion she wanted to have just yet. The room was silent as she spoke. "If someone had the ability to corral the gas pipes, they could have flooded the building with gas quickly, then ignited it. Or maybe several somebodies." She shrugged, uncomfortable with the attention. She had been the central focus of the room from the moment Ashtyn had brought her in, and she had no desire to be so.

Makkyd stepped forward, the movement reclaiming the attention from Freya. "We've always assumed that these abilities were something the Kade elite wanted to keep secret. Can you imagine trying to control a society where everybody can manipulate the world around them, and in different and unpredictable ways, too? I certainly wouldn't want to."

"But the Followers of the Dark Gods don't care about order. They're interested in chaos," Freya pointed out.

"True. Give them something that will help them inflict damage and they'll use it," Makkyd mused. "You're very sharp, Freya."

Freya flushed at the compliment. Makkyd didn't strike her as a woman who gave them out freely.

"We would call you one of us if you were willing, you know," Makkyd said. It seemed a casual comment, but Freya couldn't help but feel that this whole demonstration had been leading to her being asked this question.

She felt trapped, aware of the other people watching her, waiting for her answer. She knew that committing herself to this group was to commit herself to walking away from her constructed life of allegiance to the Kade. But she had already come so far. It seemed that there was no turning back. So she forced a smile to her face and nodded.

The next day of rest was finally the day for the memorial of all the people who had been killed in the destruction of the Healing Centre. The death toll had been enormous. Nearly all the patients inside had perished, and almost half of the healers. Several people in the immediate vicinity had been killed by flying rubble, or even from inhaling the thick, choking dust caused by so much stone being pulverised.

Freya should have gone to the ceremony. The healers who had died were people alongside whom she had worked for years. But the thought of enduring the Kade service made her feel ill, especially as it had taken so much time for them to organise it. She knew that the delay had been caused by the Kade focusing on cleaning up the city, on maintaining their appearance of competence and control, rather than paying homage to the victims of a terrible crime. She didn't want to support that. So she stayed at home, aimlessly wandering from room to room while Symon worked in his workroom on a commission for a Kade official. It seemed he was in high demand by very powerful people, especially if her glance at the robes worn by the roomful of Kade elite had been anything to go by. Symon was in good spirits during the one or two occasions he had emerged from his workroom, accepting her explanation of feeling ill as to why she did not attend the service with distracted sympathy. Success suited him.

By the afternoon she was bored, but she had no reason to leave the house. She couldn't see Ashtyn. He was busy on some Resistance matter. But even if he had been free, she knew they had been spending far too much time together. If she continued to see him this frequently, they were sure to be discovered.

Aimlessly, she went into her own workroom and tried to organise the notes on her observations of the body and various medicines that she had experimented with making or refining over the years. Looking at her diagrams, directions and notes, all made in an effort to heal people better and faster, she considered the power that she now knew lay within her. She wondered how far the limits of her capabilities extended: if she could heal broken bones with a thought, or purge poisons from someone's system merely by the force of her will. Her notes on the properties of antidotes may well be useless if that was the case. She was unsure whether to have a crisis over all the time she had wasted trying to cure people with conventional methods, or exhilarated by the realisation of how many people she could help now that she knew what she could truly do. She was on the floor, surrounded by a sea of paper, when a knock on the door echoed through the house.

"I'll go," she called to Symon as she stepped delicately over the scattered pages.

When she opened the door, she found herself face to face with the Master-level Guardian who had escorted her to the Kade interview.

"Yes?" she asked. It was not only her recent commitment to overthrowing his regime making her feel recklessly bold in the face of his authority, but the discovery of this power within her.

"I have been asked to get you to sign your acceptance of the position of head of the Merchant District's Healing Centre. You will receive instructions in the next few days regarding your new duties, but you will start work at the commencement of the next fiveday," he told her, a dislike reminiscent of Lyssa's radiating from him.

Freya led him inside, rolling her eyes once her back was to him. She took the document, noting it was on vellum rather than paper, and read through it as she went into her study for a scribe's pen with which to sign it. She returned, her signature on the bottom of the page, and proffered it to the Guardian.

"This is a contract which also requires your thumbprint," he said, pulling a thin knife from his belt and offering it to her.

"Thanks," Freya said sarcastically, wincing as she drew the blade across the soft pad of her thumb, allowing the blood to well before pressing it to the page. "I suppose if I do something wrong now, my blood will boil in my veins?" she said as she handed him back the blade and the contract.

"Just because you now have a position of some authority does not give you the authority to mock the Kade," he said, the faintest whisper of menace in his tone.

"I was merely asking," Freya said innocently.

"So long as that's all you were doing," he said. Before he left he gave her a long look, which she matched unflinchingly.

Freya muttered obscenities at him under her breath as she focused her attention on drawing the cut on her thumb closed. She smiled with satisfaction when she saw the cut was healed. The only indication that there had been any injury to her thumb was the red of her own blood smeared across it.

EIGHTEEN

Freya couldn't help but feel irked. When she started her new position, she would almost certainly be working even longer hours than before. She would barely have the time to see Ashtyn and she wanted to enjoy the last few days of free time that she had with him, preferably naked. But he had told her that there was a Resistance meeting and it was important that they go. So she found herself being taken back to the warehouse where she had first been introduced to them.

"How often do you meet!" she protested.

"As often as possible," he replied, pulling her into a rough embrace as they reached the warehouse entrance. Freya relaxed into his arms, enjoying the easy affection with which he treated her, even as she scanned the street for anyone who might be watching.

"Planning an insurgency makes having time with you difficult," she grumbled against his chest. His laugh echoed deep in her ears as he knocked on the door.

Bardan pulled them inside with his usual exuberance.

"Good thing you both made it," he said.

"We nearly didn't," Ashtyn commented, throwing an amused look at Freya. She stuck her tongue out at him, causing him to chuckle again.

Bardan continued as though Ashtyn hadn't spoken, although he threw an amused look at Freya. "Big things are happening. The Kade is restructuring, moving things around. We think the attack on the Healing Centre has shaken them more than we initially suspected," he explained as he led them to the hidden doorway, down the corridor and into the meeting room which was filled with the quiet hum of conversation. Once again, they were the last to arrive.

Freya had a moment to notice the curve of Makkyd's shoulders that spoke to intense scrutiny of the document in front of her before she looked up at them. "Ah, good, we can start." More papers were stacked across the table at which she stood, the piles neatly ordered. Freya was again surprised by the extent of the Resistance. Their reach was far, and the level of organisation with which they conducted themselves rivalled the Kade. It was clear that the Kade governance was still secure in its position, but it didn't seem quite as omnipotent as it had.

"How are you coming along with the swords, Ashtyn?" Makkyd asked.

He slipped his hands into his pockets in a gesture that had become familiar to Freya. "Not as fast as I'd like. I'm having trouble ensuring that I have enough material to make them at the quality and in the quantity that we need. That, and I've been preoccupied." He winked at Freya. The gesture was caught by Lyssa who made a noise of disgust. Ashtyn didn't acknowledge Lyssa's reaction as he continued. "But I think I might have found a way to make the iron even stronger. It needs to be heated to an extremely high temperature, then I blow air across it, which leaves the final product stronger and less likely to break..." He paused when he saw Makkyd's expression. "I think I can make stronger weapons with the material we do have," he surmised.

Freya swallowed a smile. Ashtyn was passionate about his work, and he had tried to explain the same thing to her on their way here She too had found it hard to follow and was not overly interested in the process.

"Well, as the Guardians are busy protecting important Kade officials from anything else that they of course have anticipated—" sarcasm dripped from the last few words and she paused to allow everybody in the room to snigger before she continued "—it means we have more opportunities to move our supplies around Oranis, and acquire new material. We shouldn't waste the chance. If you can, Ashtyn, we need more daggers."

Ashtyn's nod was pure business, the humour and laughter departing swiftly from his face. Freya watched as he received the order and felt stupid. She should have realised that Ashtyn must be one of the people who supplied the Resistance with weapons. Ownership of weapons was severely regulated by the Kade, so it made sense that in addition to smuggling them, they would be making their own, especially if someone like Ashtyn could do it without the conspicuous use of a forge to heat the metal. His position as gildsmith would give him access to the materials, and his skill would mean that the Resistance was armed with the finest-quality weapons. Now the reason he took no apprentice or other staff made perfect sense. She wondered why Ashtyn hadn't told her. Was he keeping other secrets from her?

The fluttering of panic – the product of years under the Kade rule, which told her to trust nobody – played about her throat, making her breaths an effort, but she forced herself to slow her breathing, to calm down. She had never asked Ashtyn about his role in the Resistance, and she shouldn't expect him to casually proffer the information. She looked over at Lyssa, catching the beautiful woman regarding Freya contemplatively. She wondered from where Lyssa's apparent dislike for her originated. Was some history with Lyssa another secret that Ashtyn was keeping from her?

Freya looked away first, preferring to listen to the discussion rather than lose herself in speculation and paranoia.

"There are whispers of even greater repression to come," a younger man, Grat, was saying. "Our administrators who attend the Kade officials say that they want to reinforce their power in the minds of the people by any means necessary."

"Surely they've done that in the weeks since the marketplace incident?" Bardan said.

"Yes, but it didn't work. The Healing Centre was destroyed. Even with their 'response team', it's obvious the measures they put in place following the marketplace didn't work. People are scared. There are whispers – fuelled by us, of course – that the Kade can't rule effectively. So the Kade want to crack down even harder. More patrols, new laws, an even more severe enforcement on worships. They're even going to revive the informant network."

What Symon had raised as a chilling possibility so many fivedays ago had apparently become a decision. So much had transpired in the intervening fivedays since the day after the first curfew – the day after she had slept at Ashtyn's house – that she had almost forgotten what Symon had relayed to her from a careless discussion that took place in front of him. But only almost.

"I thought the informant network still existed," Bardan said.

"To an extent, yes," Grat said. "But there has been no active attempt to recruit for several years, nor has there been public discussion of the network. The need fell away, so they stopped maintaining it. A few informants still report in, but the Kade knows a lot less about the citizens than it would like us to think...for now."

Freya shivered, thinking of the faces in the crowd at morning prayers who she'd always feared, expecting them to be watching her for any sign of discontent. It seemed that for the years when she hadn't had anything to worry about, they hadn't really been there. Now that she was a part of the Resistance and did need to worry about being observed, they would be returning. She thought of Symon and his focus on their life of comfort and safety. She wondered if he would turn her into the Kade if he found out about her secret life.

Makkyd rapped her knuckles on the table for attention, reclaiming the conversation from Bardan and Grat. "This is all well and good, but I want to focus on making the most of this opportunity. Freya, have you taken the position in the Merchant District's Healing Centre?"

Cold shock enveloped Freya, tingling along her arms, the tip of her nose. She hadn't told any of them about the Kade's offer, not even Ashtyn. Her eyes flicked over to him, but he looked entirely unsurprised to hear this information about her new position. "How did you know about that?"

"We have people working within the Kade administration, like Grat. We know a lot of their appointments and decisions. Have you formally accepted the role?"

Uneasy, Freya nodded.

"Good. Now, as part of that you'll have access to the store of herbs, medicines and other drugs, and the records they keep of those items. That's a tremendous in for us, one we've been waiting to get for a while. We need to start our own stockpile. Normally we'd liberate some from merchants, but a lot of the medicinal herbs are too strictly guarded, and their quantities are too carefully recorded, and we've survived this long by not alerting the Kade about how far-reaching our operation is."

"Wait a moment," Freya said. "You want me to steal from the stocks of the Healing Centre?"

"Of course. You're the link we've been waiting for," Makkyd replied.

"Me...specifically?" Freya asked.

Makkyd tried to hold Freya's gaze, but Freya saw the unease that flashed across her eyes.

"Yours is a name that drew our attention. The Kade has been interested in you for many years. They even seem to trust you, despite the fact that you are a Pious. They even assigned you to Zarech."

"How did you know that?" Freya's voice rose as she fought to keep calm.

"Like I said, we have people in places who know these things."

"So why does my position matter?" She had known the Resistance would ask things of her, but the way Makkyd was speaking, it was as though she were special – as though they had known about her for far longer than she had thought. The sense of being hunted crept around her.

"Because you had, and have, access to things that even our sources don't know." Makkyd's voice was patient.

"When did you find this out about me?" Freya asked. Once more, she was the centre of everybody's focus. The room had gone still, tension strung across the space. Ashtyn had paled, his expression as though he'd taken a bite of something rotten. Even Makkyd looked uncomfortable, now. Freya looked around at each silent face. Nobody would meet her eye, not even Lyssa.

"How long have you been targeting me?" Freya asked, a shrill edge to her voice.

There was no answer. Freya repeated the question, surprised by how much calmer she sounded this time, how much more authoritative her voice sounded, despite the trembling that threatened to consume her.

Still nobody answered her.

"Tell me or I'll go to the Kade and tell them everything I know right now." Only the slightest quaver shook her voice.

Lyssa said, without any trace of her customary sneer, "Several cycles now."

Freya wasn't sure if she heard sympathy or triumph in her voice. She turned to Ashtyn. "Before or after the explosions in the marketplace?"

His face was unreadable. He didn't answer her.

"Ashtyn..." Finally that initial fluttering panic claimed her throat, and she could not get the words out. She looked at him, her expression imploring him to tell her that it had been after he had first helped her up from the ground.

He swallowed. "Before." He barely whispered it. But the room was so silent it was as though he had yelled in her ear.

"It wasn't an accident that you were there to help me, was it?"

"I...had been assigned to shadow you," he admitted.

The room seemed to be shrinking around her. "I can't believe this," she said, more to herself than to anyone else. The feeling of being suffocated overtook her. She needed to get out, away from the gazes of everybody there, out of that tiny, hidden room with all of its secrets and tangled plans. She pushed past Ashtyn, evading his grasp, and ran back through the corridor and out of the building. Once she was on the street, she took deep gasping breaths. She wrapped her arms around her abdomen in some vague effort to keep herself from feeling a though she was going to fall apart. It felt like she had been stabbed in the stomach, but despite the pain that accompanied each gasp, she wouldn't let herself sink down onto the ground. If she did, she wasn't sure that she would get up again.

Ashtyn appeared, anguish written into his expression. He went to put his hand on her arm.

"Don't touch me," she screamed, not caring if anybody else heard the commotion.

"I can explain," he began, but she held up a hand to forestall whatever he would say.

"You seduced me because you wanted to recruit me." She flung the accusation at him, wanting to believe it, to be able to hate him completely. Her anger sustained the numbness that was rapidly erasing the pain throughout her body. It kept her from falling down, from crying, from completely coming apart.

His expression nearly broke her heart. "Believe what you want, Freya, but even if that were true, I grew to care about you, and how I feel about you has nothing to do with any of this." He waved his hand toward the warehouse behind them.

"You told me you wanted to go away and live out our days somewhere away from all this." She knew she was on the verge of shattering into a thousand pieces.

"I meant it. I adore you, Freya. Say the word and we can—"

"Stop lying to me!" She didn't want to hear that he cared for her. It made his betrayal hurt all the more. It was as though someone was rending her insides apart and no matter how skilled a healer she was, she couldn't put them back together again.

"Freya..." he said helplessly. He reached out to her again, but she recoiled as though his touch was poison.

The distress on his face was almost more than she could bear. She could not be broken-hearted for the both of them. For a long time they were immobile, staring at one another, his hand extended to her. She nearly broke, nearly took it. But she couldn't look at this person who had betrayed her, who had lied to her, who had kept so many secrets from her, and not feel as though he was always going to be manipulating her to serve his cause. She couldn't trust him.

"Leave me alone, Ashtyn," she said. Bitterness coated her words.

A look of resignation took hold of his features. It was almost worse than the one of pain. "All right then, if that's what you want. But know this. I will love you until the last," he said.

She all but ran away from him, resolving to put all thoughts of the Pious Resistance and their astounding abilities as far from her mind as possible. They wanted to use and manipulate her in the same way the Kade did. She had been targeted, stalked, seduced, and only by accident had she even discovered this conspiracy to recruit her. Somehow, being manipulated by her own kind seemed far worse than anything the Kade had done in the years that she had served them.

She arrived home wild eyed, like some untamed animal, shivering and barely able to speak. Symon looked at her with questions in his eyes, but she shook her head, going instead into the bathing room. She left her clothes in a disordered trail behind her, shucking them off with little thought to where they fell. She waited impatiently for the water to heat up, then she sat down and let it flow over her. The wet heat trickled over her skin, but it couldn't melt the ice that had formed within her. She felt so unbearably alone, so terribly shattered and broken. Even when her family had died, she had never felt like this, like she was never going to be put back together again. The water flowed down, covering every part of her, but still she was cold. She wrapped her arms around her legs and shivered. After her family had died, she had found conspiratorial companionship with Symon in their perfect façade of obedience. Ashtyn and the Resistance had given her a sliver of hope for a better life, of something more than simply following somebody else's rules. But she couldn't be a part of a cause that had sought to use her so callously, so secretively. She had been targeted, isolated, and when the time was right and she was receptive, she had been brought in. She felt so stupid. So betrayed.

When the hot water ran out she sat there still, shivering more and more violently until every part of her was as numb as her heart. Amid the misery that circled her, the tiny callous part of her that had forced her to show her loyalty to the Kade spoke up. She had two choices: to stay in the bathroom forever, cold and wet and naked, or survive. So slowly she began to reconstruct herself, agonisingly putting the pieces of who she was back together, promising herself that it wasn't the end of the world, it only felt that way. Finally she felt strong enough to stand, holding her head high, controlling her treacherous limbs that still tried to shake.

She emerged silent, as though nothing had ever even seemed wrong, wrapped in a fresh robe. Symon was sketching at the table. He looked up as she walked out, his eyes settling on her. She wondered what he was thinking, but as had been his way for all of the years she had known him, his expression gave nothing away. After he had seen whatever it was he was seeking, he nodded once, and stood, going into the kitchen. He returned with a plate of slices of hana and preserved vegetables. Wordlessly, he offered it to her. She slid into a seat and took the plate from him, picking up one of the hana pieces, chewing but not really tasting it.

"Is everything all right?" he asked her after he sat back down. His hand hovered over the design, the sharpened stick of charcoal elegantly positioned between his long, thin fingers.

"I'm going to need robes for the new position. Will you make them for me?" she asked.

"Of course. But can't you just get them issued to you?" If he was surprised by her lack of response to his question, he didn't show it.

"Yes. But I want to look as good as possible. Nothing surpasses your work," she replied, her voice flat, determined.

He nodded. "The tunics have Kade colours on them, don't they?"

"Yes."

"But the green stripe stays, I assume?"

"Yes."

He snorted softly. "Typical."

She said nothing.

He didn't seem to notice. "I'll have them made by the end of this fiveday. Is that all right?"

"Perfect."

NINETEEN

Freya commenced her new role with very little ceremony. As the days moved by and melted into fivedays, she was surprised by how swiftly the world of resistance and forbidden love became a mere memory and she returned to the role of an upstanding Kade citizen. It did help that she enjoyed her work. The Healing Centre quickly became her own, arranged to her specifications, her layout, her methodology. Under her leadership it flourished, a model of efficiency and innovative practices. Freya did not accept anything but the best from her people. If even a bed was crooked she would notice during her regular wanderings through the wards. She swore to herself that she would not be a leader who was barely seen. The Chief Healer had elevated herself to practically become a legend by rarely speaking with anybody within the Centre. Freya didn't like the idea that she may simply evolve into a figure entirely surrounded by mystery and hearsay. There was something about the prospect that left her feeling cold and alone. She didn't want to be any more isolated from the people around her than she already was.

As the fivedays slipped by, she was so busy orchestrating the activities of the Centre that she simply didn't have time to do any healing work. But she didn't really mind that because, as she said to anybody who asked, her position's requirements kept her totally engaged. In truth, she was grateful that she wasn't forced to be reminded of the abilities the Resistance had shown her. Deep down, curiosity to know exactly what she could do was gnawing at her with an abiding hunger, and a part of her desperately wanted to test the limits of this power within herself. But she dismissed those thoughts as soon as they came into her head – which was far more often than she liked. Those thoughts frightened her. They were dangerous. She didn't want to be tempted to use that power. If it were discovered, she could hardly begin to imagine what attention she would attract. Attention would lead to questions: Why she had not informed the Kade of her abilities as soon as she had discovered them? How had she discovered them? The consequence would of course be doubt over her loyalty to the Kade, not only because she had failed to tell the Kade of her power, but because if her ability to heal people with her mind truly did come from faith, it inevitably led to the question of in whom exactly that faith was vested. That sort of doubt only ever led to bad things for the individual in question. It was far easier to throw herself into the other elements of her role and keep as far away from the actual healing work as possible.

She worked long hours, but that didn't bother her at all. In fact, she appreciated both the demands on her time, and the fact that every moment of her day was filled with something that required her full attention. By the time she went home, often after the curfew, but with permission to be out at such an hour due to her position, she was too exhausted to think about anything other than the requirements the next day would bring. She simply ate, slept and rose again with the bells. She dutifully attended the prayers, often going to the square alongside the Healing Centre because she couldn't attend the square in her district. She was so busy that she could pretend she didn't notice the way in which the city was changing. She barely noticed the extra Guardian patrols on the streets. Her mind was so filled with running the Centre, with thoughts of how to best organise wards or what new techniques she could trial, that the stories of people dragged from their houses for not going to enough prayers, turned in by a neighbour seeking to curry favour with a Kade administrator seemed disconnected from the world of the Healing Centre. She noticed the emptiness of the streets and the fearful quiet of her own Pious district, but she could easily tell herself that she was walking through the streets late at night or early in the morning when the curfew which fell across the city kept almost everybody else inside, so of course the streets seemed more sinister at such times. She was playing her part to perfection.

And yet, in those rare occasions when there was enough space in her mind for it to wander, she missed Ashtyn. Painfully. Even though they had only been lovers for a short time, leaving him had felt as though she were tearing a part of herself away and leaving it behind. She missed the way he made her life so exciting, the way he smiled at her, the way he made her feel. She told herself that the stabbing sensation that assailed her heart whenever she thought of him would go away one day. But she feared that it would never leave, that long into her old age she would still be pining for him and the way he had made her feel. In some ways, the hurt was even more agonising because it lay alongside so many questions that arose from his betrayal. Insidious jealous thoughts crawled across her mind. How many other people had he seduced and brought to the Resistance? Was bedding her something that had simply happened or had it been a deliberate way to seduce her to his cause? When those thoughts came creeping into her mind, she dismissed them, arguing that she didn't miss him as much as she missed the feeling of being with him – the false ideal of love and happiness that he had conjured with his presence and lies. He had used her, he had stalked her, seduced her. Callously. Coldly. And that lie on which whatever genuine relationship they had built was too great to ever make it meaningful.

Those thoughts only crawled into her mind when she had a moment of spare time. So she filled her time with work. If one task was complete, she found another. She would prowl through the Centre to find something which she could fix; the method in which tools were wiped down after use, implementing a new hand-washing regime for healers, directing that the tiles in one of the wings be scrubbed so that the grout between them was white once again, even making the way in which patients' notes were recorded more precise. There was always something for which she could find improvement, and that mostly kept the thoughts of Ashtyn and the Resistance at bay, lurking in the back of her mind alongside all the other things of which she did not wish to think.

As she found more and more for herself to do, her rooms at the Centre became her second residence. Some days, she didn't even see the inside of her home. Her rooms weren't as lavish as the Chief Healer's, but they were nevertheless a beautiful space. Freya had been given the discretion to direct the specifics of the décor. After her initial thought that concerning herself with interior decoration was a frivolous exercise, Freya realised her rooms offered a message about her authority, about who she was. So, after a few consultations with Symon, she had given specific requirements for how she wanted her rooms to be furnished. The furniture was beautifully made and extremely comfortable. The rugs were lush. The scarlets, purples, and blues were vibrant, bringing warmth into the room as well as an understated yet clear display of the authority with which she was vested. Freya had eschewed the preference of many members of the Kade to decorate their spaces with small statues and trinkets, preferring cleaner, neater lines. Her shelves were lined only with the scrolls and texts she needed, nothing ornamental or trivial. To anyone who came in, her rooms were that of a woman who lived with understated luxury and authority laced through her life. Being in a position of favour with the Kade certainly had its perks.

She didn't think of herself as such, she knew the truth: she was a junior member of the Kade governance. Still, she was never made to check her name off at the entrance to the Healing Centre; the Guardians posted there recognised her and greeted her deferentially. Her position required her to remain abreast of matters pertaining to supplies and security, and to play a part in ensuring that these crucial aspects of society remained well managed. Each morning, she was given reports containing updates and requests, many of which were quite sensitive in nature. They included the estimated number of ill people across the city, the number of people who entered Oranis with noted ailments, the estimated number of days' worth of food stockpiled in the Kade storehouses, and even the exact number of Guardians within the city, with various projections on how many were available to be deployed in response to security concerns. When her first report was delivered, she had been so surprised that she assumed it was an error. But the reports had continued to arrive along with specific requests, such as to provide an inventory of the Centre's stocks. Easy, menial things. She began to assemble an understanding on how the Kade maintained their control so well – they had information on everything. The sheer enormity of the information given to her every morning was overwhelming, and she knew that she was seeing only a fragment of the information at the Kade's fingertips. The only thing that made her feel remotely comfortable about this was that, unless an individual doing something illicit – say, conducting an affair – somehow drew attention to themselves, they would be unnoticed in the torrent of information that flooded into the Kade's hands.

One morning, she was reading through the summary of what had happened overnight at the Healing Centre – a report she herself requested of her people – when a knock sounded on her door. "Come in," she called, not even looking up from her desk. She had placed it at the opposite end of the room to the door in the same way the Chief Healer had arranged her own rooms. A runner came in.

"Begging your pardon, ma'am, but I have a report for you," she said, offering Freya the Kade salute.

Freya beckoned her forward. Some reports were confidential and needed to be delivered straight to her hands. She had received her first such report two cycles ago, and it was now so routine that it had slipped into the mundane. Almost absent-

mindedly, she thanked the girl and scanned the report. She barely noticed the girl's departure.

The report stated that the Kade suspected civil unrest was
being fomented. In addition to the list of events being viewed
with suspicion was a request: Freya was required to draft a response to an uprising by 'misguided dissidents'. If such an event
occurred, which the report assured was unlikely, the Healing
Centres would need to remain under Kade control at all costs,
ready to tend as many wounded as possible to facilitate their
swift return to defending the Kade's rightful authority over the
Third Country. The report ended by reiterating that the eventu-
ality of such a conflict was unlikely, but such plans were crucial
to ensuring the certainty of the Kade's position.

Freya sat unmoving for several moments once she had re-
read the report. She wondered if the dissidents were Ashtyn's
Resistance. Makkyd had seemed so certain that the Kade knew
almost nothing about them. But if Freya had learned anything
during her brief time in her current role, it was that the Kade
knew a great deal about what went on in Oranis.

After several more moments of deliberation, Freya picked up
a piece of paper. Her hand was trembling. Scowling at her
treacherous body, she willed her hand to be still and began to
write, outlining instructions to be carried out in the event that an
attempt was made to topple the Kade.

Formulating the plan was complicated and took her nearly
the whole day to complete. It was so complex that she didn't take
her usual daily stroll through the Centre. As was typical of her,
Freya was thorough, leaving nothing to chance. She wrote instructions for any and every scenario she could envisage, detail-
ing how every part of the Healing Centre, from the store rooms to
the administrators, should respond in each contingency. She finished just as the sun was beginning to set, putting down the
scribe pen and stretching out her aching hand. She considered
doing a quick round of the Centre, but the prospect of doing more

work just didn't appeal to her, and so she gave herself the first early finish since she had assumed the leadership of the Centre.

When she walked outside, the amber light of sunset bathed the buildings. Freya stood on the steps of the Market District Healing Centre, looking at the beauty of her city. Then she noticed the people. She couldn't remember the last time she had been outside when so many people were on the streets. With that many people, the change to the city wasn't something she could ignore, or pretend to not notice. Everyone was subdued, nobody talked too loudly; the only way she could describe it was as though the city were hidden. The streets were as clean as ever, but there was something sterile about them. Despite its beauty, the city seemed cold and unwelcoming. It was so unlike the Oranis in which she had lived her whole life that it felt like a stranger.

She had overheard snippets of conversation about the Kade crackdown, but she hadn't paid them much attention. Her head had been filled with thoughts of how to make the Centre more efficient, how she could trial new techniques. The truth was that she hadn't wanted to hear those conversations. They seemed too steeped in malcontent, too subversive, and she had no desire to be associated with anything that could possibly be deemed rebellious. However, as much as she might not have wanted to take part in such conversations, she could not deny that the city was not the same.

Even though it doubled her journey home, she could not restrain the impulse to detour by the site of the Central Healing Centre. The rubble had been neatly piled. What had been of use had been transported into a warehouse for rebuilding efforts – so her daily reports told her. Some of the walls had survived, but what remained was a shell of a once magnificent structure. It filled her with an incredible sadness to think that such a beautiful place of healing had been destroyed. She thought about Zarech, willing to martyr himself in the name of the cause in which he believed. So much destruction all wrought in the name of a cause. Better, Freya told herself, to think only about one's own life rather than exist to fulfil a grander purpose. That way people didn't get hurt. Especially not her. Abruptly, she realised she was the only person in the area. Everybody else was moving through or around it as though the very ground were tainted. Unwilling to draw too much attention to herself, especially given this fearful atmosphere, she moved on.

"You're home early," Symon commented as she came into his workroom.

"I wanted to come home," she replied.

"One of the perks of being in charge," he noted, his eyes never leaving the cloth in his hands.

"Only if I don't abuse it too often." She sat beside him.

He was sewing two panels of cloth together.

"It reminds me of when you made my joining robe," she said, running her hand over the material. It was of the highest quality. He must be making a robe for a member of the Kade elite.

"That was hardly my finest work," he said.

"But it was nice that you made it," she protested, trying to nudge him into the rarely visited territory of sentimentality.

"It would have been nicer if I hadn't had to rush it. Do you remember how much of a hurry you were in to join?"

She tried to discern if she could hear a faint note of accusation in his voice.

"Can you blame me?" she asked, trying to inject playfulness into their exchange.

He didn't reply, but he smiled as he focused on his work. It was as playful as he would get. He finished the section he was working on. "I was given some barat flowers today by a customer," he said.

"Really?" She was surprised. Barat flowers, while used to distil the potent poison, were also exquisite to behold. They were strictly controlled due to their lethality, so the only people who were able to use them decoratively were extremely highly ranked members of the Kade.

"They're in the living room," he said as he picked up a new panel of cloth. Even now, he was focused more on his work than the conversation.

Freya took her leave, not even certain he noticed her go. As she walked from his workroom into the living area, she realised she could indeed smell the sweet fragrance of the flowers. She had noted it when she first came in, but not paid it much thought. She inspected the beautiful flowers. As the blooms wilted, the fragrance would become overpowering and sickly sweet, but for now, they were fresh and the perfume was a delight.

"You must have a rather important customer," she called to him, admiring the curl of the petals, the contrasting intensity and subtlety of the hues across their surfaces.

"Several." His call sounded after a brief pause in which he actually registered she had left the room and was speaking to him. He sounded smug.

She could hardly blame him. She returned to his room. "Well, they're beautiful."

"How is work?" he asked, his tone making it clear that the question was one of polite conversation more than anything else.

"It's fine. There are rumours of unrest, though," she said, curious to see his reaction.

He actually turned his focus from his work. "Who would have thought it – people unhappy with the chafing collar of the Kade."

"Are you? Happy?" It wasn't a question she was willing to ask herself, so she asked him instead.

He put down the material he was holding. "We've worked hard to ensure that we have a comfortable life, haven't we?"

She nodded.

"I've worked hard to be one of the best tailors in the Third Country. You've worked hard to be one of the best healers in the Third Country. But it's not just our professions. It's also the way we've lived our lives. Carefully. Diligently. Do you think that we've been rewarded for that?"

She nodded again.

"Life wasn't perfect before the Kade, you know," he said.

"But maybe it was better," she suggested.

"For some. Not for everybody. I don't think either of us could have succeeded in the way we have without the Kade."

"I wouldn't know," she said.

"Well, I'm content to exist with the way things are, and I hope you are too." His tone suggested that he was done with the conversation.

"What if I weren't? Would you report me to the Kade?" She asked the question with a note of teasing in her voice, but she felt anything but light-hearted as she awaited his reply.

"Don't be ridiculous, Freya. I know you'd never do anything so silly as to jeopardise the stability we've created for ourselves. We can question privately, but I know you never would outside these walls."

"Have you eaten?" Freya tried to sound casual, to speak past the sudden sharp pain in her throat.

"Yes. There's some food in the kitchen if you'd like some," he replied, seemingly content to forget about the conversation of only a moment ago.

As she left his room, she took a deep breath. Symon was right about her, even if there was a time she thought that he hadn't been. She didn't want to question the Kade. She didn't want to challenge or destroy the life she'd built for herself. Ashtyn and the Resistance had been a dalliance that she was lucky to have escaped from quickly and without any lasting harm.

She went back into Symon's workroom, bowl in hand. She sat next to him and ate, watching him work, entranced by the rhythm of his fingers as they nimbly coaxed the cloth into the shapes he wanted.

Symon was intent on his work. She tried to think of something to say. Her mind remained stubbornly blank.

The silence stretched between them.

TWENTY

The fivedays marched on. Despite the Kade's continuing assurances, Freya couldn't deny the insidious combination of curiosity and apprehension about whether the coming day would bring an uprising. The atmosphere of anxiety had only intensified, seeming to perfuse the city and seep into the very stones of its buildings. Freya felt that such an unstated sentiment sprawling across Oranis could only be sustained for so long before something happened. That feeling grew as she overheard conversations expressing sentiments just shy of discontent with the Kade during her routine rounds through the Centre. She tried hard not to listen, not to become entangled in any criticism of the Kade. Contrary to Freya's expectations, however, the tense peace remained in Oranis for first one fiveday, and then another. Slowly, she began to relax once more. The Kade's very public decision to begin using the network of informants instilled just enough fear in everyone. Nobody dared openly voice an opinion of genuine protest or malcontent. Freya was able to tell herself that what she sensed on the streets on the rare occasions she was outside during daylight couldn't possibly be the sullen resentment that fermented rebellion, but was instead begrudging submission.

One overcast day she left the Centre just as sundown fell across the city. The sun had ignominiously slipped below the horizon. It reflected the mood of the city. Guardians stood silent and foreboding on the Centre's perimeter.

She walked across the street, her mind occupied with one of the many small problems that had arisen as part of any normal day. From the shadows of a nearby street, Ashtyn suddenly emerged. She gave a small scream of surprise. He grabbed her arm and shushed her.

"What do you want?" she hissed in anger once she had recovered herself.

"To talk." His eyes implored her not to leave, throwing little shards of pain across her.

"I have nothing to say to you," she snarled, anger springing to her defence. She fought to lower her voice, afraid of being overheard. The fact that she was even speaking with him was already dangerous enough.

"Please, let me explain," he begged.

"Why? What even is there to explain?" She hated him for his intrusion into the world she had rebuilt. She had forgotten how good he looked; she tried to dismiss how she felt as drawn to him as she had on that very first day. She hated him for that, too.

"Everything, anything. Just please don't walk away." He made another grab for her arm as she pulled it free.

"There are twenty Guardians who would come if I yelled," she threatened.

"Freya." He said her name with such intensity that her breath fled.

"Please, just leave me alone," she begged him, overwhelmed by a sense of fatigue. It was exhausting trying to resist the warmth of his skin, the way his eyes seemed to bore into her soul. She didn't want to feel so drawn to him, so torn. She didn't want to miss him as she had.

"I'm sorry I lied to you."

"I'm sorry I met you," she retorted.

"Are you really happy living like this?" he asked, his voice soft. Had he made it a challenge, she could have given him a direct refutation, but his demeanour of supplication had wormed its way behind her defences. It seemed that no matter what she did, he was always able to get around the ways she used to keep out everybody else in the world.

"Why are you here?" She avoided his question by challenging him, caught between a desire that he simply leave, and desperation to prolong the exquisite agony that his presence evoked.

"You aren't happy, are you? I can see it. Over the last few fivedays, you've looked as sad as you did when I first saw you. You broke my heart with your sadness, Freya, and I didn't even know you."

"Have you been following me?" Her mind flicked back through the late nights and early mornings walking through the streets. They had been so empty that surely she would have noticed Ashtyn skulking after her.

His lips pressed together as though she had caught him entangled in another lie. "Am I being followed?"

"Only to make sure you weren't going to tell the Kade about us." He was so desperate in his earnestness, but it didn't stop anger from rising at the fact that the Resistance it seemed was unwilling to just leave her be. She opened her mouth to say as much, but he spoke before she could unleash the profanity-laden tirade.

"They stopped following you two fivedays ago. I convinced them that you wouldn't turn us in. I know that you would never do that, regardless of whatever you may think of us...of me."

"What do you want?" She told herself to block out his world, that he was manipulating her, only telling her what she wanted to hear.

"All I want is for you to be happy. I *was* meant to recruit you, but..." He was unable to hold her gaze and the vibrant green of his eyes was instead directed at the ground.

"What about what Makkyd said? About how your charms worked on so many others?" she challenged. She had held onto that comment. It had reassured her that leaving him and the Resistance had been the right choice. She had thought Ashtyn was someone she could build a life with away from the ruins of her childhood, away from the violence of the Kade and the suffering within Oranis. But to think that she had only been one woman in many made her as desperate to reject him as it made her feel foolish.

"So what if I've been with other women?"

"How many of them did you recruit?"

"That's unfair." His voice had dropped so low that she almost couldn't hear.

"You manipulated me." She pulled the strap of her healer's bag higher on her shoulder and folded her arms across her chest in the same motion. She needed the distraction of the movement. She needed to stay in the moment rather than drift into a realm where desire and regret danced endlessly together.

"I adored you," he countered. "Adore," he corrected himself.

"You lied to me." She wanted to yell at him, to put all of the awful, bubbling, exquisite sentiment to which no words could do justice into one long primal scream. But that would attract attention, and her life was safe because she avoided just enough attention.

"Yes, I lied to you. But never about how I felt." Now he looked up again, and she bit her lip to to stop herself from crying. Why were his eyes so green? Why did one look from him tear her apart in the way that nothing else in the world had ever managed to do?

"Tell me that you'd still be willing to go and just live on that farm with me." She challenged him despite herself. The most slender thread of hope uncurled inside her, defying what she knew his answer would be with a certainty that drenched the very motes of her being.

"I would want nothing more in the world than to live out the rest of my days with you in quiet seclusion. But I would never forgive myself for leaving here. What Makkyd is doing means something."

She turned away, feeling her heart wrench in two. His blind devotion to this cause would forever relegate anything and everyone else to second place. She didn't want to be a part of his cause. She didn't want to believe in something so deeply that she would die for it, would forsake her own happiness for the possibility – not even the certainty – that it may be one day realised. She just wanted to be happy and safe. It was all she had ever wanted.

"Freya, please." His voice put sound to the rending of her heart.

"Please what? Come back to you? Or come back to the Resistance?"

"Both."

He had only come to make one last try at recruiting her. She felt a tremendous bitterness well up inside her, making her insides feel as though they were about to curl in on themselves. "Goodbye, Ashtyn."

"If you change your mind we're meeting in three days at Bardan's warehouse. You would be welcomed."

She was already walking away from him so fast she was practically running.

She despised herself for the hope that had flared inside her at the sight of him. She had believed for a foolish moment that he might have wanted her and not what she could offer his cause. She chastised herself for allowing him to affect her so profoundly when she should have known better. She had rebuilt her life to what it was before he had destroyed all of the beliefs and ideas she had so carefully constructed and maintained, and now he had tried to do it once more.

She had locked away her grief and anger after the takeover, knowing that it would only lead to her own harm, and he had come with a key, letting all of that emotion come pouring out, using it, directing it so that she could and would aid his cause. She felt as though he had looked into her soul and found the parts of herself that she kept hidden from everybody. He had coaxed them out gently with words of kindness and compassion, and then he had used them to control her. Not even the Kade had done that to her.

Unusually, Symon was not there when she arrived home. But she was thankful for his absence. She was so badly shaken by her exchange with Ashtyn that she wasn't certain she would have been able to pretend everything was fine. As she entered the door, her senses were assailed by the cloying sweetness of the barat flowers' fragrance. After so long, they were finally wilting.

It was the suffocating sickly sweet scent of death that finally overwhelmed her. She began to cry, the tears welling in her eyes and crawling down her cheeks.

She allowed herself to feel the intense emotion course through her before she wiped away the tears. Taking stock, she told herself that nothing had changed since that morning. Ashtyn had still lied to her when he first met her, when she had entered his bed, even when he had brought her to the Resistance. She had still made the right decision to commit herself to the Kade's way of life. If anything, her most recent encounter with Ashtyn had only affirmed that. She was a citizen under the Kade. Her diligence and hard work had been rewarded. Life as a part of the Resistance would bring war and death – far more death than under the tight control of the Kade. Her distress, she reasoned, was only a residual emotion from her moment of rebellion, simply fear that her indulgence would be discovered and bring everything for which she – and Symon – had worked, crashing down. It was nothing more. It could not be anything more.

She soothed away her fear that her indiscretion might be uncovered by reasoning that this, too, was unfounded. Ashtyn would be careful to ensure their affair went undiscovered. It left a bitter trace across her mind to know that Ashtyn would never draw such attention to himself lest it may reveal the existence of his precious Resistance, and he would never do anything to endanger them. She told herself to let it go. She was safe, and that was the important thing.

Finally certain that she would not lose her composure, she went into her workroom and sat at her table, pulling out the notes that she had been working on for a new treatment. This was all that mattered: doing her job and doing it well. This was all she'd been put on the Godskissed Continent to do. Not to partake in some failed rebellion, not to carry on chasing a tempestuous love affair. Simply to heal, as well and as much as she could.

The smell of the dying flowers sat heavily in the house.

TWENTY ONE

Three days later, Freya was scanning a report while she paced around her rooms when a knock sounded on the door. Rather than call for whoever it was to enter, she simply opened the door. That was how she found herself face to face with the Chief Healer.

"My lady," she stammered in surprise. Belatedly, her clenched fist came up to offer the Chief Healer the Kade salute.

Her deference was waved aside by the Chief Healer, who strode into the room. Freya glimpsed elite guards take up positions on either side of the door as the older woman closed the door.

"Freya, how are you?" she asked. She spent a moment surveying her surroundings before she nodded slightly; an approving gesture.

"I've been well, thank you, my lady."

"I've just come from a meeting in which we were discussing the fine work that you've been doing here."

"Thank you." Freya blushed at the depth of the praise, offering one of the chairs to the Chief Healer. The older woman sat down, letting out the slightest sigh. "It seems all I ever do is go from one meeting to another," she said tiredly. "I haven't actually done proper healing work in the longest time."

Freya wondered if the Chief Healer was of strong enough faith to be able to heal in the way that Freya could. She suspected that she was. She shooed the thought away.

"I haven't been doing that much actual healing myself lately," she admitted, pushing the thought aside before it took root in her mind and she considered the implications to such a truth.

"That's what you get for being good at your job," the Chief Healer said wryly. "They promote you, and stick you in an administrative position in the hope that you can share your genius."

"And were you able to share your genius?" Freya asked. She realised with some astonishment that the overwhelming terror she had initially felt at speaking with the Chief Healer had dissipated. Certainly, she was still intimidated by the woman, but not in the way that she once had been.

An almost wistful note entered her tone. "Unfortunately for me, I was able to share my talents. In some ways I'd have rather been demoted, gone back to healing. The body, Freya. That's what I've always felt most at home dealing with. Overseeing a group of individuals who can't do what I can, and will never be able to? It's frustrating. But sometimes you have to give up what you love in order to help people, help your cause."

Freya watched the older woman with a curious fascination. This was a glimpse into the person behind the familiar hard and efficient persona. She hadn't even considered that the Chief Healer did not necessarily want her job or the responsibilities that came with it. Freya had simply assumed that she had unhesitatingly followed the Kade order to replace the old Healers' Guildmaster after the takeover.

"Anyway," the Chief Healer said, the tone of efficiency and purpose returning to her voice. "The reason I'm here is in relation to the increased reports of subversive activity. The plans you drafted were excellent. So excellent that we instructed all the other Healing Centres to use them. Strictly between us, the reports that we're sending out are a lot more optimistic than we're feeling. This resistance movement is proving far harder to find than we first expected. Even though they haven't done anything significant, it's only a matter of time before they make some move against us and announce their existence to the people. And after the actions of the Dark Gods' Followers, we're quite concerned about the security of the city. The greatest points of weakness are warehouses with strategic supplies and Healing

Centres. Not only do we stockpile many potent substances in the Centres, but we would also be crippled in the event of an attack if we weren't able to quickly heal our wounded. Despite the plans that we've put into place – and the ones you created – we're worried that the Centres may not be safe."

"There's a chance of an attack?" Freya had been so certain that even if there was an attack against the Kade, the Kade would be able to quickly and completely crush such dissidence. She had warred with a sense of sadness at the likely deaths of the members of the Resistance whom she had met, but ultimately reasoned if they made decisions which got them killed, it was their choice to make.

"We aren't sure. Either way. That's the problem," the Chief Healer replied. "So we've decided to double the protection around your Healing Centre. I wanted to advise you in person. We would also ask you to be particularly cautious in your own movements. You're a relatively prominent member of the Kade government, and some...discontents may find your Pious origins reason to single you out."

Freya shivered, disconcerted to hear herself called a prominent member of the Kade governance. She barely considered herself part of the Kade governance, let alone someone with any seniority. But then again, she'd come face to face with some of the highest ranking members of the Kade. Most who were Kade by birth hadn't achieved that.

"If things escalate, we may even assign an escort to you when you walk in the streets," the Chief Healer added, seeing the look on Freya's face. She likely meant it to reassure, but, facing the prospect of being constantly under the watchful eye of a Guardian left Freya feeling trapped.

"Thank you," she stammered, even though she felt anything but grateful at the promise.

"You are a valuable asset to us, Freya. We don't want to lose you," the Chief Healer said, the faintest hint of warmth in her voice.

"I don't know about that, my lady." Freya looked down, not sure if she was blushing from the compliment or from a deeper shame at being an asset to the Kade.

"I'm impressed you never asked about Zarech, you know," the Chief Healer added.

Freya's head snapped up at the mention of Zarech. "What do you mean?"

"Don't be coy, Freya. It's unbecoming," the Chief Healer admonished her with the thinnest of smiles. "You knew what was happening to Zarech, and yet you tended to him without comment, over and over again."

"It wasn't for me to question your instructions, my lady. I could only assume that you and the Kade had your reasons," she answered, letting none of the churning reaction to what the Chief Healer was saying show on her face.

"I knew you would do well. I said that you would pass."

"Pass, my lady?" Freya queried.

"Yes. Zarech was a test."

"A test?" Freya echoed stupidly.

"Yes. Of your loyalty. Of your willingness to obey our orders without question, trusting that we had a plan. And you demonstrated a brilliant willingness to do so."

"I don't know what to say, my lady." Freya wondered what the Chief Healer would have said had she known the content of the conversations between Zarech and Freya.

"You don't have to say anything. You have proved yourself." With that, she stood and offered Freya the Kade salute. It was an extraordinary mark of respect – subordinates offered it to their betters, and equals offered it to their equals. Never did those of higher rank offer it to people below them. Freya got to her feet and returned the gesture, remaining mute as the Chief Healer crossed to the door and opened it, nodding once to Freya before leaving.

Alone, Freya mulled on the notion of being an asset. It was an impersonal term, but perhaps the Chief Healer had simply been careless with her choice of words. But the Chief Healer didn't really strike Freya as a woman who would do anything imprecise. Moreover, being offered the Kade salute wasn't something that was offered to an impersonal asset. She picked through the conflicting emotions and arguments that the Chief Healer's visit had evoked, unable to arrive at a clear conclusion regarding how exactly she should feel. She was still standing there, her report forgotten in her hand, when one of the Centre's runners burst into her room without knocking. She stood, ready to yell at him for his impertinence, but through the open door she heard the sounds of her Centre in chaos.

"What's wrong?" she demanded, anger morphing into urgency.

"The Chief Healer was attacked in the quarter. Several bystanders have been severely injured. They've been brought in – all need immediate attention. The Chief Healer is unharmed but has returned to the Centre. She requests your assistance," the runner gasped.

Freya motioned for the runner to lead the way and followed at a run.

The Chief Healer stood in the middle of the general ward, calmly giving instructions. Amid the moans of pain and frantic movement, her implacable aura of command was indisputable.

"What happened?" Freya asked, her eyes snapping around the room to take in the surrounding chaos.

"A cart came careering toward me, and then it exploded. It must have been packed with bits of metal and stone, because the air was filled with flying debris, which hit everybody nearby," the Chief Healer said with a calm that belied the fact that a very brutal attack had just been mounted against her life.

Freya looked around at the chaos. She wondered how the Chief Healer had escaped with no wounds when everybody in the area appeared to have suffered some kind of injury. "Are you certain it was intended for you?"

The Chief Healer's eyes tightened into something that seemed almost malevolent. "The cart came straight for me, just as I turned a corner. It seems too convenient to be mere coincidence. But enough chit chat. We're going to have to do some healing, Freya." A smile made its way across the Chief Healer's face. Freya wondered how the powerful woman could be so casual about the attempt on her life, and then so excited at the prospect of healing. It made the Chief Healer seem not overly concerned about the people around her. Freya hoped she would never become like that.

"Who are the most critically wounded?" Freya asked, surveying the ward full of broken and battered bodies, with more people being brought in with each passing moment. She saw a young girl, no more than seven years old, lying on a pallet. She moved to her side, sensing the extent of the injuries before she even got to the girl's side. She began an examination, pulling aside the girl's tunic to reveal a gaping wound, and noting the telltale strip of green cloth sewn into the girl's sleeve.

"Get me bandages," she instructed a passing healer, resisting the urge to force the girl's wounds closed with the power of her will. That would call too much attention to herself and stop her from being able to help the other people who needed her.

"Freya, what are you doing?" the Chief Healer called from another bedside.

"She's going to die if I don't help her," Freya replied, cursing as she realised the wound was deeper than she'd first thought.

"I need you to here work on this Guardian with me."

"But look at her, she's badly injured," Freya protested.

"So is he. He's more important," the Chief Healer said.

"What?"

The Chief Healer strode to her side, impatience radiating across the space between them. "Freya, this is merely a Pious child. He is a Master-ranked Guardian. I thought you would understand how important they are, not only to the security of the city but to the Kade."

Freya took another reluctant look at the girl, then called to one of the healers. "Trem, tend to this girl." Her steps were heavy as she accompanied the Chief Healer to the bed where a Master-ranked Guardian lay. She glanced back over her shoulder, wanting to make sure that Trem was attending to the girl. But before she could get a proper look, The Chief Healer spoke, demanding her attention.

They saved him. Even without any gods-granted abilities, the two finest healers of their time were working on one person. He would have needed to have been in pieces for them not to be able to save him.

Freya turned away, exhausted by the intense effort of will she had expended to not once lift her eyes from the Guardian before her to look over at the girl. She started to go to check on the girl, but the Chief Healer called to her again. "Freya, where are you going? I need you to work here." There was a touch of impatience in her voice.

It had been a long time since Freya had been ordered around by someone when it came to healing. The fact that she was now being made to heal people who she knew didn't need her help as much as others made her feel as though some angry animal were prowling inside her chest. Perhaps this was another test of her loyalty, making certain that she could put aside her own instincts and obey the instructions of a Kade. If it was a test, she passed, grimly following the orders barked at her by the Chief Healer, her hands bandaging, suturing, soothing, almost without her mind realising what she was doing. Well-honed instinct took over, and amid the clashing chorus of wounded bodies that clamoured in her mind, she obeyed the training that had been instilled in her for years to simply do her work with as little flourish as possible, drawing only the barest amount of attention to herself.

Finally, the worst of it was over, and Freya was released from the obligation to do only as she was told. Freya made her way through the ward, looking for the young girl. Something about the girl had reminded her of her sister. Perhaps it was the way she looked, perhaps it was simply her age. Even though Rohana had been several years older when she had died, the mass of dark hair and the innocence of her rounded face meant Freya was inescapably reminded of her sister. Regardless, she couldn't put the girl from her mind, and her agitation mounted with each bed that contained the wrong person.

The severity of the girl's wound meant that she had been half expecting it, but the shock when she saw the girl's body laid out waiting to be taken to the hall for the dead still crashed into her, fizzling along her limbs, through to her very core.

"Trem? What happened?"

He hurried over at her call, a look of genuine contrition on his face. "I...I just don't think I was good enough. She was so badly injured."

Freya put aside her distress and placed a hand on his arm. "You can't save everybody. All you can do is try to get better for the next time." With a start, she realised that she was giving him the same advice that Makkyd had given her. She hadn't agreed with it at the time; she wasn't even sure if she agreed with it now. But she had to reassure him, to offer him comfort. That was her duty, and she knew she had done the right thing when she saw the line of self-recrimination across his face ease.

She waited until the ward had cleared a little, then she sank down beside the girl's body. Only then did the soft tremors overtake her body. Grief and rage were inseparable, both yoking her in equal measure. She looked down at the body. This was the truth. Anything else that she had told herself about the Kade had simply been a lie that she had made up to make herself feel better. At the end of everything, it was the girl in front of her, and those like her, who was going to be allowed to die. Not because of anything that she did, but because her life was less valuable to the Kade.

Freya saw in her mind's eye the bloody and battered body of Rohana. The bodies of her family had been released once the Kade had finished dragging them through the streets for everybody to see. They had been dumped in one of the halls for the dead, limbs askew like the discarded toys of a particularly irate child. Freya had dutifully gone to them, her body rigid with shock and grief. She did what no girl should have had to do and cleaned their bodies, readying them for the Kade death rite that would be performed on them. Nobody had dared to help her or simply be there for her. She was marked as being affiliated with blasphemers. Until she had proved that she was not a traitor, she was too dangerous to be associated with. Freya wiped the blood off their faces, cleaned away as many of the marks of the Kade's brutality as she could. Eventually, they were bound up to the necks, coarse brown cloth tightly wrapped around their limbs. Freya had dared not even think of the Pious funeral prayer, let alone whisper it over the bodies of her family. They were buried in the Kade way, but without any of the respect that the Kade would afford one of their own. Her parents' eyes had been closed, but Rohana's were open. Freya had closed them, but the dead sightlessness of her sister's eyes was like another knife to her already brutalised heart. Rohana's eyes had been full of life and mischief. Nobody should have seen them like they were in death: still, blank, glazed. For two years afterward, Freya had endured nightmares about it, waking in the middle of the night drenched in sweat. But she had never screamed, never reached out to Symon. She had put it all back in the secret place inside her, knowing that speaking of it would jeopardise everything.

She looked down at the girl's face. She hadn't given her sister the Pious prayer to the dead, but she could at least give this girl that. Her lips formed the words of the prayer, whispering them quickly. The girl probably was too young to know what it meant – all her memories would be of life in the Kade way, and yet she wore a green band that meant her life was less valued.

For a long time, Freya stayed there, looking down at the girl.

"Freya!" The Chief Healer called to her from the middle of the room.

Freya looked one last time at the girl before she slowly stood and walked to the Chief Healer's side. "We could have saved her."

"And risk losing a Guardian? They take years to train! And they are vital for the city's safety."

"But this was an innocent girl." Her voice held quiet accusation, but she couldn't bring herself to be worried about how it may appear.

"She was a Pious," the Chief Healer replied firmly, as though it explained everything.

"Like me?" Freya asked.

"You're different. You've proved yourself. Freya, being in charge means making unpalatable decisions—"

"This isn't unpalatable. This is the life of a girl who I could have saved."

"And think of all of the lives that you did save," the Chief Healer pointed out.

"Yes, Kade citizens."

"They are my priority. I don't have to defend this to you."

Catching herself, Freya swallowed the words of anger and accusation that trembled on her lips. "You're right, I'm sorry. It was just a shock."

"It's all right. Even the best of us sometimes get thrown. Take the rest of the day off," the Chief Healer suggested, her face softening ever so slightly at the excuse Freya gave. "You did some fine work. Many people are alive because of you."

Freya smiled tightly. The Chief Healer looked at her for a minute longer, then left, the remaining elite Guardians of her retinue flanking her alongside two Guardians who normally guarded the Centre; they had been co-opted to fill the space left by those of the Chief Healer's normal guard who had been injured. Freya surveyed the ward. Everybody who she could help had been seen to; the chaos had all but dissipated and been replaced by the numbed silence of shock and pain.

She called to a nearby healer. "When you have a moment, Aylah, could you please find out who that girl's parents were – one of them is probably somewhere here. When you do, please let me know who they are."

Freya looked around the ward once more to ensure there was nobody else whose life would be forfeit if she did not see to them, then she went straight to her rooms. Her fingers were the steady of an expert healer as she exchanged her bloodstained robe for a clean one. It wouldn't do for her to been seen in such a state. It wasn't appropriate for someone in her position. She almost didn't bother to change, but years of working to survive, to blend in, forced her to.

Once she'd changed, she sat at her desk, her hands folded neatly in her lap and her gaze fixed unseeing on a point in front of her. She couldn't quite muster the willpower to leave, to move, to do anything. All she could think of was the girl who had died because she was Pious; because she had been born into the wrong family. Freya wondered how many more times she would be asked to sacrifice a life because it was the wrong life according to some arbitrary measure. She was a healer. Her first duty was to heal those who were most in need, not those who were most important. It was an ethos she had grown up believing, and it was now one she had been made to betray in order to live a comfortable life – because she was afraid of what would happen if she didn't obey. But fear wasn't sufficient to excuse doing nothing. Not anymore.

ACKNOWLEDGEMENTS

As I have stated before, writing a book takes a village to support the poor, beleaguered author. This is the point where I can explicitly acknowledge the people who have been the most shining examples of support during a process in which the first draft is an act of baring yourself and the editing is an act of breaking and re-making yourself.

A million, endless thank yous must always go first to my parents for the way they nurtured my love of stories from my earliest memories. Then a million more must be bestowed upon them for the many ways in which they have supported me since I started publishing my books.

But of course, writers need the benefit of a dispassionate and external eye, and a team of people who help turn a manuscript into an actual book. Thank you to Jason for doing another fabulous job with copyediting. He definitely makes me a better author as a result of his critical eye. I'd also like to thank Sarena and Jess for their extensive and exhaustive consideration of so much of Dark Intent. I strongly recommend any and all writers join a group – the support of other writers, and their in-depth contributions is truly invaluable. For the cosmetic side, Marcus graciously reprised his role as cover designer. The depth of his patience in listening to me ramble about the story and world is only surpassed by the fact that he pulled a fabulous concept from those ramblings.

And then there is the support team.

If you are an author and not on Instagram, you absolutely should be. My thanks to the bookstagram community cannot be said enough. You guys have been so insanely, unflaggingly supportive.

To my friends and loved ones who have gone so out of your way to buy and read my work – so many of you have done it quietly, without any fanfare, but with a loving and emphatic support that truly leaves me floored. In no particular order; Jess (beta reader extraordinaire), Lucas, Angus, Lucy are the four people who make me feel like a real author when I sometimes doubt it. I truly love you guys.

Finally, I want to thank Mitch, who knew this story was going to be something special after he read the first chapter, refused to allow me to write any more until he had surprised me with Scrivener, and then took me down to the pub where he bought me a drink and forced me to walk through the story so I could do it justice. I write this while sitting next to him (he has no idea what I'm writing), as I write many things sitting next to him. He is my sounding board, he believes me when I don't believe in myself (but refuses to pander to my self-doubt and self-pity), and he is my ideal reader. Thank you is never enough.

ABOUT THE AUTHOR

Alice Jane Boér-Endacott was born and raised in Melbourne, Australia.

She certainly has a pet kangaroo which she frequently uses as a mode of transportation. She does not have a pet koala, but one does deign to live in her back yard. He and the kangaroo are great friends.

She is actually has many dollarydoos saved, and will soon purchase her fifth house – she is considering buying abroad and would welcome any suggestions.

Her first word was, obviously, "Shakespeare".

She is also a really bad liar.

You can find her on Instagram @alicejaneboere.
And on twitter @ajendacott

COMING 2019

DARK PURPOSE

"When the time comes, I know you'll be able to do what's necessary,"
she said before walking away. "Maybe that's what I'm afraid of," Freya
whispered.

The Kade rule the Third Country through terror and unrelenting oppression. To the outside world, healer Freyanna Kuch is
a member of the subjugated Pious class whose collaboration has
seen her richly rewarded by the Kade. But Freya is a member of
the Resistance. Her upstanding marriage, work, and conduct is a
front as she works to create a better, more equal world.

However, the world of intrigue and shadows requires everything of a person. If Freya is to succeed in the Resistance, she
must sort out her complicated feelings for Ashtyn, the man who
brought her to the Resistance, and try to navigate the blood-
thirsty demands of rebellion, despite her obligation as a healer to
do no harm.

As tensions rise across the Third Country, Freya must decide
who she must be in order to fight for the world she wants, even if
that means turning away from everything she holds dear.

DARK PURPOSE – PREVIEW

ONE

"Again, Freya," Astrom said, stepping back.

"I'm tired," Freya protested, rubbing the spot on her arm where Astrom's staff had smacked her.

"Do you think that the Kade will stop in battle to allow you to rest?" the other woman demanded, her voice impatient but not unkind.

"I'm a healer, not a fighter," Freya argued, tired of the endless practice she had been forced to undergo that day and on all the other days.

"The only thing that not knowing how to fight will do is get you killed," Makkyd said from her seat near the edge of the room.

Freya looked resentfully at Astrom's physique. The muscles in the woman's arms were as hard as the stone she worked. In comparison to her, Freya was uncomfortably conscious of her frailty. Healing work required a different kind of strength, but Makkyd was correct; if it came to any kind of physical confrontation, Freya's lack of training would see her dead. Taking a deep breath, she picked up the wooden staff she had dropped on the ground and settled back into a fighter's crouch, readying herself for the next beating that she was certainly she would sustain at her teacher's hands. There was something almost insulting about the easy strength and speed Astrom possessed. Especially when compared to Freya's efforts. Astrom leaned back for a moment and then almost lazily stepped forward, her staff a blur as it moved through the air. The endless hours of practice drilled into her had Freya stepping to the side and bringing her own staff up to block Astrom's attack before her mind had even registered what was happening. Her body curved to one side and she stepped behind Astrom, whipping her staff up and around to lie against Astrom's neck.

The watching room erupted into cheers and whoops as Astrom stepped aside, bowing slightly to Freya. "You always hold back until you're tired," she noted, bending down to touch her toes in a stretch.

Freya shrugged, stretching out her own arms and groaning as she felt the accumulated bruises from the session make themselves known.

She didn't like fighting, but it had become a mandatory part of her life in the Resistance. Cycles of training and practice had given her a rudimentary competence with various weapons, although she remained the most proficient at the staff, despite Astrom's chuckle that with a staff there was no keen edge on which she could injure herself. Nevertheless, her healer's teachings meant she did not feel truly comfortable with any weapon in her hands. Using them to inflict the sort of damage she had spent her life learning to fix was an anathema to everything in which she believed.

"You've come a long way." Makkyd, the leader of the Resistance, clapped her on the back. Her hand landed directly on one of the places that Astrom's staff had hit her particularly hard. Freya winced, but Makkyd did not seem to notice. Astrom did, and shot Freya a look of amusement and sympathy.

"I've been training hard enough," Freya said lightly, closing her eyes and letting her mind focus on the bruises, healing the inflamed tissue with a thought.

Noticing what she was doing, Astrom stepped forward and extended her arms in a subtle request. Freya obliged, stretching out her mind toward Astrom's body and finding the injuries, righting the discord that their presence caused. "You don't even need to touch me anymore to heal me," Astrom marvelled quiet-

A B Endacott

ly, careful not to be overheard by the other onlookers. Not everybody in the Resistance was aware of the powers that true and
deep piety could bestow. Only the most trusted members of the
Resistance, those whose faith had remained unchallenged even
during the years of Kade rule, had discovered their abilities.

She smiled. "You'd also slightly pulled a muscle from doing
something in your workshop," she whispered to Astrom.

"Did you know that all along?" Astrom laughed as Freya
grinned at her. "No wonder you won that last one!"

Freya shook her head, running her fingers through her dark
crop of hair. "Don't be a sore loser," she teased. The easy repar-
tee between them had sprung up over the fivedays that Astrom
had taken Freya under her wing and mercilessly trained her – a
special project, of sorts. While Freya struggled against a sense of
being slightly offended that her ineptitude was deemed so severe
that she required special attention, her teacher had been endlessly patient and encouraging, and she couldn't find it within herself to resent Astrom for her the endless bruises she had inflicted
upon Freya. Indeed, they had become close, friends – Freya's
first in a long, long time.

They moved to the room's edge and two others stepped forward into the makeshift ring, taking the staffs from Freya and
Astrom, settling into fighting stances. Freya sat on the sidelines,
and watched as they moved backwards and forwards exchanging
blows, but neither gaining the advantage. She quickly grew bored
and her gaze began to rove around the room. There were a few
faces there that afternoon she didn't know. The number of people
within the Resistance had swelled over the last few fivedays as
the Kade crackdowns had become increasingly severe. Despite the
fact that it had been several cycles since the brutal attacks of the
Followers of the Dark Gods, the Kade's edicts claimed that they
were taking no chances with the safety of Oranis's citizens. Yet
somehow this translated into the Healing Centre that she administered seeing more and more individuals who bore signs of the

Kade's brutality, sustained because they were deemed to be in breach of some Kade order. It was little wonder that the people were starting to seek out the Resistance.

She realised with a start that Ashtyn was sequestered into a corner of the workshop-turned-sparring space, almost out of sight. He must have seen her fighting. She was glad she had been unaware of his presence before she had stepped into the space with Astrom. Almost certainly, she wouldn't have managed to get that final victory had she known his eyes were on her every movement. As though he could feel her gaze on him, his eyes found hers. She quickly looked away, feeling heat travel across her face. Despite the cycles that had passed since she had returned to the Resistance and committed herself to liberating the city from the Kade, she still felt uncomfortable around him. She had never forgiven him for the way in which he had seduced her so he could then introduce her to the Resistance. Despite his claim that he had fallen in love with her, she couldn't move beyond the lingering betrayal that the discovery had brought. Especially because of the way he had made her feel. She pushed aside the memory of his lips on her skin, and forced her attention back to the center of the room. Some things were better left unthought, and this was one of them. Her life was already difficult enough juggling the pretence of loyal Kade collaborator against her secret life within the Resistance without reintroducing the added complication of her romantic sentiments.

Eventually, the practice finished. People left Astrom's workshop in small groups. Freya watched them as they departed, noting the fatigue or exhilaration. She no longer received looks of surprise in rely to her presence – this group of people, the more senior, trusted members of the Resistance, were now accustomed to her presence here, although every now and then, she still caught them regarding her with curiosity. She couldn't blame them. She was well-known for being favoured by the Kade for her obedience to them. To suddenly see her placed among the leadership of the Resistance might well be cause for confusion – even concern. But she was finished allowing the Kade to hurt innocent people so that she could live comfortably and safely.

"You know, there's an air of anticipation in the city that I haven't seen before," she commented as she helped Astrom push the benches back into place.

"That's true. You can only rule with the kind of force the Kade's employed for so long before people begin to start seriously contemplating an alternative," Makkyd replied, bringing over a tray of tools and placing it on top of a table.

"You sound almost thrilled that the Kade is being so vile," Freya said, struggling to pull a worktable over to its usual place.

Ashtyn came over to help her, easily moving it by himself. She refused to meet his eyes.

"I hardly enjoy the ongoing violence brought against our own people, Freya," Makkyd replied acerbically. "But I can appreciate the opportunity it presents."

Freya brought over two stools. Ashtyn took one from her, his hands brushing against her own. Her skin tingled where their hands had touched, but she told herself to stop being so silly.

"I suppose that's why you're our glorious leader," she retorted dryly, realising too late that she had echoed Ashtyn's description of Makkyd the first time he had brought her to the Resistance. Now her eyes did flick over to him, and she saw him looking at her, knowing it, too. She blushed again.

"I suppose that must be it," Makkyd said, seemingly oblivious to Freya and Ashtyn's shared look, or indeed the awkward moment that had bloomed from it.

They finished replacing the furniture and the smaller group of people – the leadership of the Resistance – gathered around one of the tables, exchanging their respective updates, and considering the new information they shared. The regular, more structured meetings of the Resistance leadership had recently been replaced by the informal updates that were given by whoever was present, so that Makkyd could be passed the information whenever the opportunity arose. She was the mastermind of the Resistance, co-ordinating the group's many arms. Freya was always amazed that Makkyd hardly ever wrote down anything that she was told – citing security precautions – yet she remembered the tiniest, most inconsequential details with apparent ease.

Over the past few fivedays, the possibility of an uprising was looking ever more likely as subversive discontent within the city grew, requiring plans to constantly be amended, and immediate responses to issues as they arose. Makkd's brilliant mind held all those plans, adjusting them and giving out the necessary instructions immediately. Freya had never seen her truly fazed by anything, not reports of a beating, nor of permits being inexplicably revoked, nor of the announcement of more severe curfews. Makkyd's mouth would simply tighten for a moment, then she would announce what they would do in reply.

"Bardan, are our supplies safe?" Makkyd asked, looking at the portly man.

The merchant who had been the first person in the Resistance Freya had ever met clasped his hands together, propping his elbows on the tabletop. "As safe as they'll be anywhere in Oranis. Raids and impromptu inspections are occurring on a daily basis. I've placed our more...controversial supplies in the secret areas Ashtyn has built, and the rest is documented as legitimate, thanks to Lyssa's talents."

Freya felt a stab of bitterness at the fact that Lyssa's alterations of ink even after it had dried on paper was thanks to her own inquisitiveness. Had she not asked whether it was possible, she suspected Lyssa would never have thought to experiment with it. Yet here was Lyssa getting all the credit for her idea. Her jealousy wasn't helped by the fact that Lyssa had, from the very first time she had met Freya, taken an instant and vehement dislike to her. Their relationship had not improved. Lyssa made snide remarks at Freya's expense whenever the opportunity arose; criticising Freya's fighting technique, the amount of medical supplies she diverted into Resistance warehouses, Freya's progress in honing her ability to heal with only her mind. More than once Freya had fought her exasperation with Makkyd for not stepping in and chiding Lyssa for her pettiness. Although she hated to admit it, Lyssa's goading had made her train harder and improve faster, determined to shut her up. She wondered if Makkyd realised it. Knowing Makkyd, she probably had. As much as she was sometimes ruthless, that was fair; her position was not to care for her people, but to get a job done. And that job could soon become quite messy.

"Freya, our sources indicate that there's a large shipment of barat coming in. How much do you think that you'd be able to get for us?" Makkyd's question cut through Freya's thoughts.

Startled, Freya looked at her. "You seem to know more than me. I wasn't even aware that a shipment of Barat was arriving." Freya's own discovery that the lethal barat flower could be used as a topical remedy for vile rashes that covered the whole body, a symptom of the sweating sickness that had recently run through the city, had led to a significant increase in demand for the dangerous plant.

"Keep an eye out for it then. Having some of it in our stocks could be very useful," Makkyd told her.

"What would we use it for?" Freya asked suspiciously. Even though she had made her decision to join the Resistance knowing that she would be helping to hurt, even kill people, she still didn't like the prospect that something as unpleasant as barat poison may be unleashed by them.

Makkyd shrugged with a nonchalance that Freya couldn't quite believe. "It's a useful thing to have," she replied. She immediately directed a question about weapons to Ashtyn – the group's armourer, which forestalled any questions Freya may have asked regarding her plans for the dangerous substance.

The meeting concluded, Freya went to the wall and took her healer's robe off a peg, slipping it over the light shift and trews to which she had stripped down for the training. As was often the case, her eyes slid down to the green band that had been sewn into arm. It denoted her status as a Pious; her undesirability. And yet she had been placed by the Kade into the highest position that any Pious had achieved. Her skill and displays of dedication to the Kade had led them to overlook her birth to promote her beyond her peers. The fact that her robes were edged with the red, purple, and blue colours of the Kade only served to highlight her unique position within Kade society. She sometimes wondered if it was another technique of control; to try and elicit disunity amongst the Pious by evoking jealousy toward one of their own. But the Chief Healer had always emphasised Freya's invaluable contributions to the Kade governance, at times even speaking to Freya with warmth and candour – or what constituted warmth and candour for her.

Freya shook her head. She didn't know what was causing this pensiveness, but it wasn't helping anything.

As she straightened her robe and checked to make sure that hear appearance was spotless, she felt Ashtyn come up behind her. Her whole body tensed.

"It's been nearly a year since we first met."

She thought she detected a note of uncertainty in his voice. At least his comment gave a likely explanation to why she was suddenly so introspective - the upcoming anniversary of when her whole life had been inverted.

"Am I supposed to celebrate?" She tried to keep her voice neutral.

"I just thought..." His nervousness threw her.

"Yes?" She turned around to look up at him. She was still as attracted to him as she was when she had first met him. Being that close to him still made her breath catch, made her stupidly conscious of how she held herself, where his body was in relation to hers.

He seemed to recover himself slightly. "I just thought you may like to know," he said.

"I didn't realise it had been that long," she replied quietly, looking away from him so that she didn't have to meet his eyes.

Before he could say anything else, she darted around him and left the room. Despite herself, she glanced back at him and their eyes met. He looked as though he was about to say something across the distance between them, but seemed to think the better of it. She wasn't sure if that left her relieved or disappointed.

READ OTHER STORIES FROM THE LEGENDS OF THE GODSKISSED CONTINENT

QUEENDOM OF THE SEVEN LAKES

"There are always those who are willing to pay for someone else's death."

Having grown up amongst the Family of Assassins, Elen-ai knows well the prices people are willing to pay to see their enemies fall quickly, quietly, and discreetly. When she is asked to preserve life rather than take it, she is surprised. Upon hearing that her charge is the Queen's only child Gidyon, who is secretly being groomed to succeed his mother, she is horrified. To ensure political stability, no man has ever sat on the throne of the Queendom of the Seven Lakes. Yet one does not easily refuse a Queen, and so reluctantly, Elen-ai accepts the contract.

Her fears only deepen upon meeting the sixteen-year-old Prince Gidyon, who treats her as no better than a petty murderer. However, following an attack on his life, Elen-ai is forced to admit that the danger of leaving this boy-prince alone may be even worse than leaving him to his own devices. Elen-ai reluctantly accompanies Gidyon across the country to identify those within the seven most powerful families who are responsible for the attempt on the Prince's life.

Somewhere in their travels from the calm waters of Lake Tak to the looming cliffs above Lake Bertak, the two form an unlikely yet profound friendship, and Elen-ai begins to see that

Gidyon has the makings of a great ruler within him. As they meet with the families of power, it becomes increasingly clear that secrets and power games run far deeper throughout the Queendom of the Seven Lakes than either of them ever suspected.

THE RUTHLESS LAND

"Lying is not simply about telling a plausible story, it's about being able to tell what someone will want to believe"

To outsiders, the Fourth Country is an unforgiving place. Under the leadership of ruthless women, powerful families regularly wage brutal campaigns against one another to increase their land and wealth, and men live in a state of complete subjugation.

Lexana, heiress to the Farwan family, is sent to the Academy, an elite institution where the daughters of powerful families learn and refine techniques to maintain and gain power. There, she finds herself attracted to Jaxen, one of the teachers who defies convention and goes about unveiled. His apparent disregard for what is expected of him leaves her both uneasy and fascinated.

Then the impossible comes to pass, and disaster befalls the Farwan family. Lexa must leave the Academy to find her mother and help restore her family to power. Jaxen insists upon accompanying her, arguing that she cannot survive without his help. Lexa can't be certain that she can trust Jaxen, but he is right; she needs his help if she is to succeed.